Sons of the *Phoenix*

Part One

by author

JOSEPH MACKAY

Sons of the Phoenix
Copyright © 2017 by Joseph Mackay
Cover Design by Niki Kangas
Edited by Travis McGaughey

Sons of the Phoenix (Part One) / Joseph Mackay – 1st ed.
Library of Congress Cataloging-in-Publication Data
ISBN-13: 978-0-9981321-0-5

To Connor and Alex
For whom there are no limits

Prologue

The world had changed.

By 2051, mankind had drained the earth of its fossil fuels. For years, humanity's best scientists looked for alternative forms of energy to help sustain life on Earth. Many technologies were created, but all were insufficient to satisfy man's rate of consumption.

In 2075, physicist Paul Samson and his team made a breakthrough in slipstream technology. Their method of increasing the speed of particles faster than light created a way to harness and stabilize wormholes through space and time. It wasn't long before the team discovered ways to follow the particles through these folds in space-time.

Probes were sent out first and, soon after, manned exploratory flights, searching for habitable planets and other viable resources. In 2095, the first colony vessels were sent through slipstream portals to various star systems to establish livable conditions on habitable planets and report on the level of available resources. Most colonies performed their function as best they could with limited interaction with the United Earth Defense Force, the collaboration of Earth's nations and governments.

Excited about the possibilities of exploring the galaxy and developing other worlds, the majority of the population became complacent, satisfied to let the global government use these worlds to help them sustain human life. Over the years, however, the people grew restless, unsure of the progress of the colonies, unsure of the future.

Then the Gortha attacked. They were a race of evil, lizard-like humanoids that possessed superior technology and a hunger for planetary resources. In 2115, in response to the Gortha threat, the UEDF was taken over by the global military under the command of General Harruhama, who sat at the head of the Earth Military Council (EMC).

The people lived in fear of humanity's new enemy, getting sporadic media reports from the front lines of the battle. In order to help battle the alien race, the EMC opened the OMBIcademy, enlisting children into military service. Children, with their developing brains, had proven much more capable in utilizing new synapse-sync technologies, which fused growing brain functions with operating computers, allowing users to experience combat, piloting, and operating functions with the speed of thought.

Humanity was all too willing to offer its brightest children to their government to protect the human race, all in the name of the greater good.

Chapter 1

Draft

"Are you sure this is what you want?" Major Sanders asked the dark figure on the other side of the video display.

The shadowed face answered in a menacingly distorted voice, "How else are we going to get at them, Major Sanders? We cannot win if they hold all the cards."

"I still don't understand how this plan is going to work," Sanders stated, more to himself than to the figure on the screen. Sanders did not like taking orders he didn't understand.

"Perform your task and we will take care of the rest. The more you know, the more dangerous it will be. Understand this is for the greater good."

"He is only ten! Christ, they're all just children!" Sanders lamented aloud. His words came out with a snarl, a last effort to appeal to any sense of conscience.

"Of course, I know that. We cannot afford to wait any longer. They grow bolder with each passing year. Just do it, Sanders." The video call abruptly ended.

Major Edmond Sanders sat staring at the video screen in his AX-11 utility vehicle for a long while after the conversation ended. He had never thought of himself as a particularly brave man, joining the military as an officer right out of college at the age of twenty-two. Now forty-seven, Major Sanders had a lot of reservations about the current string of events unfolding in the galaxy. Ever since the "2115 Incident," as it was referred to by the Earth media, Sanders had watched the military grow in power and influence. For the last six years, he had witnessed events that made him numb.

Now sitting on a quiet country road on a Saturday afternoon, he was going to deliver a draft notice to a ten-year-old boy, a boy who would become a UEDF soldier and probably go on to die fighting a war in space.

He pulled out his onboard computer and began to type. "Connor Pereira, DOB: 2111-02-05, UPIN: CMP-2111-M-02." The computer pulled up the boy's information immediately and began printing the conscription notice.

Sanders looked at himself for a moment in the rearview mirror of his AX-11 and took a deep breath. As he took the notification in hand, he growled under his breath, "God help us all."

~ ~ ~

Connor's tenth birthday party was in full swing at the Mercer Estate, a fifty-acre property sixty miles north of San Francisco, in Healdsburg, California. The estate's eight-foot rock wall enclosed the entire property, including the large main house that was often described in architectural circles as "a temple to man's virtues," using hard angles to accentuate the strength of the materials used to build it. The long driveway up to the house was adorned with large sculptures of legendary figures striking heroic poses. They were the collection of William Mercer, who purchased them almost exclusively from the Cordair Art Institute. William had designed the house and landscaping of the property with the sculptures in mind, knowing that the institute's unparalleled work would emphasize the strength and beauty of the architecture and the land. Everyone who had ever visited the estate had been left with a feeling of inspiration of man's greatest achievements or a feeling of annoyance over the owner's considerable ego.

The children at the party were playing outside near a large swimming pool, which featured a long waterslide exiting through a tall waterfall that cascaded down from a rocky swell, where a hot tub sat steaming like the caldera of a volcano.

"Their own little paradise, to enjoy all alone," one of the guests said a bit too loudly. Elena March had never been a woman of subtly or wit.

William Mercer stood by the grill, cooking hamburgers for his guests, wondering, not for the first time, why he had invited the Marches to the party. The festivities had been enjoyable until Austin March's mother started drinking and began with the snide comments and personal praise. William sighed, resolving to not let himself become irritated.

He was a lean and muscular man, with slightly thinning brown hair. The edges of his temples had become gray over the last few years, as did spots of his trimmed goatee. He would have appeared handsome except for the cold, hard edge around his dark-blue eyes. He stood out from the crowd, not because he was tall or particularly well dressed, but because of the intensity of his demeanor. He scanned the clusters of partygoers as they mingled about the grounds, measuring the way they carried themselves and listening to how they spoke with the people around them. He had a way of gauging the people he encountered, something he had learned as a boy. "Always looking for gold," as his grandfather would say. "But sadly, I'm still broke."

He stood upright in a relaxed sort of way. He always appeared relaxed, no matter where he was. It was as if the entire world had belonged to him or, perhaps, he belonged in the world.

A man of some repute in the Bay Area, William had designed several homes and buildings in the city before retiring at the age of thirty-six. The death of his wife had taken a heavy toll on him, and his priority became raising his stepson, Connor, into a man his mother would be proud of.

The doorbell took William's mind away from his increasingly irritating party guests. He deftly set the grill to an automatic function, which would flip and serve the hamburgers when they were ready. He passed by quiet groups of guests, who had just been talking about him, on his way into the house. He crossed through the long, hardwood hallway and into the foyer, to answer the knock on the large, oak door.

He opened the front door to find himself standing face to face with a man in a military uniform. The man was nearly two inches taller than William, with a head of completely gray hair and a face that appeared to belong to a wild animal more than a man. William was familiar enough with the United Earth Defense Force to be able to identify the man's rank.

"What can I do for you, Major..." William began.

"Sanders," the Major replied. "I am here to deliver this."

Major Sanders handed William a slip of green paper, officially sealed by the UEDF. William stepped outside, onto the front landing, and shut the oak door.

"What the hell kind of sick joke is this?" William asked, with tempered anger.

Sanders was not normally intimidated, but he found himself taking a step backward, unsettled by the threateningly calm tone.

"It is no joke. As you are his legal guardian, I am here to inform you—" Sanders began.

"I can see that it's a draft notice, but what makes you think I'll let you take him?" William interrupted, anger building in his voice. "—that your ward, Connor Matthew Pereira, is to report for duty on Saturday, February twelfth, by order of the Earth

Military Council of the United Earth Defense Force," Sanders finished, despite the interruption.

"And if he doesn't?" William said in an icy tone.

Major Sanders remained silent.

"I am going to say this once and I want you to really listen to me, Major. God damn the UEDF and the council straight to the pits of Hell. When I see you there, I will make you pay for this for an eternity."

Major Sanders accepted the idle threat without flinching, even though technically it was illegal to speak of the council in a negative or aggressive manner.

Sanders locked eyes with William and said quietly, "I'm sorry," before turning and departing the estate.

William fought back the wave of despair that followed the feelings of bitter helplessness. He had no idea what he was going to say to Connor or what he was going to do without him. For William Mercer, the galaxy was closing in around him too fast and he wondered how he would survive the collapse.

~ ~ ~

"I'm not going!" Connor shouted from the hallway.

"I don't think they are giving us a choice, Connor," William said with a disheartened look in his eyes. "This is a mandate from the council."

"I'm still not going!" the boy screamed back with a shake of his head that tossed his mop of brown hair from side to side.

It was all a show, of course. Connor's chocolate-brown eyes betrayed his acceptance of the fact that he'd be gone within a week and nothing he, nor his stepfather, could do would change that.

He had been listening at the door since it closed, his anger building as the conversation between his stepfather and the Major concluded. Left inside, he felt a hot rage at the idea that someone other than he would decide his fate.

Connor's mother had died six years prior, while on assignment. Captain Marlena Mercer was flying an Anubis Class Fighter, escorting the colonization freighter, Andromeda, to the Hourglass Nebula colony when they were attacked by the Gortha, an evil race of "cold-blooded humanoids," as the evening holotube reports had explained.

That attack started the Gortha War and had led to a military coup of the UEDF government, which the majority of the citizens had supported.

The day after Marlena's funeral, Connor's older brother, Alex, enlisted into the UEDF at the age of ten. William would have tried to stop him, but after the funeral, weeks had gone by before he could pull himself out of despair enough to function normally. Alex had told them both that he had something to prove to himself. Their father left when Alex was five and, after his mother died in the line of duty, no one doubted that Alex had some demons. It had been a tragic day for the family in so many ways that neither William nor Connor had ever fully recovered.

William had been left to raise Connor alone and had done so as if the boy were his own son. He had made raising that child his life's work, out of love and as a way to cope with the pain of losing his wife to a faceless enemy and one of his adopted sons in the aftermath. He had done everything he could to prepare Connor for the day he would leave to be his own man. He did not, however, expect that day to come on Connor's tenth birthday.

Several years before, the Holotube news had announced that the military would be drafting high-ability adolescents due to the neural growth patterns. Growing minds proved more receptive to mental augmentation and virtual battlefields. William had explained to Connor, while watching that report, that the government was using technology to grab more power and reach further into the lives of the citizens.

The fact that his birthday party was interrupted with the delivery of a draft notification left Connor hating the world.

"I don't know what to say to you, Connor, but I know that you are going to make your mother proud," William said, with a subtle wince at the mention of his wife.

Connor noticed the wince and felt his anger quickly melt into sympathy for his stepfather. "I will make her proud," he said quietly. "I would have, even if I didn't get drafted."

"I know it. Who knows? Maybe you will run into Alex. The last time he wrote he was on Station Sigma, orbiting Mars."

Connor thought a moment. "By the time I am in orbit, Alex will be out of the academy. Besides, I can't even remember what he looks like," Connor said sadly, while looking over at an old photo on the wall of the two boys playing baseball together.

It was almost more than William could handle. "Let's get back to your party."

"Okay," Connor said, remembering that he had kids over to play with. The idea that they started playing games without him only aggravated Connor's irritation.

~ ~ ~

The tone of the party was somber after the draft notification arrived. Most of Connor's friends didn't know what to say to him and he wasn't offering any explanations. At that moment, he hated the Earth Military Council and everyone in the room. He especially hated his friend Johnny Perez, whom he suspected took back the gift card that his parents had brought. Connor could just hear the excuse, "Well you weren't going to get to use it anyway."

Seeing Connor's tension grow, William suggested that they play a game of Hide and Seek.

He watched the kids take their positions while halfheartedly listening to the other parents talk about the unfairness of it all. Johnny's parents were the worst, complaining about how the election process of councilmen had been rigged to give the military more power and how they would never allow Johnny to be drafted.

William watched curiously as Connor hid under a gazebo in the backyard of his estate, followed by Johnny. They had known each other since their first year of school and Johnny always seemed to follow Connor around. As Marlena used to say, "Everyone is drawn to that boy's light."

"We should petition the council. Surely they won't force us to give up our children if we all write letters together!"

The tirade was lost on William as he watched Connor settle into position opposite Johnny under the gazebo. Meanwhile, Mary Atherton, who was "it," was finishing her countdown.

"Yeah … maybe," was all he replied, not really interested in rants that offered no viable actions.

"Maybe?!" came the predictable retort. "My brother-in-law is an attorney for the state and he can present our case! His fees aren't too high and I won't charge much for introducing you two!"

An unremarkable comment lost on uninterested ears. William did not normally tolerate insincere claims from anybody, but he let the other parents go on anyway, focusing intently upon the game in the yard.

His eyes were fixed upon Connor's hiding spot where he had lost sight of him. Only by luck did he see that the boy had exited out the opposite side of the gazebo and up the backside of a nearby tree that had a strong, low branch that hung out over the house. Smiling, William wondered what Connor was up to.

Finishing her countdown, Mary began systematically checking the yard's most predictable hiding places. Her first stop was the gazebo.

"I found you!" Mary shouted at Johnny, who had his eyes shut while he ducked down, as if closing his eyes would make him harder to find.

Johnny's first reaction was to shout out, "Connor is hiding on the other side!"

Johnny had adopted the philosophy, "If you can't win the race, break the legs of those who run faster than you." William found it distasteful.

While Mary was annoyed when Connor wasn't there, Johnny was furious. They complained to each other and then went to tell on Connor for making them look stupid. William was all too happy to point out that they had made themselves look stupid.

The kids spent the rest of the afternoon unable to find Connor while their parents made shallow observations and threats on William's behalf. Grateful for Connor's disappearing act, William let the party end shortly after, without bringing out the cake or unwrapping the presents.

After the guests had departed, Connor emerged from a cupboard in the kitchen that he had managed to sneak into, eating a slice of cake that William hadn't noticed was missing until now.

"Pretty sneaky, I saw you though," William said, wearing a sincere smile that lit up his eyes with pride.

"I wasn't trying to fool you, I was trying to fool the fools!" came Connor's reply, laced with irritation over the day's unexpected turn.

"I would scold you for being disrespectful to your friends, but you did save me from hours of being hounded about what I ought to be doing."

"You should really thank me, how long before they would've started asking for donations or loans?"

"Ha! I guess I owe you one for that. Did you notice that almost everyone took back their presents?" William asked.

"What? You better be kidding!" Connor exclaimed.

He was kidding. As Connor ran to check his presents, William lamented that these precious times with his adopted son were fleeting and would soon be over. He had no idea what he would do without Connor in his life, but he suspected that it would be too quiet and painfully lonely on the estate.

"Listen, promise me you'll write," William said soberly when Connor came back into the room, opening the largest gift.

"I will write you all the time!" Connor said, throwing aside the unwrapped box of dress shirts. "You're my best friend." With that, Connor dashed up the back stairway to his bedroom for the evening.

That night, William wept until he fell asleep.

~ ~ ~

Connor couldn't hear the sounds of agony from his stepfather's room. Had he heard it, he may have spent the night in tears himself. But as soon as Connor closed his bedroom door, he turned on his datapad and began looking up information on what to expect from the OMBIcademy.

The web results left him with more questions than they answered, offering only vague references to the apocalyptic war raging throughout the galaxy and how enlisting would give Earth a fighting chance against the Gortha hoards. According to the official page, the United Earth Defense Force was now at sixty percent strength, having lost the third and fifth fleets in the original assault against the Gortha and several more ships in following years.

Connor suspected that the entire page was set up to be inspiring, but it only made him feel sick to his stomach. He looked out his bedroom window at the lights of Healdsburg in the distance. He wondered, not for the first time, what it would like to be away from home. With the fear of being away from all that he knew, mixed with the hint of excitement at a new adventure, Connor fell asleep backwards on his bed.

Chapter 2

Goodbyes

She was a rare beauty, with eyes the color and shape of almonds, and a smile so radiant stars would be jealous. The dark colors of her flight suit only served to accentuate the curves of her slim body, as her dark-brown hair flowed gracefully down her back. She was Captain Marlena Mercer of the United Earth Defense Force's third fleet, and, unequivocally, the best pilot in the UEDF.

The mission was nine weeks into the ten-week schedule. Marlena was ordered to escort the colonization freighter, Andromeda, to set up a colony on Aeris VII in the Hourglass Nebula. The freighter and its escort had come out of the slipstream jump and were now using their momentum to move toward their objective.

Her eyes were sharp, no detail missed as she scanned the endless darkness ahead of her ship. She had been on many missions in deep space and nothing escaped her attention. She saw the distortion in the stars ahead before her sensors detected the objects and she immediately understood the danger. Responsible for the lives of two thousand sleeping colonists, she didn't hesitate moving her Anubis fighter, the Tizona, into an aggressive position ahead of the Andromeda.

"Unidentified vessel, you are interfering with an official UEDF mission. Withdraw immediately," Marlena ordered into an open com, before the vessel had completely manifested before her.

The ship materializing ahead of her was massive, almost twice the size of the colonization freighter she had been escorting over the past nine weeks. She had never seen its likeness before. Many jutting tendrils emerged from the tubular hull toward the aft of the ship, whipping forward and back, reminding Marlena of an angry squid. The ship was longer than it was tall, with no markings to identify its origin.

She watched as the tube on the port side of the ship opened and launched a succession of projectiles toward the Andromeda. Marlena's hands immediately went to her weapons, locking on to the projectiles and launching her own counter measures. Confident that her auto-drones would handle the fire against the Andromeda, she turned her focus on the enemy ship itself. It was massive and heavily armored, with no visible weaknesses.

Undaunted, she hastily launched a barrage of heavy cannon fire at the larger vessel, aiming at the base of one of the thrashing tendrils, followed by anti-armor missiles that blazed forward in a steady stream of destruction. By her estimate, it was enough firepower to level any ship in the UEDF's fleet. The heavy salvo proved to be enough against the squid-like ship, which had the misfortune of materializing in front of the Tizona. It imploded quietly in the vacuum of space, popping like a bubble and sending debris in every direction.

Marlena didn't have time to celebrate her victory as several other strangely shaped ships began to appear around her. She knew that, despite her skill and the firepower of the Tizona, she would not be able to sustain a lengthy battle alone against so many heavy battleships.

Keying in the evasion codes of the Andromeda, Marlena begin the process of sending the colonization freighter into a slipstream back to Earth, before it could be captured or destroyed. While her left hand worked the coding sequences, her right hand continued the offensive against the superior enemy force, launching everything the Tizona had toward the larger vessels.

She was thankful that her weapons were doing significant damage, as another strange squid vessel exploded in a massive fireball, the oxygen inside it igniting from internal damage. The Anubis Class Fighters were highly regarded as the strongest defensive fighters in the fleet, and Marlena's personal modifications to the Tizona had made it unequaled.

Despite her early success in the battle, Marlena knew she couldn't continue defending the Andromeda and keying in evasion codes with the sheer number of enemy ships appearing ahead of her. Making the situation worse, many smaller fighters that moved like a school of angry piranha began to launch from the large ships. She stopped counting targets, knowing that it didn't matter, as she began to feel overwhelmed.

She rapidly exhausted her ammo supply with the non-stop suppressive fire she continued to direct toward the nearest vessels. Her mind was spinning as her targeting computer audibly identified new targets appearing around her, followed by red flashes from her control board lighting up to show which ordinance was depleted. She saw two enemy vessels moving to block the Andromeda's egress as it maneuvered around for its slipstream jump.

Turning her remaining weapons on the closer of the two enemy vessels, a finned monstrosity that looked more like a shark than a spaceship, Marlena knew she didn't have much time. As her last anti-armor missile plunged into the shark-like ship's head, she smiled. The missile burrowed deep before detonating, causing an implosion that surged from the head to the tail.

"Just one more," Marlena said quietly to herself.

Her eyes went to the picture she kept on her instrument panel. The caption at the bottom read, *My Boys.* It was an old photo she took at a picnic with her family years before. She looked at her sons' joyful smiles; Alex's green eyes looking down at the ground while he was laughing and Connor was grinning, looking off toward some unknown adventure. William's dark-blue eyes focused straight ahead, looking into hers as they always did. She loved her husband and her sons. The thought of them brought a small grin to her face even as her fighter took a hit on the starboard engine.

Marlena kept her eyes locked on her husband's as alert lights flashed around her console. The instrument board audibly identified damage her ship was taking in an impassive voice as she aimed her fighter toward the star-shaped vessel that blocked the Andromeda's retreat.

As the Tizona's engines increased to full power, Marlena Mercer kissed her gloved finger and pressed it to the photo of the people she loved most.

"Take care of them, baby," she whispered.

The Tizona smashed through the hull of the enemy battleship. Several small explosions instantly disabled the vessel and veered it off course. With clear space ahead, the Andromeda's slipstream drive activated, sending two thousand sleeping colonists safely back to Earth.

~ ~ ~

Connor woke up with tears in his eyes. He'd dreamt of his mother's last mission many times before, but never in so much detail. Turning to the clock beside his bed, he stared at the pale-green

"4:22 AM" glow that softly illuminated his room. He would not be shipping out for another three hours but he lay awake, staring up towards ceiling somewhere in the darkness above him.

The last week had gone by quickly, Connor and William spending as much time together as they could. Connor's favorite beaches, amusement parks, they grasped at each precious minute like it was their last.

Every night William made Connor's favorite dinner, breaded chicken and trees (Connor's term for broccoli), and they talked about any and everything they could imagine. The boy always asked questions when he didn't understand something and William always seemed to have a good answer. Connor never needed to be told something twice, he had always absorbed knowledge quickly.

As if at a frantic pace to assimilate what should have been a lifetime of information, Connor absorbed the knowledge quickly, from the reasons behind cellular decay to the origins of star names, from shape of galaxies down to the intricacies of microscopic organisms. He was glad every day that William was in his life; he was, as Alex used to call him, "a Human Encyclopedia." Connor often wondered if he would ever know as much as his stepfather did. On that level of musing, he also wondered if that brilliance might have been the light that his mom had loved so much in the man.

It was becoming painfully obvious that this parting would be difficult for them both. Over the past six years they had developed an extremely strong bond. As the clock ticked closer to the inevitable departure, Connor began to grow nervous about the experience. He tried to calm down with breathing exercises that his Mom had taught him years before; she always said to take a few deep breaths, slow down, and imagine the outcome that he wanted in as much detail as he could.

With that in mind, Connor imagined himself at the head of his class, a great commander and pilot, just like his mom. He pictured himself as the paragon of all cadets and ended his thoughts imagining putting an end to the war so that he and his brother could come home.

Eyes closed and focused, Connor fell back to sleep.

~ ~ ~

The sound of the alarm clock surprised Connor. He didn't realize at first that he had fallen asleep. He could hear sounds coming from the kitchen below. Bleary-eyed, he hopped out of his bed and looked at his clock; 6:30 AM. Glancing around his room, he slowly absorbed the details he'd taken for granted the majority of his life – the action figures on his bookshelf, the threadbare carpet, the captain's bed positioned in the corner. It dawned on him then that this could be the last time he got out of that bed, onto this floor.

He felt sincerely loved by his parents as he looked around at all the nice things they had given him. His captain's bed was comfortable and his green sheets were incredibly soft. He never thought about it much, but he realized that they must've been expensive. On the opposite side of the room lay an unused matching bed that was always made perfectly. Alex's bed. Alex had his own room in the house, but soon after settling in he had moved his bed into Connor's room so they could be closer. Alex always said it was because Connor was afraid of the dark, but Connor had suspected that it was Alex who was afraid.

Between the two beds was an old desk William had given to Alex, which had been both of their desk in its time. Connor used it for drawing schematics of inventions he thought the world would benefit from. The latest schematic featured a wristwatch that would always point to a counterpart it was calibrated to, so that any two people could find each other anywhere in the world. Connor smirked at his own work as he looked above the desk, out the window.

The view of the backyard caused Connor to ache with memories. The volcano-looking pool with the slide that he had always enjoyed descending, splashing into the warm water below; the stone pathway that lead back to the oriental-style gym that William and Marlena had used to exercise in together; the woods beyond the fence where Connor and Alex used to explore and fight fantasy battles with mythical creatures.

The rest of Connor's room was a clutter of toys he hadn't bothered to put away after his birthday party. He left them there, hoping that someday he might have a childhood to come back to.

Connor dressed quickly in his camouflage pants and a blue T-shirt then left his room, shutting the door and not looking back.

~ ~ ~

Connor found William in the kitchen, making what appeared to be extra-crispy bacon as the man stared intently at the sizzling pan. His eyes were glazed over as if he were staring across a thousand miles at some far-off memory. Connor didn't disturb the reverie at first, but when he noticed that the bacon was smoking, he cleared his throat loudly.

William looked up and smiled at him. It was apparent William didn't realize that he had burnt the breakfast he had been staring into.

"That smells like it would have been awesome," Connor quipped sarcastically.

"Huh? Oh. Yeah..." William replied nonchalantly as he dumped the bacon into the sink, not seeming to care that he had wasted it. "What can I make for you?"

"I don't know," Connor offered his usual reply.

"I can make you cereal, oatmeal, scrambled eggs, cinnamon rolls, chocolate chip pancakes..."

"Yeah, yeah, yeah!" Connor excitedly replied at the mention of chocolate chip pancakes.

"Those were Alex's favorite too," William remarked offhandedly. "God, and hers..." he continued nostalgically. "You are a lot like them."

Connor wasn't so sure about that, but let the comment go as William began to gather the ingredients for his pancakes.

"What are you going to do now?" Connor asked, changing the subject from the past to the future in an effort to avoid crying.

"You mean without you to babysit all the time?" William said with a painfully forced smile.

"More like me babysitting you," Connor rebutted indignantly.

William looked at Connor, suddenly stern. "You have your mom's temper. That short fuse will get you into a lot of trouble if you don't learn to keep it in check."

Connor remained silent, thinking about the implications behind the warning. What was William really trying to say? The man had always preached the practice of living consciously and paying attention to the real meaning behind people's words.

"What do you mean?" Connor asked after a moment, unsure he understood.

William looked at Connor right in the eyes as he said, "When you give people power over your emotions, letting them make you angry or sad or whatever it may be, they will be able to use it against you, to control you. Regardless of how you feel, don't be so quick to show your hand."

Connor looked at his hands in response.

"Eh, a poker term..." William said smirking as he flipped a pancake in the air, catching it with the pan. William went about making breakfast while Connor mulled over what his stepfather had told him.

"If anyone tries to see my hand, the next thing they'll see is my fist," Connor said thrusting his fist forward, proud of himself for formulating his own cliché out of unfamiliar terms.

William burst out laughing at an answer he should have expected from his stepson. His laughter subsided and he continued thoughtfully.

"That's actually really clever. I'll have to remember that."

William had always been an advocate for appropriate violence. He had once given Connor advice on how to deal with a bully at school who had been stealing Connor's lunch. He had said, "If that boy takes your chips, go tell an adult. If the adult does nothing, you punch that kid as hard as you can. Don't stop hitting him until a teacher or somebody pulls you off him, and I promise they will pull you off quickly."

Connor had asked, "Won't I get in trouble?"

To which William replied, "At school, maybe, but when you get home, I'll buy you ice cream every day you're suspended, and buy you a new game too. I won't let the school punish you for standing up for yourself when your teacher won't."

Connor had always liked William's sensible advice; it made him feel in control of his life. Connor especially liked it when he'd found out that 'suspended' was apparently an extra weekend.

William served Connor his pancakes and set about cleaning the kitchen while Connor ate. Connor noted with a twinge of concern that William hadn't made any breakfast for himself, but lost the thought in the deliciousness of the chocolate chip pancakes his family loved so much.

Connor was nearly done with his breakfast when he was interrupted by a knock at the door. William went to answer it and called Connor into the foyer. Major Sanders was standing at the door in his pristine military uniform.

The car had come thirty minutes early to take him away. Later they would find out that this was a common military tactic to help ease the pain of long goodbyes. In this case, it made it worse. It seemed to go by so quickly. One minute he was eating breakfast with his stepfather like he had every morning and the next he was being taken away by a stranger, against his will, to go fight in a war.

"It's time to go, Connor," Major Sanders said coldly.

More than anything Connor wanted to stay. One more minute, one more day, with the man who had raised him for the past six years. William was obviously feeling the same way as he hugged Connor tightly.

"Be your best self out there," William said to him. "You were born to shine, so go blind them with your light." It was what William had said to him every morning when he dropped Connor off at school. He added, "I love you, son."

Connor looked up at William and said, "I love you too, William."

Major Sanders stood watching the exchange with uncharacteristic patience.

After the goodbyes, Sanders took a step in front of Connor and lead him to a black bus that was waiting for them outside. Connor didn't look back. He knew that his life had just changed forever.

Major Sanders, however, did look back as Connor boarded the bus. What he saw was not the impassioned man who threatened him after receiving the conscription notice, but in his place a very dangerous man on the edge of breaking.

Chapter 3

Initiation

Connor didn't have much to say once he was on the bus, so he quietly looked out the window while the bus rolled along the streets where he grew up. He tried not to think of the past too much as he traversed through areas that were thick with the memories of his childhood. He didn't have to fight it for too long, as the bus soon took him beyond the streets he knew and out his window lay only the unfamiliar.

The bus smelled like dried sweat and the seats were well worn. Connor sat in a middle seat near an emergency exit, always wanting to be prepared, just in case something happened. Alex had always told Connor to think ahead like that.

The grilled windows made the bus feel like it was taking him off to prison. He also noted dryly that someone had carved, "You suck, Fish-mouth," on the back of the seat in front of him.

The bus continued for almost an hour by Connor's estimate, heading south from Healdsburg toward San Francisco.

Other than the driver and Major Sanders sitting at the front of the bus, Connor was the only passenger aboard. He wondered if they would be picking up any other kids along the way, and asked Major Sanders how many stops they would make. The man didn't reply to Connor's question, but turned around to regard him for a long while.

Taciturn people annoyed Connor. Soon he started looking for ways to annoy the Major back. Connor settled on singing a repetitive jingle he'd heard from the military recruitment ad that he had seen on the holotube. Of course, Connor put his own spin on the song.

"We are the last line of defense" became "There is a long line to take a dump."

"No force has ever matched us and never will" turned into "Our toilet was stopped up by our stinky pill."

Connor didn't have time to finish the song as the bus pulled up to a military airbase. He made a mental note to write complete lyrics and teach them to all the recruits if the instructors were as annoying as Major Sanders was.

Connor's attention was pulled away from annoying Sanders as the bus entered the grounds of an old base through an armed checkpoint. There were no signs, but judging by the distance and direction they had traveled, Connor figured it was probably Travis Air Force Base. He had come here once a few years before to an air museum.

"No going back now," Connor muttered to himself.

He had always been fascinated with military aircrafts, both atmospheric and space-faring. His mother had flown solo in an Anubis Fighter in the UEDF, which normally required a pilot, a navigator, and a gunner of exceptional skill. He looked from his window around the airfield but, to his disappointment, no battle aircraft were around.

The bus continued onto a long runway and turned sharply toward the far end, where a small twin turbine SLX-Condor was waiting. These were primarily used for VIP transport across international waters. They were one of Connor's least favorite aircraft that he could name. He had a model of it that he had never played with, except to send it crashing down.

As the bus pulled up to the Condor, Connor said discouragingly, "Not even the LX upgrade model, must have been built before 2107. And here I thought I was getting special treatment."

He noticed Major Sanders looking back at him with what must have been the man's version of a grin, although to Connor he more closely resembled a snarling wolf. Had the man heard him from the front of the bus?

"Or maybe you aren't as important as I thought you were," Connor said loudly.

Sander's grin made a slight twist and became an actual snarl.

"Now that's an improvement," Connor said a little quieter.

Connor walked to the exit as Sanders was getting up and the both of them exited the bus when it fully stopped. Walking with weighted steps across the runway toward the Condor, Connor took several deep breaths to calm himself down. Although he acted impertinent, he was afraid of leaving home and of the man who was taking him away.

The bus pulled away behind them as they got to the foot of the open stairway. His hands shaking, Connor proceeded up the steps ahead of Major Sanders with trepidation. He did not like any part of what was happening.

When he got on board he settled into a comfortable leather seat while Sanders spoke a gruff word to the pilot that sounded like it could have been an order. Sanders then entered the cabin, stopping at a small refrigerator to pull out an unlabeled bottle of what looked like water. He set the bottle on the table in front of Connor and sat down.

"I can tell that you're afraid," Sanders said quietly.

"You're just saying that because I'm a kid. I'm supposed to be afraid."

"Your hands are shaking, kid."

"And you're sweating. I'm the one who should be afraid, what's your excuse?"

Sanders glared hard at Connor before pushing the bottle of clear liquid toward him.

"Drink it," Sanders barked.

"You drink it, I'm not thirsty," Connor quipped back turning his head away.

Sanders' eyebrow rose in disbelief before saying, "Drink it or I will make you drink it."

Connor believed that Sanders would try, but just the same decided to drink it. The water had a bitter aftertaste, which Connor soon realized was a sedative.

"So I don't know where we're going, right?" Connor said sarcastically, trying to fight the effects of the potent narcotic. "Very … cloak and dagger."

Sanders' mouth formed a wolfish grin. "Nothing gets by you, does it, kid?" The man's voice oozed with condescension.

Connor did his best to mimic the man's absurd smile while black spots began to fill his vision. It wasn't long before the drug took effect completely.

As his consciousness slipped away Connor thought he heard Sanders say, "Annoying little kid."

With Connor unconscious, Sanders pulled a handkerchief from his pocket and dabbed his forehead until he realized he hadn't been sweating at all. It occurred to him that the kid had forced him to show his hand without much effort. He quietly decided to be more wary of this kid in the future.

~ ~ ~

"I hate this," a girl's faint voice complained. "What do you think is out there?"

"Oh man, half these kids aren't even awake yet," a whiny-voiced boy replied.

Another boy chimed in lewdly, "This bracelet is tighter than my brother's girlfriend; how do I get it off?"

"Maybe you can cut it with your razor-sharp wits," Connor murmured, as he began to awaken. That brought nervous laughter from the other kids who were awake.

The lewd kid sitting across from Connor glared at him, but remained silent, obviously embarrassed.

Connor looked around the room he was in. It appeared to be some kind of holding cell for the group of kids he was with. Connor did a quick count of forty boys and girls all around his age, sitting across from each other in two long rows. A pair of large doors loomed at the far end of the cell with a trace amount of light coming through the opening between them. The motion was faint, but Connor could tell the cell was shifting as if it were swinging slightly.

When Connor tried to move, he realized that the bracer attached to his arm was locked in place on the armrest next to his seat. The bracer itself occupied the majority of Connor's forearm and felt tight against his wrist.

From where he was sitting near the back of the containment cell, Connor could see that most of the kids were awake now and all of them seemed to be as confused as he was.

"Hey, Connor!" he heard a voice cry out from his left.

To Connor's surprise, Johnny Perez was sitting across from his row near the back of the container.

"Johnny, do you know what's going on?" Connor asked, not particularly happy to see his friend, since the events at his birthday party a week before.

"I have no idea, I just woke up!" Johnny replied. "My dad enlisted me the day after you got your draft notice."

"I wonder why?" Connor asked sarcastically, which only prompted an awkward shrug from Johnny.

The cell lurched suddenly and locked into place. The abrupt movement seemed to wake up the rest of the kids in the room. A voice boomed out from a single speaker on the wall.

"You are the United Earth Defense Force OMBIcademy class of 2126. In this academy, you will learn how to think quickly, how to fight hard, how to win decisively—"

"How to take a majestic dump," Connor added flippantly, which drew another laugh from the kids around him.

"—and when to stay quiet," the voice continued, as if responding to Connor directly. Connor grimaced slightly.

"Because it is your first day, you get to meet the class that is graduating in 2121 and see what they have learned over the past five years. Have fun!" the voice finished menacingly as the double doors began to open.

Connor was on immediately alert. After being treated so coldly in the bus, he did not expect a warm welcome from the class of 2121. In the back of his mind he wondered if he would see his brother. The thought of that both excited and terrified him.

When the doors finished opening, the bracers unlocked from the arm rests and began to light up with different colors. Connor's bracelet glowed dark blue and he noticed the number thirteen scratched into the side of it.

"Just my luck," Connor said with a heavy sigh.

The other kids began to shuffle toward the exit when Connor heard a slight whine behind him.

"Mine is stuck," Johnny cried. "Help me, Connor!"

Connor turned to help Johnny out of his seat while the other kids exited the cell. After a couple of seconds Connor got Johnny's glowing red bracer to release by slamming his fist into the armrest. As he helped Johnny to his feet, he heard a scream from the yard beyond.

The scene outside was chaos as the boys walked out of the cell. Connor and Johnny stood at one end of what appeared to be an obstacle course that was occupied by older kids with glowing, colored weapons in their hands and thirty-eight screaming ten-year-olds running to avoid them.

The older boys were laughing as they used their weapons to slice and hack away at the younger children. When the first kid went down, a short kid with thick glasses, Connor had thought he had been killed. But seeing the kid seize up rigidly, Connor realized that he had been stunned by the weapon instead.

Connor tapped Johnny's shoulder and ran up a small hill toward the edge of the battlefield to take in the scene around them. The younger kids were falling fast to the onslaught of the older while Connor did a quick count, but he only spotted about fifteen opponents. As some of the younger kids got past the older group on their way up the short hill, Connor noticed the weapons the older boys were using were appearing out of the bracers on their arms.

Connor looked to his own bracer while Johnny frantically looked around the grounds, which was mostly comprised of ramps, tunnels, odd structures, and sand. The arena was narrow, extending over a hill beyond their sight.

"Let's get past them and get out of here," Johnny said, moving ahead of Connor.

Connor nodded, but was focused upon his bracer. The letters "O.M.B.I" were clearly stamped into one side and his bracer seemed well-worn. Connor even thought he saw dried blood on one side. Not pausing to think of the implications of secondhand equipment, Connor began tapping on the display, which opened a holographic menu system.

Connor followed Johnny up the edge of the course, while staying low and out of sight as much as possible, cycling through menu options. He noticed that most of the menu options had a "locked" icon next to them and were grayed out, categories like *HUD, Neuro-Sync, Vehicles, Aircraft,* and *Melee.* Connor stopped reading, not finding an option that was unlocked.

Connor and Johnny ducked behind a large concrete pipe that sat on top of the ground while Connor selected the weapons tab on his OMBI. Only one option was unlocked: *Dagger.*

"Well, it's gotta be better than nothing," Connor said quietly, selecting the weapon. A glowing blue dagger manifested in Connor's hand.

"Don't do that! You'll get us in trouble!" Johnny squeaked from their hiding place.

"I think we're supposed to use what they give us," Connor cut back with a harsh whisper.

Connor could hear screaming and crying from beyond the hill, farther into the arena. Most of the other kids in the starting area were already down and the few who had gotten past the "welcoming committee" were obviously regretting their progress. Some of the kids had tried to get back into the cell, which had closed behind Connor, and were not putting up much of a fight against the bigger kids who were taunting them.

Connor heard the older boys shouting things like, "Take it, hisser!" and "Die, lizard lips!"

"Let's go through the tunnel so they can't see us," Johnny said as he moved into the enclosed space.

"Lead the way, Johnny."

While Johnny started through the tunnel, Connor moved around the side closest to the center of the arena, between the pipe and a ramp offering some cover from the older kids who were intently approaching the small group trying to run back to the cell. As Connor approached where the pipe ended, he almost walked into the back of an older kid who was hiding, intently eying the tunnel's exit. From where he was, even in all the commotion, Connor could hear Johnny scuffling through the tunnel, talking as though Connor was still with him. Connor noticed the boy in front of him tense up, ready to strike with what appeared to be a glowing yellow battle axe.

Connor moved first, stepping to the boy's side, and jabbed his glowing dagger into the older boy's throat. The boy seized up and fell to the ground, muscles going stiff with the disabling strike. The battle axe dissipated as the boy fell hard to the ground.

Connor felt a slight vibration in his wrist and noticed out of the corner of his eye some glowing blue numbers flashing in rapid succession. He didn't stop to read them as he grabbed Johnny and started to run forward up a small incline.

"Stay quiet, idiot," Connor snapped at Johnny, who mumbled off what sounded like an insincere apology, clearly not understanding what Connor just did for him.

Nearing the center of the course, Connor noticed a large four-sided screen that looked like some kind of a scoreboard up in the sky. Apparently there was scorekeeping happening and, although they appeared to be outside on a sunny day, the flickering scoreboard indicated virtual elements to the arena.

Connor's jaw dropped as he read the score, *39 | 2*, with a countdown clock at thirty-seven minutes. He wasn't naïve enough to believe that he was the only one who could see the scoreboard. His fear was confirmed when he heard someone shout out, "Only two left!" followed by, "Hiding like mice, probably. Find them!"

Connor pointed at a nearby tower structure that stuck up from the sand at an skewed angle. Quietly, he and Johnny ran toward the structure, hearing the older boys closing in all around them. Connor went first into the tower and immediately turned to Johnny, grabbing his wrist.

"What the heck are you doing?" Johnny said abruptly, trying to pull his hand away.

"Shut up!" Connor said working through the menus until a red-colored dagger appeared in Johnny's hand.

"Oh, cool!" Johnny said, a little loud.

Connor quickly moved under a nearby stairway and out of view from the main entrance. Connor made sure Johnny saw him go in, as Johnny hid behind a pillar across the way.

"When they come in, let's ambush them before they get us!" Johnny whispered loudly from his hiding place.

"Okay," Connor whispered as he moved out of his hiding place and up the stairway as quietly as he could manage. Connor had just rounded the corner to the second floor when he heard the group of older boys enter the room below.

"Come out little mice!" a low voice taunted, followed by the laughter of what sounded like a half-dozen other boys.

Connor moved toward an open window and peeked out to see a dozen more boys in uniforms coming toward the tower. One boy stood out from the group wearing what appeared to be an officer's badge and walked with an air of authority, casually issuing commands to the boys around him. Connor stepped back into the shadows of the second floor and took a deep breath.

Below, Connor heard Johnny attempt an ambush, yelling out the word, "Now!" followed by a high-pitched scream.

"We caught the mouse! Now, who needs the points?" the low voice taunted.

"Connor is hiding under the stairs!!" Johnny squealed, as if his attempted betrayal would earn him some mercy from the older boys.

"Go get him!" the low voice said. "I'm taking the points."

Connor heard Johnny fall to the ground and looked out the window. *39 | 1* was on scoreboard's display hovering above. The officer and his team moved confidently toward the tower's entrance with the battle nearing its end. Some of them were even putting their weapons away as they got close to the entrance. Connor took another deep breath and began running toward the window.

"Wait! That lizard-loving mouse lied! No one's here!" one kid shouted from the back of the downstairs room. He hadn't finished his sentence when Connor landed on top of the dark-haired officer, stabbing down hard with the dagger in his hands. He felt the satisfying vibration of a clean kill before turning and stabbing a surprised-looking, unarmed boy in front of him. Connor's bracer vibrated again, followed by the steady flow of numbers rapidly moving across the display.

The older boys began to reactivate their weapons in an angry panic. They shouted curses at Connor as he turned to run up a nearby ramp and back down the other side. He knew he was moving toward the opposite side of the arena from where he had entered and could only hope there was some sort of exit there.

A greenish arrow smacked Connor's right arm, causing it to go limp with a jolting pain. He hadn't realized that the virtual weaponry would hurt so much, and didn't care to learn how badly a kill felt.

Connor began running a serpentine pattern over and under obstacles, moving toward an exit he could only hope was out there somewhere. He could hear the older boys shouting at him, closing in on him. They were bigger and likely faster, so Connor used his smaller size to squeeze through portals that the older boys would have to slow down to navigate. Thinking the fight was over, the older kids were out of their defensive positions and formations. They didn't even take any serious defensive positions this far into the course to begin with, being put there to bully the new kids.

Connor crossed an open area and saw a long ramp ahead of him that led toward a red door. Connor put his head down and sprinted forward with all the speed he could muster. The older boys closed in from behind him and from his flanks. As his feet hit the ramp heading toward the exit, he noticed a tall figure ahead of him who seemed to come out of nowhere.

One more obstacle on his path. He moved to attack with his dagger, swinging it furiously from side to side. The figure ahead of him dodged and moved just out of reach of the dagger with practiced ease, producing no weapon to counter Connor's attack.

One arm limp and with the sun in his eyes, Connor pressed the attack until he felt his wrist caught and twisted behind his back. Connor tried unsuccessfully to punch with his other hand, fighting against the numbing pain the green arrow protruding from his shoulder produced.

With a grunt by his captor and increased pressure to his held arm, Connor was turned around to look out across the course he had just completed. Thirty-five or so older boys stood glaring up at him. Their dirt and sweat covered features, reddened by a mixture of embarrassment and frustration, twisted into scowls and barred teeth. Their still-activated weapons glowed ominously in the sunlight, as their muscular arms were raised, prepared for a fight.

"You guys suck, letting a ten-year-old get this far!" Connor yelled out defiantly, prompting several shouts and cuss words.

"Scale-skin!" one boy called out at Connor.

Connor heard a familiar laugh behind him. "You're not going to make a lot of friends with that attitude, Tonns," the voice said quietly. "Good job though."

Connor was stunned at the use of his childhood nickname and tried to turn to see the speaker, but could only turn his head enough to see the boy's call-sign, "Mephisto," displayed prominently on a commander's uniform.

"Easy, kid, just wait," Mephisto said to him, as he struggled to get free.

"Another batch of little baby lizard-lovers falls to the 2121 Elite!" Mephisto shouted, still holding Connor in front of him. The crowd of older boys below yelled back in unison, although with an acute lack of enthusiasm, "Yes, sir!".

"Four shutouts today! You must be tired to let one kid prevent our fifth shutout by three kills!" Mephisto continued. The boys below put their heads down, except for the one with the low voice who yelled back, "So who gets the points?"

"Not you, Vector! In fact, none of you deserve this kill! You all ought to be embarrassed!" Mephisto shouted, as he deactivated Connor's OMBI with a tap from his own glowing, black bracer. As soon as Connor's OMBI deactivated, the holographic elements of the arena began to disappear into the ground, including all the weapons the older kids were holding. Connor also noticed the green arrow, and the pain it caused, faded away.

"Commander Mephisto tapped out a lizard baby?" Vector yelled out angrily. "What the hell? Who is this stupid hisser anyway?"

"This stupid hisser is the next best commander in the academy," Mephisto said to the stunned crowd, "and he is my brother."

Chapter 4

Here and There

"**Y**ou're the stupid hisser. Who deploys their troops like they are trying to lose?" Connor said with a smile.

The boys shared a quick hug in front of the bewildered crowd. Looking at him, Connor didn't recognize his brother right away. When he had left, Alex was an athletic, lean kid with a mop of brown hair. The person in front of Connor now was a clean-cut man, whose muscular frame betrayed a subtle grace.

"Last time I checked, I won," Alex replied with his own smile that lit up his bright, green eyes, eyes that Connor remembered well.

"Yeah, only because my team sucks. They're a bunch of babies!" Connor retorted.

"I think that's the point." Alex chuckled. "Everyone starts out the same way here–dead. They say that when you're already dead, you've got nothing to lose. Besides, you lizard babies need to be taught to adapt quickly or you will always get beaten this badly. You got lucky."

"How was I lucky?" Connor asked, taking it all in as Alex led him up the ramp toward the red door, leaving the groups of others behind.

"Because you're the only kid to ever start the OMBIcademy alive." Alex grinned as he spoke, "My little gift to you."

Beyond the red doorway, at the end of the arena, Connor and Alex emerged into a hexagon-shaped area with six doors, five red and one white. There were forty chairs around a center island that held a large glowing scoreboard, which stood prominently in the room.

Connor cocked his head as read the scoreboard:

#1: Mephisto: Alex Pereira 1246 Kills / 1 Death
#2: Vertigo: Austin Hughes 723 Kills / 7 Deaths
#3. Slayer: Anthony Ramirez 668 Kills / 19 Deaths

The list showed seven other names followed by impressive scores.

"The list shows the top-ten student battle scores in the OMBIcademy since its formation in 2115," Alex explained.

Alex moved Connor's arm to a slot on the side of the scoreboard and placed the OMBI into it. The screen darkened and read, "New student: Connor Pereira. Enter call-sign…"

Alex entered the word "Raptor" on a virtual keypad. "The graduating class of the OMBIcademy has to show the new kids the ropes. Since my class was the founding class, we've done this every year so far. We always give the kids call-signs instead of letting them pick—it's tradition. Either you earn a respectful title or a humiliating one. Yours is one I've been saving, in case you ever signed up. Normally we give them out during the first week sometime, but you earned yours today with that jump. It means bird of prey."

Connor accepted the compliment with a beaming smile. When Alex pressed "accept" on the keypad, the scoreboard refreshed.

#1: Raptor: Connor Pereira 3 Kills / 0 Deaths.

#2: Mephisto: Alex Pereira 1246 Kills / 1 Death.

#3: Vertigo: Austin Hughes 723 Kills / 7 Deaths

#4. Slaycr: Anthony Ramirez 668 Kills / 20 Deaths

"Some gift!" Connor exclaimed. "All the other kids are going to be gunning for me now!"

The smile on Alex's face disappeared instantly. "Then be better than them, Connor. I know you've got it in you; we have the same genes! You proved that out there."

Connor thought for a moment and said, "I will keep that score perfect. I'm going to make Mom and William proud."

Alex's lip tightened at the mention of their mother.

Connor continued, "If you were the founding class, who got the kill on you?"

Alex's expression changed to one of amusement as he explained, "On the first day, the teachers were our opponents—military officers! The weapons they used were made from wood." Alex unconsciously rubbed a spot on the back of his head.

Connor was about to ask who the teacher was when the door opened from the arena and more kids entered. The kids were paired up, young to old, and the older were explaining various topics to the younger.

He watched as each of the older kids eyed the scoreboard and then look him, some snarling. Clearly the idea of a perfect kill/death ratio on the scoreboard didn't sit right with them at all. It was supposed to be impossible. Connor heard the discontent in the angry mumbling.

"Are they going to be mad at you for that?" Connor asked, pointing to the scoreboard.

Alex laughed. "Probably, but who cares? No one can beat me anyway."

Connor went to follow Alex out of the white door on the far side of the room when he heard a loud wail from the opposite doorway.

"I'm not top ten?!" Vector screamed in his hearty, baritone voice.

The entire room went silent as Vector marched up to the screen and shouted again, "That stupid hisser took Mephisto out of first and me off the board!? I earned that spot!"

Vector locked eyes with Alex and quickly turned his attention to Connor. The room was silent and the air was thick with tension.

After a quiet moment, Connor announced, "Maybe if you weren't a scaly-skinned baby, you would still be on there."

Connor heard Alex let out a resigned sigh from beside him.

The insult was more than Vector could take. His face flushed maroon with anger as he grit his teeth. He closed his hands into fists and rushed full-speed toward Connor, a glint of fury and malice shone from his narrowed eyes. Panic welled up inside of Connor as he braced himself for the charge. His mind quickly played out the scene; he'd wait and jump away at the last moment. Before he could move, he felt Alex's hand on his shoulder as his older brother stepped in front of him, accepting Vector's challenge.

Alex reached out fluidly with his left arm and caught Vector's wrist. The boy's face contorted in agony as Alex turned his momentum to the side and put pressure on his wrist.

Vector stopped cold, his face inches from Connor's with the look of pain etched across his eyes.

"Apologize," Alex said quietly.

"Forget you, hisser! Let me go!" Vector cried out.

Alex applied more pressure. "Apologize to Raptor for making a fool of yourself. He earned his spot."

Alex's declaration didn't make much sense to Connor, but Vector did squeak out an apology. Connor even thought he heard Vector call him, "Sir."

Alex released Vector, who left from the farthest exit within the room without another word to anybody, leaving his new student confused and alone.

"That goes for all of you," Alex said announced to the room. "You will respect the OMBIcademy hierarchy."

The room was stunned and Alex led Connor out the room's white door into the hall beyond.

~ ~ ~

On the opposite side of the Milky Way Galaxy, in the Eagle Nebula, on planet Atmos XI, Adam Malavich stood in a vast cavern, tending to his crops. The atmosphere on Atmos XI was not as friendly to humans as it was on other colonies, with high winds and extreme temperatures part of daily life. The six-hundred and eleven people who lived in Colony XB742 had grown accustom to the harsh conditions, building most of their structures underground, where frozen lakes were turned into potable water. The massive solar energy of the binary star system, combined with the irrigation that the hydrologists provided, gave Adam and his family plenty of resources to grow a multitude of crops.

Adam had been a part of XB742 since the colonization freighter had begun flight preparations back on Earth in 2107. He had gone to school for horticulture and studied harsh climate farming in anticipation of colonization. Being one of the primary providers of food in the colony, Adam had earned a solid reputation and was elected leader fourteen Earth years prior.

They called the planet "Hades" when they first arrived, because the first man off the ship had been incinerated after getting caught out a double-sun, noontime firestorm. The man was the United Earth Defense Force representative assigned to lead colonial growth in the system. Many more would have died, had his reign lasted more than three hours. Adam often thought about that little man, whose undeserved ego could fill the shoes of a man twice his size. It had been fourteen years and Adam still couldn't remember his name.

After moving underground, the people had dismantled their ship, the Argos, to build homes in the large cavern that made up the bulk of the colony. Natural crystalline structures extended down from the ceiling like great stalactites. They glowed brilliantly from the refracted surface light. Today the cavern was bathed in a solid green phosphorescence, indicating that the blue and red stars Atmos XI orbited were both visible in the bright skies above. Adam enjoyed the different colors that the days underground would often take. Rarely was the sky above totally dark and in the various color combinations, Adam's crops thrived.

As he neared the area of his garden, where he was attempting to grow sugar cane, Adam paused to reflect upon all the changes his family had to endure as part of the UEDF's mission. Looking across his subterranean fields toward his home, Adam resolved that it had been worth all the trouble to be away from the UEDF and the oppressive leadership of the Earth Military Council.

"Father!" Adam heard his oldest son call from the other side of the cavern. He watched as the sixteen-year-old boy looped over hay bales and sprinted toward him.

Adam stood up from his stooped position upon Jordan reaching him, and searched his son's eyes for why he had hurried toward him. Sweat glistened from the boy's crimson face, heated from his sprint. His son held up a finger, as he bent over, panting, trying to catch his breath.

"What is it, Jordan?" Adam gently patted his son's back and felt him quiver. "You look exhausted."

"You have to come; the old Argos sensors are acting up. Mom thinks there's another ship in the system!" Jordan explained.

Adam stared at his son, wondering if this was some kind of an elaborate prank to get him to come in for a meal. But after seeing the distressed look in his son's eyes, Adam figured it was likely sincere.

"Let's get back to the house. It's probably just a glitch," Adam said, attempting to hide his concern from his son.

They jogged back to the house where Adam's wife, Melanie, was waiting for them on the front porch. The house had been built only six years prior out of metals from the Argos and stone slabs from the quarry, around one of the giant crystals found in the colony. Adam was fond of the house that he had designed after reading one of the few books that was brought to the colony, *The Integrity of a Building* by William Mercer. Adam loved the natural light that the crystalline portions of his house refracted into the many rooms. Melanie, a former engineer, had even developed a way to focus the crystalline light they had on most days into a metal oven she had built for cooking.

The day's green light only made the lines of worry more apparent upon Melanie's face as she led the way into the house's study, where most of the supplies intended for colony leadership were kept.

Adam looked at the pieces of equipment carefully, trying to remember what he had learned about them all those years ago. He hadn't used them in more than ten years and had long since stopped sending one-way transmissions to Earth.

The data upon the sensor screen taken out of the Argos' navigation core indicated a vessel in the system moving toward them. The system was estimating the vessel's arrival in eight short earth hours.

"I will try to get more information about this ship," Adam said to his concerned wife. "You and the boys gather the people and see if any of them have any kind of weapons."

Melanie's face was pale with worry.

Noticing her concern, Adam added, "Just in case."

Over the hours that followed, Melanie, Jordan, and their youngest son, Abraham, managed to gather nearly five hundred of the colonists. Some carried old Earth firearms and others had weapons modified from the tools of their various trades. Each of them looked distressed, the implications of an unidentified vessel heading toward their home weighing heavily upon them.

~ ~ ~

In the officer's observation lounge that sat above the school's five battle arenas, Major Sanders and Colonel Victor Roden sat quietly observing the events below. Roden was the current head commander of the UEDF OMBIcademy. He was a quiet man, choosing to speak only when it was necessary or relevant. Plagued at a young age with male-pattern baldness, Roden almost always wore an immaculate, red UEDF air beret that marked his rank. He was a career officer and, at the age of sixty-eight, had made a decision to semi-retire by taking a position training recruits at the OMBIcademy. The scowl he wore on his leathery face betrayed his distaste for children. The thought of it almost made Sanders laugh.

"Something amusing, Major?" Roden asked in a gruff voice while sitting at a dark, oak desk in the center of the room.

Major Sanders didn't realize that his mirth was obvious as he replied, "My apologies, sir. Nothing is amusing."

Roden didn't bring the subject back up as he moved toward the window of the observation lounge.

"That one could be a problem. Skilled like his brother and, hell, like his mom, but he has no respect for authority," Roden said in an even tone, pointing down onto the melee field.

Sanders knew who Roden was referring to and thoughtfully added, "Neither Alex nor Marlena respected authority."

Roden responded with a laugh that sounded like a bag of gravel landing on cement. "Indeed," was all he said.

Roden had known Marlena while she was alive and had great respect for her skill, both as a pilot and commander. Roden had been one of the many officers at her funeral.

"According to the preliminary data we received, the council believes that Connor will take to the OMBI training even faster than Alex did," Sanders explained.

"That explains why they recruited him, he could be an asset in this war," Roden stated, as much to himself as to Sanders.

Sanders nodded.

~ ~ ~

Connor hugged Alex as they parted ways in the corridor beyond the scoring room. Alex had promised that he would see Connor again for training before returning to Station Sigma, and that they would have more time to catch up.

"Keep your chin up and watch your back, kid," Alex had said to Connor before departing.

Other kids were beginning to filter into the cold, metallic hallway, which split off in several directions. Nothing was marked or labeled here, so Connor followed Alex's instructions on where to go next by activating his OMBI's only current available function: *Return*.

A blue light appeared on the ground in front of him that stretched ahead and led off around a corner. He could see other kids activating their Return functions, but did not see the lights appear for them. Resolving to figure out that little mystery later, Connor began to follow the illuminated path before him. As he walked through the gray, metal halls, Connor felt very alone for the first time in his life.

He saw other kids wandering around, some that he thought he recognized from earlier that day, but he made no effort to talk to any of them. He was unsure of how they would react to the kid who had not suffered a humiliating death like the rest of them had.

As Connor continued following the blue, holographic line, he took short steps, unsure of what to expect from the OMBIcademy. The thought that he would be there for four years overwhelmed him to the point where tears began to rim his chocolate-brown eyes.

As he crossed a side corridor, he heard the sound of sniffling, which caught his attention. Connor couldn't see who was making the sound at first and asked, "Who's crying down there?"

"Shut up!" a girlish, high-pitched voice replied in an accent Connor couldn't quite place..

"Fine, I won't help you," Connor shot back angrily as he took a step away from the hallway.

"Wait—"

Connor paused.

"Come here."

"No," Connor retorted. Remembering the way the other kids were looking at him in the scoring room, Connor wasn't about to wander off down a dark hallway at the first cry for help.

"If you want my help, you can come out here."

A girl about his age shuffled her way around the corner toward him, her red, curly hair covering her face as she stared down to the floor. She lifted her trembling chin slightly, causing her hair to fall to the side, revealing a set of green, puffy eyes which stared up at his. Her damp, freckled cheeks confirmed she had been crying. He didn't recognize her from the battlefield or score room, and figured it was safe to stay.

"What happened? Did someone hurt you or are you lost?" Connor asked, his tone one of annoyance rather than concern.

"I don't know where to go and I hate this place," the girl whined in an accent that Connor finally placed as Irish.

"I am starting to hate it too," Connor agreed. "What's your name?"

"Amanda."

"Okay, Amanda, did you turn on your OMBI's 'Return' thing?" Connor asked.

"My what's what?"

Connor sighed and took Amanda's wrist, activating the function.

"There," Connor said with a satisfied grin.

"Oh, woah! I can see a blue line," Amanda said with wide eyes. She looked up at Connor and smiled, her once tear-streaked face lit up in appreciation.

"I guess that means we're both on blue team. I think we're supposed to go where it's leading."

"Lead on then…"

"Connor. My name is Connor Pereira."

"Amanda McTaggart, pleased to meet you!"

The two continued down the cold, metal hallway listening to the sounds of their boots echo ahead of them.

"Where are you from?" Connor asked quietly.

"Belfast, in Ireland," she answered. "You?"

"California."

"Oh wow, were you conscripted or did you enroll?"

"I was drafted. You?"

"Aye, drafted."

Connor nodded, expecting that answer. He couldn't fathom any kid, or their parents, signing their childhood away willingly. The two continued down the cold, gray halls at a slow pace, unsure of what to expect at the end of the long, blue path ahead of them.

Chapter 5

Soldiers

The large, blue sea serpent affixed to the door made it easy to identify the Blue Army barracks. The sight of the door also caused the OMBI's *Return* hologram to dissipate. As Connor and Amanda approached the entrance, the door slid aside, allowing their entry.

The barracks were like nothing Connor had ever seen. The common room was octagon shaped with several couches, chairs, and tables placed around the space. In the back of the common room was a kitchen area, where several boys were hanging out, eating chips out of small bags. Doors were evenly spaced around the room, clearly labeled 2123, 2124, 2125, and 2126, the last of which looked new.

Connor began to walk toward the 2126 room when an older boy moved in front of him, blocking his way. The boy had dark hair and deep brown eyes, which he used to glare down at Connor.

"What?" Connor asked with a sense of panic welling up in his chest, afraid he was going to have to fight.

The boy didn't reply, but he continued to stare down at Connor, his upper lip twitching slightly.

From behind Connor, someone shouted, "Blue Army, attention," as the barrack door slid open. Children of all the classes filed in to stand at attention for a dark-haired, older boy in a commander's uniform. Connor did his best to mimic the others around him, standing perfectly still with his arms at his sides.

The commander walked in with an air of authority, stopping to survey new recruits in the room. He took a deep breath and a slight frown etched the corners of his mouth. Connor turned absently to the boy who had blocked his entry, realizing how closely he resembled the commander. When Connor turned his head back, the boy in the commander uniform stared straight at him.

"I am Slayer, Commander of Blue Army, class of 2121 and a 2121 Elite," the boy announced, all the while scrutinizing Connor. "You've been vetted and recruited or joined the UEDF OMBIcademy because you stood out. You were better than the rest. You're going to have a chance to prove it over the next six years."

Ending his short speech, Slayer walked over to Connor. As he moved closer, Connor recognized him as the officer he had landed on in the Arena. The anxiety he felt before grew in his chest as the older boy stopped in front of him. Slayer's eyes bore into Connor's as he stood there without saying a word.

Connor stared back with as much intensity as he could muster.

"My brother," Slayer stated, "was supposed to take my place on the leaderboard when I graduated."

The boy next to Connor looked away, face flushed with embarrassment.

"But it looks like you'll be holding one of the top spots for a while. If you can keep up that perfect score, that is." Slayer's tone was a cross between curiosity and irritation, mixed with what Connor thought might be respect.

The other kids were watching intently as Connor quipped, "Well, perfection does run in my family."

Silence dominated the room while Slayer looked at Connor and grinned slightly.

"We will see, Raptor," Slayer said softly.

"The rest of you need to be taught tactics, combat skills, and how to use your OMBI," Slayer declared. "You will have your first peer battle in one week, which I will supervise before going back to Station Sigma. Older classes, get back to your studies until I have time to give you your new schedules. Any questions?"

Amanda raised her hand slightly.

Slayer looked at her expectantly.

"What's an OMBI, uh, sir?" she said after a moment.

"That is a good question…" Slayer began.

"McTaggart, sir. Amanda McTaggart," she declared proudly.

"McTaggart, the OMBI stands for Omni-Manifold Bracer Implant, and it is your life now. It is a device that syncs your motor reflexes with your brain in order to make you a better soldier. This process takes a few years to complete and it is the reason only intelligent kids are allowed into the OMBIcademy," Slayer explained as if he were reciting from a book.

"The OMBI will be your personal datapad, your arena score tracker, and your weapon arsenal. It will help you upgrade your combat efficiency in melee, ranged, and vehicular combat. But— and I cannot stress this enough—you have to work very hard to earn the points required to unlock its various functions.

"Most of your education will be about how this works," Slayer said, holding out his glowing blue bracer, "and how to work with it. Any other questions?"

"Have you unlocked everything?" Connor asked.

Slayer turned to regard Connor for a moment, before replying, "No."

"Has anyone?"

"Your brother is the closest, at about halfway," Slayer said, the respect evident in his voice.

Connor pressed the issue, "Why would they make something like this, that we can't finish unlocking while we're in school?"

Slayer replied, "If you find out the answer to that, you let me know. We've talked a lot about it and, the best we can figure out is, it's to see what kind of person you are by what choices you make."

"But—"

"Enough! There will be plenty of time for you to figure that out. For now, you need to go familiarize yourself with the basic functions in your barracks," Slayer asserted.

Slayer turned to his brother, whom he called Flayer, while Connor was left to his own thoughts as he walked towards the door marked 2126. The barracks were no more than a bunk room, down a hallway that reminded Connor vaguely of the cell he had been brought into the arena from earlier that day. The ceiling in the barrack was tall, as if to accommodate a larger structure than bunk beds and some foot lockers.

He walked into his barrack to see most of the beds were occupied by other kids who were sitting on them, talking with other kids, and playing on their OMBIs. Connor spotted an available, single bed at the end of the room with the word "Commander" above it. Seeing that no other kids were going to attempt to take the responsibility of that title, Connor took a deep breath and shut his eyes, imagining himself as the best fighter, best pilot, and best commander in the academy. When he opened his eyes, he strode forward to his bunk.

~ ~ ~

Connor was exhausted from the day's battle, but he couldn't resist his OMBI now that he had some idea what it did.

Upon activating the screen, a familiar interface came up with the list of features. Connor noted that the other kids seemed to be staring off into space, until he realized that their holographic displays were only visible to them. The concept confused Connor at first, as he had seen Johnny's display in the battlefield when he touched the other boy's OMBI, and Amanda's, when he had activated her *Return*. Connor made a mental note to give the subject of touch interface some thought later, but for now he delved into his menus.

The main menus appeared as floating icons above Connor's left hand. He used his right hand to select and cycle through them.

"Not so bad, six options here," Connor said to himself as he cycled through the icons.

The crossed swords were an icon Connor knew from the arena that would access his available weaponry. The mail icon seemed obvious enough. The cross-hair icon came up as *Optimization*, which Connor decided to revisit soon. The spaceship icon was labeled *Vehicles*, the numbers were *Score*, and the arrow was the *Return* function that would tell him where to go in the academy.

It wasn't long before Connor realized there was a sub-menu available in most of the features, although most of the functions were still grayed out. Connor's interest drew toward the flashing numbers that indicated his score section, and he decided to start there. *Battle*, *Test*, and *Points* were the available sub-categories that came up for him. Connor selected *Battle* to start, which gave him a visual display, "Raptor, Rank 1, Score 3:0."

Connor smiled and moved on to *Test*, which he skipped after his OMBI informed him in large red words, "YOU HAVE NOT TAKEN ANY TESTS." Irritated by the all-capital letters, Connor moved on to *Points*, He was surprised to see that he had accumulated 7000 points from his victories earlier, and wondered how they were related to ranking. It was difficult to believe he had more points than the older students, so he assumed it didn't have any bearing on ranking.

Confused over what the *points* function meant, Connor looked to the kid in the bunk next to his, a kid whose only remarkable feature was his large glasses.

"Hey, how many points do you have?" Connor asked.

"I don't know," the kid answered, puzzled.

Connor walked over to the kid, grabbed his OMBI, and began to cycle through the menus. *Zero* points. Connor was even more confused.

"Thanks," Connor said as he walked back to his bed.

On a hunch, Connor went back to the *Battle* menu and to the sub menu, *Melee*. *Dagger* was still the only available option, but Connor selected *Spear*, even though it was grayed out and had a lock icon on top of it. Words above the icon appeared and said, "Unlock *Spear* for 1000 Battle Points?" along with a green, 'Yes,' button and a red, 'No,' button.

"Ah, so they unlock stuff. Cool," Connor whispered to himself.

Connor resolved to save his points for now, figuring none of the other kids in his class had any to start with anyway, and decided to explore the other icons in his OMBI. Connor's attention went to the mail icon, which gave him the choice between *Internal* and *External*. Connor started with *Internal*. In the 'To' field, Connor wrote, 'Mephisto,' hoping that the mail would reach his brother. In the message field, Connor wrote, "You suck," and pressed the send button.

Pleased with himself, he selected the external mail option, which brought up a template to draft a letter for family or friends outside the UEDF. Connor filled in the fields.

To: William Mercer
Subject: OMBIcademy
Message: Dear William,

Today is my first day at the OMBIcademy. It is so strange here. Stupid Johnny somehow was allowed to come out here and already tried to rat me out to older kids, but you won't be surprised to hear that I outsmarted him. I also got 3 kills in my first match against 'Elite' older kids and I have the best score in the school, no joke!

Guess what? I saw Alex today! He was my opponent in my first battle and afterwards he gave me a call sign and showed me a few things about the school. My call sign, by the way, is 'Raptor', pretty awesome, right?

So far I have met a few kids, and they seem ok. I really miss being at home and talking to you. But if it's this easy to send you mail, maybe I can write to you some more, so it will be like I never left? Write me back soon!

From – Connor
PS: You suck fish mouth.

Connor thought keeping his first letter light would be a good thing, just to see how it went. Upon hitting send the message was highlighted orange along with the words, "Pending review." Connor assumed the EMC had to censor outgoing mail, to make sure military secrets were not released. Connor toyed with the idea of sending fake emails, with fake military secrets from other kid's OMBIs while they slept, but dismissed the idea. He resolved instead to try to make friends, not enemies.

His thoughts were interrupted by two boys arguing on the other side of the room. The argument appeared to be about who got the top bunk of a particular bed.

"Great," Connor said to himself as he got off his bed and walked toward the two kids.

"What's the problem?" he demanded.

"What does it look like? This hisser wants my bunk!" the taller of the two kids explained.

"It was my bunk first! I set my things down and, when I got back from the toilet, my stuff was on the floor," the other kid whined in what sounded like a South African accent.

"What are your names?" Connor asked quietly.

"Wade. Marshall Wade," the taller boy said.

"Aaron Michaels," the shorter one followed.

"Well...," Connor said slowly, "you both seem to be focused on crap that's not important. Regardless of who is telling me the truth, neither of you has earned a kill in the arena, so neither of you gets a bunk."

Connor didn't feel good about ordering kids to sleep on the hard, metal floor, but he wanted to make sure that whining and complaining were not commonplace in his barracks.

"What?" both boys exclaimed together.

"In fact, that goes for all of you!" Connor said proclaimed. "When you earn a kill, you can pick the bunk you want. Until then, you will all sleep on the floor."

The kids of Blue Army class of 2126 all moaned and began to move their things off the bunks.

"What gives you the right to demand that of us?" Aaron Michaels scoffed.

"I am your commander," Connor said, pointing at the plaque over his bed. "If you can beat my score, you can take over. Until then, you will do what I say."

Bold aggressiveness was not in Connor's nature, but he had heard enough whining from his team. He figured, by giving these kids the impression he was as deserving of respect as his brother, he could convince them to believe it.

To his credit, without exception, the other kids all moved to the floor, taking pillows and blankets off the beds to accommodate themselves. Amanda looked at Connor with a newfound respect. He had shown her compassion in the corridor, but now he had drawn the line between a boy, looking to make friends in a new place, and the commander that he had visualized himself to be.

Looking around at the kids in his barracks, Connor tried to gauge each one for potential.

"Searching for gold—" Connor mused under his breath. Looking at the way Aaron Michaels glared back at him with hatred, he continued, "—but sadly still broke."

~ ~ ~

In the Black Army barracks on the other side of the OMBIcademy, Alex Pereira was going through the motions of introducing the new recruits to their OMBI and its basic functions. Black Army had established a dominating position in the Academy from the day Alex assumed leadership. There had not been a battle since the beginning that Black Army did not win or bring to a draw. Alex Pereira did not play for second best, and he was not interested in soldiers who accepted less.

Alex knew that the first week was critical to the success of his army, since he would have to go back to Station Sigma for the remainder of his education. Alex had always worked directly with the new recruits, identifying the hierarchy that he would put in place before he left.

As Alex continued his instructions on basic weapon functions, his mind wandered to his brother. Connor had performed exceptionally right out of the gate, adapting quickly, and using his head. Alex always thought that Connor would be a good commander, but he was far beyond what he was supposed to be on his first day. Alex mused to himself that, had they been the same age, he probably wouldn't have had as good a battle record.

Alex's OMBI vibrated while he was finishing a lesson, indicating he had new mail.

"Vertigo, take over the introductions, Alex instructed to his second-in-command, Austin Hughes. Austin was a good commander and a good soldier. In the beginning, he had tried to keep up with Alex's score and had, at one time in their first year, almost assumed the role of Black Army commander. In combat, he was almost as good as Alex. Tactically, however, he wasn't even close.

Austin continued the lesson from where Alex left off, having assisted in teaching many times before. Alex left the barracks, into the common room, and sat down at a table to read his message.

—*Message Received*—

"You suck"
Delivered 09:37 2121-02-13
From: Pereira, Connor (Raptor).

Alex's face lit up with a rare smile as he replied.

To: Raptor
Subject: I won

Message: If I suck so badly, how was it I dominated you in the melee arena without a weapon?

—Message Sent

Alex always loved to banter with his little brother. It had been six years since he'd sparred this way against a worthy opponent. Connor was only four when Alex left, but, even so young, Connor was quick-witted and never backed down from a fight. Although he hadn't thought much about his childhood before OMBIcademy, interacting with his brother brought back a lot of great memories of his youth. With the good memories, however, sometimes came the bad.

Connor hadn't yet been born when their dad left. Alex barely remembered the man, but he did remember the day that he didn't come home from the bar. Ethan Pereira had been a hero among the local fire protection service back home. He had earned numerous commendations for bravery, and had designed the 311 Anti-Fire and Medical Robots to assist with fire control and medical response times. Ironically, his design was so efficient that the 311AFMR ended up costing every fire and medical professional their job when the UEDF began mass production.

His father had never been right with himself after putting his friends out of work. While the world was safer, thanks to him, he could never forgive himself for letting his friends down. The money his father had made from his design, was spent trying to help those who had lost their jobs. Eventually, though, his addiction to alcohol took over, and a disconnect formed between him and their family.

Christmas morning, while his mother was seven-months pregnant and on leave from service, Alex awoke to discover his father had not returned from the bar. He would later learn that his father, in his guilt and belief it was for their own good, had abandoned them to join a colonization freighter and had left without a goodbye.

The memory still brought tears to Alex's eyes, which he did not attempt to hide. Alex knew that no one would dare say anything to him about it, especially after he had sent Vector to the infirmary with a broken wrist not an hour before.

It was the following August, when Connor was six months old, that Alex's mom had met William. A year later, they were married. Alex took a long time to warm-up to the man who had adopted him and his brother. Deep down, Alex was afraid to experience the pain of losing a father again. William was always extremely patient with Alex though, and eventually Alex started thinking of him as the big brother that he had never had.

The memories of the few years they had together as a family were some of the best Alex had. They had traveled together to different parts of the world, had designed and built a house together, and always made happiness a priority. When the OMBIcademy had opened in 2115, Alex hadn't considered it for himself, wanting to become a professional athlete. The day the black car arrived and the men in uniform delivered the notice of his mother's death, Alex changed.

Alex, William, and Connor all handled the news differently. Connor had run to his room crying, and didn't eat or drink for two days. William collapsed to his knees and didn't speak or eat for a week; the news had almost killed the man. Alex, tears in his eyes, began looking for retribution within an hour. He signed up for the OMBIcademy, forging William's name as legal guardian. The day after Marlena's funeral, Alex was gone. With hollow goodbyes to his family and fury in his heart, he sought the means to get back at the monsters that had taken his mother away from him.

He didn't know how long he had been sitting there thinking about the past when his OMBI's mail vibration broke his reverie.

MELEE ARENA?! Why was I hit by an arrow then? Your team cheated! Next time fight me when I have both my arms working and we'll see how lucky you are! CHEATERS!
Delivered 10:12 2121-02 13
From: Pereira, Connor (Raptor).

Alex laughed at his brother's ire. It hadn't occurred to him in the arena that his elite team had indeed cheated, although their victory was assured. The things that these kids did for OMBI points never ceased to amaze Alex. The arrow was green, however, and Alex should have known to expect a Green Army soldier to pull something like that. How they cheated would be a mystery for Alex to solve another day.

To: Raptor
Subject: Green Arrow
Message: Green Army always cheats. Slayer should be explaining this to you right now. He is a pretty good commander and will teach you a lot, if he can get over the fact that you crushed him. You might have wounded his ego today a bit by jumping on top of him from that tower, so you better watch yourself. He has some brothers in this school too, and who knows what they will try to do to get back at you.

If he doesn't tell you, remember: Green Army will try to bend the rules to win. Red Army has a reputation for being VERY aggressive; expect them to charge in quickly. Yellow Army is patient and will try to draw you in until the timer runs out in some arenas. Black Army (MY Army) doesn't lose, so the best you can hope for is a tie, you're going to want to be smart and quick to have a chance. Blue Army is known for adapting quickly to changes and typically puts up a good fight, but now that you're in charge I want to see something new!

—Message Sent—

Something on Alex's OMBI caught his eye. He noticed, in addition to his *Return* function, there was an option to *Locate*, as well. Alex selected *Locate* and sent Connor a request to sync OMBI locations. Something about knowing where his brother was made Alex feel better about going back to Station Sigma in a week.

Alex had experienced random unlocking of OMBI features before, but the addition of *Locate* was unexpected. He guessed it was exclusive to family members, but he had no way to be sure. When Connor's acceptance came through, Alex felt at ease. The glowing, black arrow pointed off through the wall, in the direction of Blue Army's barracks, a straight line between them.

Smiling, Alex returned to the class he was supposed to be teaching, and began measuring up his new recruits.

~ ~ ~

Back in Blue Army's class of 2126 barracks, Connor was watching an arrow point back toward his brother with a sense of comfort. The mail conversation with Alex made him happy. He had forgotten how much he missed him.

Connor looked around the room at the kids sitting on the floor and wondered why his battle commander was not teaching them anything. He walked across the cold barrack floor and peeked into the common room. There he saw Slayer, sitting and talking quietly with his brother.

"Hey! Aren't you supposed to be giving us some kind of instruction on what we're supposed to do?" Connor asked, irritated.

"You seem to know how to handle yourself, having the top score and all. Figure it out, genius," Slayer replied, his voice laced with sarcasm.

"Fine then," Connor said to himself, turning back around.

Connor addressed his class, "Since no one is going to bother showing us how to use our equipment, we are going to have to figure it out on our own. Other armies right now are getting all the information they need to kick our butts in the arena. Our expert is sitting around, doing nothing, and wondering why he cannot beat a ten-year-old in the arena." The last part Connor said loud enough for Slayer to hear in the other room.

The kids in Connor's class laughed a bit at Slayer's expense and listened to Connor intently.

"I have figured out how to send mail, how to use weapons, and how the scoring works, but I don't know anything about any of the rest of it. Has anyone figured out anything else?" Connor asked.

The room was quiet at first.

Amanda spoke up, "I don't think anyone has any points to do anything with."

Connor nodded at that. "Well, until we take some tests or start figuring things out, we're not going to get any. We have a battle, I guess, in one week, so let's start talking about what you guys can do."

Connor walked around the room introducing himself to the other thirty-nine kids. He asked about where they came from, what they did there, and how they came to be in the OMBIcademy. He made mental notes on which kids he wanted to start out as officers, and which kids he thought might do better taking orders. At the end of an hour, Connor had the roster in his mind and began figuring out how it would play out.

He made Amanda a lieutenant (not knowing the term he was supposed to use), along with Marshall and Aaron, whom he'd met earlier. They seemed to have strong personalities that Connor thought he might hone. Besides, he was tired of Aaron glaring at him, and thought a little promotion would help make him feel better.

"So when we get into our first battle, we'll break up into four teams of ten, led by me, Amanda, Marshall, and Aaron. Lieutenants, get to know your squads and learn about what they can do."

Connor felt good about taking control of his army and wondered how he would do matched up against another squad. Talking with the nine other kids he had assigned to his lead, Connor started measuring up their abilities. He visualized himself as the best commander in the academy and he was not going to give up on that without trying his best.

Figure it out as he went along, Connor planned out how he was going to make the best army the school had ever seen.

~ ~ ~

As the first week rolled by, Connor frequently had dreams about his mother's death. He would wake up in a cold sweat and almost call out for William, as he had when he was younger. Night after night, he would lie there and think about what he had seen. They were never quite the same, but he always had to watch her die.

The first week of school passed slowly for Connor. Long nights of little sleep left his mind muddled, and the classes on military terminology, history, and equipment were boring. Even among the supposed genius recruits of the OMBIcademy, Connor was a fast learner. Most military history, vehicles, weapons, and equipment were well-known to him, having studied them as a hobby back home. He spent most of the time in his classes trying to figure out different ways to utilize his OBMI.

The teachers were pretty mellow, mostly semi-retired officers who would put on videos and sit back while they played. The videos were the direct curriculum of the EMC and, rather than try to teach the kids anything themselves, the teachers seemed content to let the video do the teaching for them.

It was agonizing to Connor.

Ever since Alex had sent him an unlocked feature, he wondered how he could reproduce the effect. Alex and Connor discussed it briefly one morning in the hallway, and even Alex, after six years, wasn't exactly sure how the OMBI functions worked.

The brothers would meet up as often as they could, ignoring their respective armies, to talk about what had happened over the last few years and also to discuss their childhood. Neither boy talked about their mom very much, only to occasionally remind the other that, "Mom would be proud."

Alex would show Connor a lot of different OMBI functions he was aware of. He said that he preferred to specialize what his squads would unlock to be adaptable, since the battles were always different and changed often. He showed Connor his favorite weapon choices, and what weapon trees he had unlocked over the course of the years. He unlocked a variety of different weapons in each category, as well as many of the optimization features that gave him more information on the battlefield. It was strange to Connor how different his OMBI seemed compared to Alex's.

As the first week ended, the distance and years that had separated the boys seemed as though they'd gone away. They were as close as ever before. Connor wrote William many messages, all of which were still pending review, which made Connor angry every time he looked for an update.

One night, after waking up to a dream about his mom, Connor sat up awake for several minutes, unable to calm down. He wasn't sure why, but, he sent the message:

To: Marlena Mercer
Subject: Hi Mom
Message: I miss you. – Love Connor.

—Send—

Oddly, that message was not labeled "pending" the next day, but rather "sent." Connor figured whoever was monitoring his mother's old accounts would probably delete it. Or maybe it was processed through some computer filter and marked obsolete.

By the time his first battle rolled around, Connor didn't feel ready. He still hadn't spent a single point to unlock anything, even though he figured that it would probably give him an edge. He wanted to rely on his army, who he had been discussing tactics with at length after his conversations with Alex.

He even showed them all a few edge weapon techniques he had learned by looking them up on his OMBI while he wasn't sleeping. Since the dagger was every recruit's starting weapon, being trained on it seemed like a good idea to Connor.

Chapter 6

Blue Army

C onnor awoke on the morning of his seventh day in the OMBIcademy with a sense of dread. It was the day of his first peer-to-peer battle. Unlike the battle on the first day, the students were supposed to earn kills and begin to establish rank. Connor really didn't know what to expect. His first day had been driven by instinct and reaction, while today he would have to work with the team that he had trained.

He did the best that he could with them over the week. But he felt that they were unpolished and he had no idea how the older kids had been training the other armies. Connor was glad for the time he got to spend with Alex and wished that it would never end. Slayer was supposed to be teaching the new kids of the Blue Army. Instead, he would stand in an open doorway watching with his arms folded across his chest, his gaze focused, and features expressionless, offering no help while Connor ordered the new recruits through their exercise and tactic routines.

Connor put the thought out of his mind and took seven deep breaths. Seven deep breaths, a trick that his mom had taught him when he was three, as a way to calm down and get control of his anger. Connor visualized the battlefield as well as he remembered it, thinking about the ramps and structures, the sand beneath his feet. He imagined his team performing well and winning the battle. When he opened his eyes, he felt calm.

As his OMBI vibrated with new mail, Connor casually opened the notification.

"TO: RAPTOR, BLUE ARMY COMMANDER
BLUE ARMY 2126 IS TO REPORT TO ARENA LOBBY AT
0800 FOR BATTLE WITH YELLOW ARMY"

Before closing his OMBI, Connor went back to the mail Alex had sent him on his first day about the different tactics each army was known for.

"Yellow Army is patient and will try to draw you in until the timer runs out …" it read.

Connor wasn't sure what they'd try on the first day, but if they were going to focus on defensive positions to force some reckless decisions, he was not going to give them the chance.

"They want to play chess with me…" Connor said quietly to the dark room, "…I'll just change the game."

Connor activated the barrack's lights at 0600 as usual, waking up the kids who had been sleeping on the floor all week. Connor was dressed in his blue commander uniform before anyone else was awake.

"All right, everybody, wake up! You have five minutes to get dressed and meet me in the hallway for a run to the gym. Twenty-minute workout today, then get cleaned up and ready for battle. If you hurry, you may even have time to eat before we go into battle."

"Who are we fighting?" Marshall Wade asked.

"Yellow, if that matters." Connor replied. "We're gonna kick their butts!"

That brought a smile to Marshall's face and a slight cheer from the rest of Blue Army, everyone except Aaron Michaels, who had been combative toward Connor every step of the way. Connor was still not exactly sure what to do with Aaron. He wasn't a bad lieutenant once he stopped complaining, the problem was the complaining rarely stopped. Connor knew that he was going to have to trust the other kids here to do their part if he was ever going to make something of Blue Army.

Connor ran at the head of his column of soldiers, as he had every morning since his second day. He thought it was good to get them up and working together before anyone else had gotten up. Connor didn't sleep much anyway and he figured that it should seem like it was on purpose.

During their workouts, Connor would have the kids focus on endurance training. A virtual dagger would earn a kill without much strength behind it, but fighting a forty-minute battle in the arena may cause his army to wear out before the fight was over. Connor never saw any of the other 2126 armies working together or working out at the OMBIcademy gym, which made him feel better about his leadership skills. In fact, other than a few groups of kids working out together, Connor never saw other armies doing much of anything together.

By the time 0800 rolled around, Connor's army was ready for their first battle. The door to the arena lobby was closed when Blue Army arrived ten minutes early. A tall man with a shock of gray hair stood in front of the door stoically as if waiting for something.

"Blue Army reporting for battle," Connor said to the man coolly.

The man stepped aside and waved Connor's army through the portal.

The arena lobby was the same that Connor remembered from a week before. Quietly in the center of the room, Connor watched his name flicker above the rest in the first position with his three kills and zero deaths. The other kids noticed it too and while some smiled, feeling reassured that their commander was apparently the best student in the school, others smirked at the scoreboard.

Connor knew he was going to have to go a long way before he would earn all their respect. But he also felt good about his start.

The scoreboard flickered and the red words, "BE SEATED" flashed across the screen in all capital letters. Connor read the message out loud by yelling, "Be seated!" as loud as he could. Making the other kids laugh usually calmed them down.

When the other kids were sitting, Connor himself sat down and the red message faded to a blue screen. The words, "BLUE ARMY" appeared as the room began to shift. Connor felt the room sink slowly like an elevator and then spin clockwise. It was over quickly though, which was good, because it had nauseated Connor a bit.

The screen read, "WAITING FOR YELLOW ARMY," and Connor screamed that out as well. Some of the other kids joined in the reading and laughed out loud at their own enthusiasm.

Blue Army sat waiting for about five minutes. All the while Connor walked around the room, reassuring the other kids that this fight would be fun. He also told his lieutenants to expect Yellow Army to fortify and try to wait them out. He quickly shared a plan he had been devising since he had heard who Blue Army would be battling.

The screen changed once more, reading "MELEE ARENA SELECTED, BATTLE BEGINS IN 10...9..." The countdown seemed slow to Connor, who was used to counting seconds while he was waiting for his classes to end. He activated his OMBI and got ready to select his dagger. He was somewhat re-lieved to see that they would be battling in the melee arena, since he hadn't worked out any tactics for the ranged or vehicle arenas.

When the countdown reached one, the red door nearest Connor opened and a familiar arena lay beyond. The virtual elements had changed, as well as the layout of the structures, but the arena was much the same as Connor remembered it.

Connor proceeded down the ramp at the head of his squad. He motioned to Amanda to take squad 2 up the left side of the arena quickly and to Marshall for squad 3 to quickly move up the right. Connor had to assume that Yellow Army would be attempting to take up fortified positions, so he led his own squad up the center at double speed, running as quietly as they could.

When Connor reached the bottom of the ramp, Aaron and squad 4 followed the plan and began yelling and screaming excitedly at the top of the ramp, proceeding slowly into the arena, making as much noise as they possibly could.

As Connor ran forward, staying low with the nine other kids under his direct command, he produced his glowing blue dagger from his OMBI. The other kids followed his lead as they ran low through a pipe near the center of the arena. Connor could hear Aaron talking loudly, exchanging dialog with some other kids about which buildings they should hide in. It was all part of the ruse, a diversion to blindside Yellow Army before they were ready.

As Connor neared the end of the pipe toward the opposite side of the arena, he saw that it was working. Yellow Army had been moving toward various buildings, but was stopping to listen and adjust their hiding spots to ambush Blue Army as they loudly announced their approach.

Connor never slowed as he came out the exit side of the pipe he was in, walking right into a whole Yellow squad. He noted that they were dressed in similar uniforms, but the only way he could really identify these kids as enemies was the glowing yellow daggers they had protruding from their OMBIs.

Connor put his left hand behind his back, hiding his OMBI as he ran toward the surprised squad. Thinking quickly and three steps ahead of the rest of his own squad, he began to shout.

"Blue Army is advancing, fall back!" Connor shouted at the nearest kid.

Almost all of the scared kids of the Yellow Army squad actually turned to run, and the ones who stared questioningly got a blue dagger jabbed quickly into their chest. Connor himself had earned five kills before anyone else on his squad joined the fray.

With no casualties on his own squad, Connor had effectively eliminated an entire enemy squad. He knew he couldn't keep up the momentum though, as the scoreboard hovering above changed to show Blue Army in the lead. Connor moved forward, hoping to find another surprised Yellow Army squad to dispatch easily.

As Aaron led his advance from the rear of the arena, Marshall met resistance on the right flank in the form of a partially fortified Yellow Army. Amanda fared no better on the left flank, moving into a fully fortified Yellow Army position. Yellow Army had dug in quickly and was gaining advantage on the flanks.

As Aaron's squad joined up with Connor near the center of the field, Connor ordered them to move off to the left flank to outmaneuver the Yellow squad Amanda was fighting.

Aaron didn't move.

"What is your problem?" Connor asked furiously.

"You're going to get all the points while I sit back and get none," Aaron replied, matching Connor's anger.

"Are you kidding? We get points for winning too, idiot!" Connor shot back. Not really sure that was the case, Connor vaguely remember Alex saying something about team points.

"Well you should have told me that!" Aaron cried defiantly.

"Whatever! Just do your job!" Connor shouted, pointing toward a left flank that was making no progress.

Aaron's squad pushed into the left flank with an appetite for battle. Aaron was knocked out quickly after climbing aggressively over a wall into a trio of well-fortified Yellow Army soldiers. Most of Aaron's squad fell shortly after, but the distraction gave Amanda the opportunity she needed to push forward.

Connor shouted, "Squads 2 and 4 join up under Amanda and sweep around the backside of the Arena. Find that other Yellow squad! But be careful!"

Connor looked up at the scoreboard, 32:17 with a countdown of thirty-eight minutes to go.

"Not bad" Connor said under his breath. He held the center of the arena with his full squad, while Marshall and squad 3 were in a stalemate for position on the right flank. Connor knew he had time to wait it out, since there was a missing Yellow squad still out there. Connor was not going to get outmaneuvered.

He didn't end up waiting long as he noticed movement ahead of him. Amanda's large squad had rooted out the missing Yellow squad from a square building structure ahead of his position. They were shifting to intercept and ambush her. Connor tapped the two nearest boys, Toby Jenkins and Liam Butler, on the shoulder.

"You two with me, the rest of you flank that squad attacking squad 3," Connor ordered.

Squad 1 began moving toward squad 3's position on the right flank while Connor, Toby, and Liam moved ahead toward the square structure.

Connor could hear Amanda's squad moving up the left flank toward the building, and knew the ambush would happen soon. Connor motioned Liam and Toby to move low around the left side of the building, while Connor moved around the right himself. Near an opening in the wall, he could hear the quiet countdown of a squad commander preparing for the ambush.

"Five…" the boy said in a whisper.

Connor moved around to the front of the building.

"Four…"

Connor could see Amanda moving quickly with her squad right into the choke point between this building and the wall next to it.

"Three…"

Connor activated his OBMI and selected *Battle: Melee: Fist Weapon.*

"Two…"

'Unlock fist for 500 battle points?' the OMBI read. Connor selected, "Yes" as quickly as the prompt would let him. Connor noted in passing that he had only earned 100 points per kill against Yellow Army as he spent the 500 points he had earned from his first ambush.

"One…"

Connor's glowing dagger disappeared as he selected his fist as his primary weapon. No glow, just like Alex had told him.

Connor ran into the room with a look of terror on his face, as the Yellow Army commander was about to charge forward.

Connor whispered loudly, "They're coming up the other side!"

The few seconds of hesitation cost the squad commander as Connor punched him right in the throat. Connor whirled back around on the other nine kids, who were stunned by the savage act of violence. He began punching kids, pushing away dagger strikes and biding his time, settling into a rhythm of defensive fighting.

It wasn't too long before all Connor could do was block the daggers being thrust his way. But with each passing moment fewer daggers made the attempt as Liam and Toby stabbed the confused Yellow squad kids in the back. When the last Yellow soldier fell, Liam and Toby wore big smiles on their faces.

Connor smiled back at the boys. "Nice one! Saved my butt!"

Liam and Toby grinned at each other as they followed Connor outside where he met up with Amanda.

"One squad to go," Connor said enthusiastically.

Looking at the scoreboard, he realized that it was far less than that. 30:4 with the countdown at around thirty-five minutes.

Amanda flashed a pretty smile at Connor and said, "Spectacular win!"

"It isn't over yet, let's go crush those last guys!" Connor said, smiling back.

The last four members of Yellow Army were fortified in a tower. They were blocking the stairs, looking frantically from the swarm of Blue Army troops to the clock floating quietly above.

Connor noted how few troops it took to block a stairway in this arena, and was a little irritated by the cowardly tactic. Not wanting to rush in and risk losing more troops than he had to, Connor began to think of ways of getting to the second floor of that tower.

Waving to Marshall, Connor asked him to kneel down near the wall that was beneath a window overlooking the field below.

"When I say so, just stand up so I can see what is going on in there," Connor ordered with growing confidence.

Marshall nodded and went down on his hands and knees. With the help of Amanda and Liam, Connor climbed up onto Marshall's shoulders and as Marshall, the tallest kid in Blue Army, stood up, Connor found himself peering into the room above. Of the last four kids in Yellow Army, three were guarding the stairway, swinging their daggers furiously at any one who got close. The fourth kid was standing near the window, looking back at his friends rather than the battlefield.

Connor didn't not waste the opportunity, reaching out with his empty hand and chopping forward into the boy's chest. The kid made a loud cough as he went down hard. The distraction caused the boys at the stairs to lose their position and they retreated into the room.

The Blue Army kids swarmed into the room as Connor got down. The second Connor's feet hit the ground, the virtual elements of the battlefield diminished and the scoreboard read, "BLUE ARMY VICTORY 30:0."

Blue Army cheered loudly. As the stunned kids got up off the ground, they too joined in the celebration. Although Connor did note the sour look on Aaron's face.

Connor went about helping the kids from Yellow Army off the ground and soon Blue Army was following his example. To each kid, Connor said, "Well fought," while looking the kid in the eyes.

Connor wasn't sure who the commander of Yellow Army was, and knew it was about to change due to whoever had the higher score. Connor didn't really care as he headed for the exit to upload his score and thought about the ways he could do it better next time.

Walking up the ramp, exchanging notes with Marshall and Amanda, Connor was feeling like he was on top of the world. The scoreboard update made him swell with pride.

#1: Raptor: Connor Pereira 10 Kills / 0 Deaths

Connor immediately selected his OMBI mail and began to write:

To: Mephisto
Subject: I win
Message: This is too easy. We beat Yellow 30 to 0!

—Message Sent—

With a smile on his face, Connor walked back to his bar-racks, thinking about how proud his brother would be of him, how proud his mother would've been, and how proud his stepfather would be.

~ ~ ~

"The kid shows incredible potential. The brain sync readings to his OMBI are even stronger than his brother's," Major Sanders said to the shadow on the screen.

"I have no doubt about that, Major. It is as I said," the distorted voice replied with an eerie crackling.

Sanders continued, "I am eager to test him on his other abilities as well."

"All in due time. For now, just watch his progress and report back to me."

Sanders hesitated.

"What are you trying to hide?" the voice said as if the dark eyes on the other side of the screen were reading his thoughts.

Sanders shivered at the idea.

"I…" Sanders began with uncharacteristic uneasiness. "It's Connor's stepfather. The man is on the edge. I think that he might do something … rash. We have been blocking Connor's letters…"

"Unblock them," the voice replied coldly.

"I don't think that it's a good idea. If this is going to happen as planned, there cannot be a connection," Sanders said.

"I won't repeat myself. Do as you're ordered." With the level tone hanging in the air, the transmission ended.

Major Sanders was left with his thoughts, sitting in his dark room watching the battle feeds from the school below. He wasn't sure why he couldn't shake the image of a man on the edge of sanity, those cold eyes glaring back with rage and fire.

Hesitantly, Sanders grabbed his datapad and unblocked Connor's letters.

~ ~ ~

Four thousand miles away from the UEDF OMBIcademy, William Mercer sat alone staring at the pages of a book he had stopped reading hours before. The ice in the cup beside him had long since melted as the new message alert on his datapad flashed, interrupting his trance.

William smiled for the first time in the week since Connor had left when the messages popped up from his stepson at the OMBIcademy. William read through each one carefully and smiled as he read Connor's description of his experience and his interaction with his brother. William scribed a quick reply.

To: Connor Pereira
Subject: I knew it
Message: Well of course you have the best score. You are definitely your mother's son. I am surprised you haven't sent pictures of your scores to all the world's newspapers by now.

If you see Alex, tell him I said hi. I am proud of you boys. Home isn't the same since you left, except that it's finally quiet around here. Write me again soon. – William

—*Message Sent*—

William read through Connor's messages two more times before setting his datapad down. Suddenly feeling hungry, William left his study to head for the kitchen. Before he could leave, he caught sight of a light coming from a drawer that was slightly ajar. Opening it, he saw an old datapad he had forgotten about.

It had been a gift he had given his wife, for no particular reason seven years before. William was surprised that the old thing even worked. The light coming off the screen indicated a new message. Curious, William typed in the password and read Connor's message to his mom.

"I miss you. –Love, Connor"

William quietly shut off the datapad and set it back in the drawer. Tears welled at the corners of his eyes and the smile disappeared from his face.

"I miss her too, kid…" William whispered to the darkness as he sat down in a nearby chair, lost in a memory of the woman who had stolen his heart all those years ago.

Chapter 7

Departure

C onnor woke up to his OMBI's messaging system vibrating. The pale-blue light from the clock on the wall read 0400. The message read:

Hey Connor, we are heading back to Sigma this morning. Great job out there yesterday! I knew you had it in you, but you don't need to take so many risks. Forty minutes is a long time, use the clock. Love you bro.
Delivered 0359 2121-02-18
From: Pereira, Alex (Mephisto).

Connor immediately went to the location application on his OMBI. It pointed toward the opposite side of the OMBIcademy. Not bothering to suit up, he ran as fast as he could in his underwear and T-shirt through the empty metallic halls of the academy.

He ran for what seemed like forever. His lungs struggled for air and his legs ached from running without shoes on the hard metal floor. Connor passed through an exit near the arena lobby and out onto a landing strip he'd never been to before. The weather was balmy and the wind had kicked up, but it was warm outside for February. It occurred to Connor just then that the arenas were not outdoors, but simulated outdoor environments. It was the climate control that clued him in.

It also occurred to Connor that he had no idea where in the world the OMBIcademy was, but judging by the February weather he felt like it was tropical. Spotting the shuttle on the far side of the landing strip, he began to run barefooted across the metal runway. Connor recognized the PLS-Thunderbird shuttle as the appropriate vehicle to launch students into space, back to wherever "Station Sigma" was. He had played with a toy Thunderbird a few times and always threw it as high as he could to simulate the rockets working to break orbit.

The older kids hadn't finished boarding the shuttle yet, but they were nearing the end of the line that had formed. Connor caught sight of Alex at the end of the line and ran as fast as his legs could carry him to see his brother.

Alex caught sight of Connor too, and ran to meet him on the runway.

"You're not supposed to be out here for another couple years, you'll get in trouble," Alex said, smiling at his brother.

"Why? They left the door open for me," Connor lied, smiling back at Alex.

"I knew you'd beat Yellow. They always try to play hide and seek instead of war. Nice job though!" Alex said, shouting over the sound of the engines warming up and wind howling.

"It was cool to see you, Alex. Thanks for all your help! I've missed you!"

Alex flashed a boyish smile that reminded Connor of when they were young. He picked his little brother up in a tight bear hug and gave him a hefty squeeze that made Connor grunt.

"I missed you too, kid. You keep your eyes on the ball and write me whenever you want," Alex said, fighting back a tear.

"I will, Alex!" Connor replied, and as an afterthought asked, "Why do they call you Mephisto anyway?"

Alex burst out with a laugh and replied, "Ask your history instructor!"

"Sergeant Mullick?" Connor asked.

"That's the one!" Alex said, putting Connor back on the ground. "I gotta go, kid!"

"Be safe, Alex!" Connor yelled.

Connor waved to Alex and spotted another face he recognized looking back his way.

"Hey, Slayer!" Connor belted out. "Thanks for nothing, you lizard-loving, scale-skinned hisser!"

Slayer yelled something back toward Connor, but it was lost in the noise of the engines. Connor stood back as the Thunderbird took off through the wind, watching as it flew high in the sky through the clouds, until the orange glow of the engines faded from sight.

As Connor walked back toward the OMBIcademy, he felt lonely again. A week with his brother had made him feel whole, like a part of him that had been missing for a long time was back. Now that emptiness in Connor's heart weighed heavily as he moved slowly through the darkness.

The rain began to come down before Connor reached the door he'd earlier rushed through, the weather a cold and harsh reminder that he was now in a place with no family, no one he loved. He imagined how Alex might have felt in his first few weeks at the academy. Surely it had to have been worse for him, so soon after their mom died.

The door was open when Connor got back to it, and an angry-looking guard was glaring at him.

"You're not supposed to be out here," the airman said sternly.

"Then lock the door next time, idiot," Connor quipped back, in no mood for anyone's attitude.

Clearly not used to being talked down to, the airman puffed up and growled at Connor, exclaiming, "It's always locked, brat!"

"Clearly," Connor said sarcastically, walking through the exit back to the halls that were to be his home for the next four years.

Connor didn't give the airman another thought as he wandered through the well-lit metallic corridors, wondering what the next few years were going to be like.

He didn't head back to the Blue Army barracks right away, instead walking a circuitous route near the other army barracks where all was quiet. Other than the airman at the door, Connor hadn't seen another person awake in the entire academy. So he walked until he felt calm enough to try to sleep again. When he finally did, he went back to his bed.

Connor was glad to see he had finally gotten a reply from William, and instead of sleeping he stayed awake reading it. The playful banter between him and his stepfather always made Connor feel better.

~ ~ ~

In an observation room in the halls above where Connor walked, Colonel Victor Roden was also roaming instead of sleeping. He had watched the brothers' touching goodbye on a monitor in his quarters after the system alarm on the landing strip door had caught his attention.

Roden didn't like kids much, but he felt a sense of sympathy for the two boys who had lost their mother so early on in this war. He knew those boys were special, because he knew that their mother - even without the benefit of OMBI technology - was the best pilot to ever fly in the UEDF.

In his heart, Roden still believed in the UEDF's mission to protect the lives of the citizens and colonies. So when he got the alert that colony XB742 "Hades" had been attacked, Roden felt regret that he was not on the front lines anymore. The secure channel would inform him of the attack that was underway, but the news on the holotube would give him different details.

It didn't take long for the news to pick up what was supposed to be classified information. Colonel Roden watched the images of smoking underground structures and the bodies of XB742's citizens lay strewn about the caverns with a sick feeling in his stomach. The news would report twenty-five thousand casualties and total seizure of the resources on Atmos XI.

Never one to let emotions cloud reason, the Head Commander of the OMBIcademy opened his dossier on the colony.

Colony XB742 "Hades"
Location: Atmos XI, Eagle Nebula
Established in 2097
Colonization Freighter Argos: Crew: 7, Colonists: 600.

Without reading further, Roden set the folder down and poured himself a glass of whiskey from a crystal decanter he acquired thirty years prior from his sister who left to become a colonist on Atmos XI.

Comparing the discrepancies between the news report, the secured message he had received, and the dossier, Roden's eyes grew cold and he began to wonder what was really going on.

~ ~ ~

Later that morning, after news had spread throughout the school about the attack, Connor walked somberly to his classes. He'd never been off Earth, but he felt sympathy for the kids who might be trying to fight and watching their parents die. The thought would haunt Connor for the better part of the week.

The only levity came on the day when Connor went to military history class and got to ask Sergeant Mullick about how Alex got the name "Mephisto."

Mullick ignored the question the first time it was asked, but soon all two hundred kids in the classroom were asking him about it.

"Back in 2121, before the OMBI's potential for children was discovered, we started the academy to train intelligent kids how to be leaders and commanders," Mullick explained with an air of pride.

"We didn't have virtual weaponry until later that year, so on the first day the class of 2121 arrived we used wooden weapons to greet them. Mind you, I thought it was a harsh way to bring kids into this school at the time. But orders are orders."

"Alex and a couple of other kids got past the first few teachers and made their way through the grounds of the melee arena before making a run for the exit. I stopped them."

"So you hit my brother with a stick," Connor stated more than asked.

"Well, understand that it was my job. Anyway, Alex did not stay down for long, he stood back up and tried to hit me."

"Tried?" Connor asked, sensing the man's discomfort at the story.

"I guess everyone knows the story. Let me just say that your brother gives as good as he gets, and we both spent the first day of the OMBIcademy in the infirmary with the 311 AFMR stitching up wounds. After that, I gave him the call sign, 'Mephisto.'"

The entire class had a good laugh at Sergeant Mullick's expense, including Mullick himself, who clearly had a lot of admiration for Alex after teaching him for four years.

Connor wanted to hear more stories about his brother, and got in the habit of asking teachers after class what they could tell him about how Alex had done. Most of them had an anecdotal story or two about how Alex would behave in class. Most of his teachers held him in high regard, but all said that he carried with him a lot of weight and worked hard, like he had something to prove to himself.

Appreciative of the encouragement he got from stories of his brother, Connor felt like he could ignore the distance growing between him and the other kids at the school. His mother was a legend in the UEDF and his brother was a prodigy. Connor had big shoes to fill and the other kids seemed to expect him to sprout wings and fly. The older students at the school were especially harsh, always calling his score some kind of a glitch. Most of them didn't know why he was the top-ranked student, but a few Blue Army soldiers were quick to spread the story.

Marshall Wade, who had earned the call sign "Ladder" because he was tall, had helped Connor climb the tower to defeat Yellow Army in their first peer match, and had an uninspired mentor from the class of 2121, would often tell stories of how Connor fought the older kids, even though Marshall wasn't in that fight on their first day.

Toby Jenkins, who was now called, 'Manzar' for no apparent reason, except that it sounded cool, would embellish how Connor single handedly fought off ten kids in Yellow Army with his fists and probably would have beaten them all alone if his squad hadn't come in. This story often earned Connor scowls from the kids in Yellow Army.

Liam Butler, call sign 'Skulls' would back Toby up in the telling of the dominating match between Blue Army and Yellow Army and often change the number from ten to twenty.

All the fame would increase the tension between Aaron Michaels and Connor, to say nothing of the humiliatingly mundane call sign he received: 'Carl.' Connor was never sure if it was one syllable or two.

Amanda the 'Cat' was always there to top the boy's stories of Connor's exploits in the first week with embellishments about his leadership and poise.

Connor's fame was rapidly growing and so was the pressure he felt to perform. He continued into his second week by allowing the kids who had earned their first kill in battle to choose their bunks. About half the kids still were on the floor, but their spirits were high with their crushing victory.

Connor also continued his army's daily workout routine and extra study on tactics and combat. The extra 500 points Blue Army got for winning were quickly spent by most of the kids on nominal upgrades. Connor saved his.

By the end of the second week Connor knew he had enemies and fans, but also that he might never have any real friends here. With his next match approaching, Connor focused more on trying to find the good in the talent that he had, especially from what he had seen in the arena.

On the morning of his second match, Connor received the notice:

"**TO:** RAPTOR, BLUE ARMY COMMANDER
BLUE ARMY 2126 IS TO REPORT TO ARENA LOBBY AT
1000 FOR BATTLE WITH RED ARMY"

Connor smiled at the thought of battling his one friend at the OMBIcademy that he had known prior to his military career.

He hadn't seen Johnny at all since their first day, and was wondering how he was doing. Mostly though, Connor wanted a chance to beat him for what he did on their first day.

With extra time in the morning, Connor used the common room of the Blue Army barracks to run some formations with his commanders. Despite not getting a kill in their first match, Connor left Aaron 'Carl' Michaels as the leader of squad 4, figuring he had performed well in the opening match until he got knifed rushing over a wall.

Carl had been combative with Connor since the match, not satisfied with his 500 points for the win and irritated that he still didn't have a bunk. Connor wasn't sure how to handle him just yet, but he figured that as long as he kept Carl close, he could at least temper the damage done to Blue Army.

After their morning workout, breakfast, and suiting up, Connor led his troops down the hallway toward the arena lobby. With a few minutes to kill, Connor worked out last minute strategies his lieutenants.

"It occurs to me that we have not done anything but melee so far, so this might be ranged. One of the older kids mentioned something about vehicles that I overheard, but when I asked him about it, he said it was for grownups, not babies." Connor said the last part with a sneer.

"My OMBI only lets me access 'bow' for ranged," Cat said quickly. The name Cat suited Amanda pretty well, Connor thought while nodding along. She was quick on her feet and moved with a subtle grace that hinted at some form of practiced balance.

"So it looks like we have bows, any ideas?" Connor asked quietly.

Carl responded sarcastically by asking, "Aren't you supposed to be the commander?"

Connor ignored the impertinent question and looked to Ladder for an answer.

Ladder was wearing his title well, standing a head taller than Connor, who was the second tallest kid in Blue Army.

"We could volley when we get in there," Ladder said thoughtfully.

Connor was nodding his agreement before Ladder had finished.

"That's a good idea, but they will probably think of it too. Red Army is supposed to be extremely aggressive, so they might try to close the distance quickly. So squads one and four, let's aim long and try to hit them when they come out. Squads two and three, close some distance and try to take some high ground for the ranged battle. If we end up in in the melee arena again, we'll go back to our standard tactic." Connor spoke quickly to his team, laying out plans before the battle began.

The wheels in his head were spinning while the arena lobby spun to where the battle would begin. As with Yellow Army, Blue Army had to wait for Red Army to get in place for a couple of minutes.

Looking around the room, Carl caught Connor's eye. It was rare to see that boy smile, but he wore a devilish grin on his face while he looked back at Connor.

The uneasiness of the exchange passed as scoreboard lit up that they would indeed be fighting in the ranged arena. Excitement welled up in Connor and he was eager to see how he adapted to a new army in a new arena.

When the door opened, Connor's plans changed. This arena was nothing like the melee arena, which had the feel of a coliseum from the Roman Empire. The ranged arena ramp looked like something out of a story about ancient China. A vast wall with various ramps and stairways marked the center of the arena.

Each side also possessed a tower near the back corner, holding what looked like a flag at the top.

Confirming Connor's thought, the scoreboard floating silently above the arena read, "Capture the flag." Adapting immediately, Connor began to yell out orders.

"Cat, squad 2 volleys then take the wall up high, left flank. Hold it!"

Cat nodded and moved her squad into position for a volley over the wall before charging forward.

"Carl, squad 4 defends the tower and the flag!"

Not waiting to see what complaint Carl would come up with, Connor moved to squad 3.

"Ladder, volley over the wall a few times then head up behind Cat and move across the wall." Ladder nodded along and moved off with his squad.

The volleys went out successfully, scoreboard showing three kills from the early attack. The expected return volley never came and Connor wondered what Red Army's commander was thinking.

Connor held squad 1 back to evaluate where he was needed but kept them firing volleys over the wall to keep the pressure on Red Army. Cat met resistance near the top of the ramp leading to the left flank of the wall but, to her credit, held her ground without giving up any soldiers or her position. Ladder moved up behind her and began firing across to the right flank where Red Army soldiers had begun taking the wall.

"Squad 4, suppress the left flank!" Connor cried out as he led squad 1 to cover at the base of the wall, where slight overhangs offered protection from arrow fire from above.

Looking up at the scoreboard, Connor was shocked.

31:37 Time Remaining: 36 Minutes.

Confused as to where he had lost nine soldiers, Connor looked back to the tower where Carl was standing alone smiling back at Connor.

"What did you do?" Connor yelled.

"Ha! I got myself some points!" Carl yelled back angrily.

"What? How? You can't team kill!" Connor stated while looking at Manzar next to him to verify. He only shrugged.

Carl ducked back inside the tower as troops from Red Army poured down the back of the ramp into the tower while laying down fire toward squad 1. An entire Red Army squad had moved into Blue Army's base, and another began trying to move around the back side of the arena to flank Cat and Ladder.

Pinned down and losing his position fast, Connor started to get angry.

"These kids can't be good with stupid arrows yet ... When I say go, run around the corner and up the ramp. If any Red Army kid gets in your way, hit him!" Connor said to Manzar and Skulls, who had both learned to trust their leader in the last fight that they had.

"Squad 1, get to the top of that wall and then start shooting the kids you knocked down and everyone else. I am going to stop this crap," Connor said confidently. "Go!"

The kids moved quickly, trying to dodge the virtual arrows as they came in. A few of the boys took hits on their arms as they reached out to block arrows that would have otherwise incapacitated them. Connor noted that it would be impossible to fire back for those kids and made a mental note to include a "human shield" element in future ranged battles.

Connor went to work on his OMBI, selecting armor first, followed by right arm - unlock 500 points. He selected "yes" as fast as his OMBI would let him. Connor bypassed the early ranged weapons and went to firearm, which unlocked at 3,000 points. Connor grimaced, not really wanting to spend that much on anything so early, but a bow and arrow wouldn't do, not now.

With firearms unlocked, Connor saw an assortment of options light up his screen for him to purchase. Irritated that he had spent 3,000 points to unlock the potential of having a firearm, Connor selected the first weapon the list: 92FS 9MM. William had that gun in his collection, Connor had shot it before and knew it well.

As the weapon appeared in Connor's left hand, he focused on what he had to do. Connor had always been a good shot, but he had never tried shooting while dodging arrows.

Steadying himself with a deep breath, Connor quickly visualized himself turning this fight around. Already, one Red Army squad was almost in position behind Cat and Ladder, and squad 1 was getting pinned down on the stairs.

"First thing's first," Connor said to himself as he bolted across the grassy ground toward the tower that housed his flag. He ran full speed, dodging arrows from the sides and above as quickly as he could. It wasn't too hard; the glowing red arrows stood out to Connor and he could see where they would be going just as they were being shot.

Running the serpentine pattern that had served him in the opening match against the older kids, Connor entered the tower to find himself face to face with a very surprised-looking Johnny, who was holding the Blue Army flag in his hands.

"Uh, Connor…" was all Johnny managed to sputter out before Connor blasted him in the face with a virtual bullet. Johnny fell stunned to the ground and the squad that had followed him in fell back on their heels.

Connor pushed forward, firing the glowing blue gun as fast as it would let him, hitting arms and legs as much as bodies or heads. The kids in Red Army couldn't ready their bows fast enough before Connor was there with a barrage of glowing blue bullets.

Connor thought he might turn the fight around right there until Carl came down the stairs. Unable to do any damage to his teammate, Connor kept the pressure on the Red Army soldiers, who were scrambling to take cover behind anything they could find. One got behind Carl and tried to use him as a shield from Connor's bullets.

The kid readied and arrow and let it fly at Connor's head. Acting on instinct, Connor threw his right arm into the arrow's path, deflecting it harmlessly away. He felt the armor fade away with the strike, but was grateful for it. Not hesitating, he ran forward toward Carl before the Red Army soldier could ready another arrow.

"You cheater!" Carl screamed as Connor closed the gap.

Connor didn't bother with a reply as he punched Carl in the face as hard as he could. Carl fell down bleeding and screaming as Connor used his virtual firearm to finish off the rest of the kids in the room.

After trying to return the flag - only to discover it was intangible to him - Connor moved upstairs and surveyed the scene below him. Cat and Ladder had both been stunned and the remnant of their squads, some five kids, were pinned down from two sides. Squad 1 had fared better, actually physically punching more kids than they were stunning with arrows. Connor did note that Skulls was following up and stunning the kids that they put down while dodging fire from above and on the sides.

Connor steadied himself and began picking his targets in the group that had come in behind squads 2 and 3. It didn't take long, the pistol easily overpowering the arrows. Red Army didn't even know what was happening as Connor removed them one after the other from the fight.

When Red Army had been cleared from his side of the wall, Connor noted that the scoreboard showed thirty-two minutes remaining and only three Red Army troops. Blue Army had eight kids active, of which three could still shoot arrows.

Leading what was left of his army around to the enemy tower, Connor figured out why Red Army had any troops left at all. Two had been hit in the legs in the initial volley and were stuck on the battlefield in front of their ramp, and another one had taken an arrow in both arms and was hiding near his flag. Connor let his team finish those kids off for the points while he grabbed the red flag.

With plenty of time to kill, Connor walked slowly back toward his tower. He didn't want to leave Blue Army stunned on the ground any longer than they had to, but he wanted Johnny and Carl to know that they had failed in their plan to betray him for an easy win.

Arriving back in Blue Army's tower, Connor stopped in front of a quite stunned Johnny and waved the red flag back and forth over his face.

"It was a nice try for an easy win, but you forgot that I will always beat you, no matter how hard you try or cheat. Idiot," Connor said with a snort. The kids behind Connor laughed as well. Carl was still unconscious and Connor noted that he had bruises forming under both eyes from getting punched in his face.

Connor thought about kicking dirt in their faces or doing equally torturous things to them for the next thirty minutes, but he was eager to get out of the arena. He carried the red flag up the stairs and onto the podium, setting the flag down and ending the match. The virtual weaponry dissipated along with the visual effects along the wall and towers.

Connor could hear Johnny complaining before he even got back down the stairs.

"You had way too many points! You had a gun! It wasn't fair!" Johnny whined.

Connor walked up directly in front of him and pushed him to the ground. Johnny fell on his butt and stared back up at an angry-looking Connor.

"I had points because I'm awesome. You try to cheat, and you're still going to lose," Connor declared.

"Well don't tell anybody what I did," Johnny said with a hint of anger.

"I'm sure they'll all know eventually. Hard to keep secrets when eighty kids all know you're a fraud," Connor replied with a smile.

Blue Army cheered for Connor as he exited the tower. Asking around, he found out that Carl had pushed the other kids in his squad into oncoming arrows.

Connor marched out of the arena, followed by Cat, Ladder, Manzar, and Skulls close behind. Carl would awake some time later in the infirmary.

As Connor uploaded his score, he smiled at his continued perfect record that was growing more quickly than he had thought it would. 30 kills, 0 deaths. With his army performing well and gaining confidence in his own abilities, Connor walked out of the lobby looking for the head commander's office.

~ ~ ~

With his OMBI guiding him to the doors that led to the upper levels, Connor didn't have a hard time finding Colonel Roden's observation lounge. He was surprised that none of the doors were restricted on this level as he marched in to find himself standing face to face with the imposing figure of Victor Roden.

After a few moments of shock that a student was in his lounge, Roden spoke gruffly, "Well?"

"Sir, I am…" Connor began.

"I know who you are, Pereira. What do you want?" Roden barked.

"I want a transfer of one of my soldiers," Connor said with an irritated edge in his voice.

"No," Roden said simply.

"Sir, he betrayed his army and ought to be thrown out of the academy. Unless traitors are something you want?" Connor asked, thinking he had the found a way to convince the man.

"I saw the whole thing. You handled it, just like your brother did in the same situation," Roden said forcefully.

"I'm not going to argue with you. Transfer him or he will be living in the infirmary for the next six years," Connor said in no uncertain terms.

Roden could hardly believe that a ten-year-old kid was talking to him this way, with such fire. The colonel just laughed.

"So much like your mother. Now get out of here," Roden said after the moment of nostalgia had passed.

Connor shrugged, accepting that he may have to hospitalize a kid day after day if that is what this head commander wanted. Not satisfied by the exchange at all, Connor walked quickly back to his barracks to figure out a squad 4 lieutenant replacement.

~ ~ ~

After the boy left and Roden had stopped laughing, he said out loud, "That kid has some spirit."

Sanders, who had been standing quietly in the corner through the whole exchange, nodded his agreement.

"He really might hospitalize that kid, you know," Sanders said quietly.

"I think that he might," Roden said. "Maybe that's how to deal with traitors."

Sanders stiffened at the statement.

"Sanders?" Roden said, suddenly very serious.

"Sir?" Sanders said passively.

"Who the hell is responsible for the door locks in this place?"

Chapter 8

Opening Doors

After talking with Manzar and Skulls, Connor decided to put them both in charge of squads. Rather than four ten-man squads with a commander and four officers, he created three nine-man squads and one eight-man squad, which went to squad 2; Cat's squad, with Connor in charge; and three bodyguards to carry messages and perform special tasks.

Connor knew he couldn't count on Carl to be of any help and actually believed he might have to keep him in the infirmary, rather than have a traitor on his team. He also let Cat, Ladder, Manzar, and Skulls take over the majority of the leadership of daily combat and physical training for their squads.

Connor focused his attention on group formations, specializations for OMBI upgrades, and working on the personal combat skills of his bodyguards. For the guards, he chose the soldier with the highest score from each squad. He represented squad 1 himself.

He knew those soldiers to be loyal so far and would work on developing a rapport with them as he had with his officers.

After their morning routine and breakfast, before classes began, Connor sat down with his three guards.

"I am thinking, spears for melee. I see a lot of kids unlocking longer daggers, swords, or double weapons. I don't see a melee weapon available that would be better than a spear if we get good at it," Connor said thoughtfully.

Tim Sanz, call sign Dice, who had already earned seven kills in their first two peer battles, nodded his agreement. He was a quiet boy who wore a buzz cut like he was a seasoned veteran. Tim had come from Southern California and was admittedly incredibly smart. Connor thought that Tim might be a good person to share ideas about tactics with, except that he rarely gave feedback other than nodding along or shaking his head. Taciturn people still annoyed Connor.

Connor's second bodyguard, Wade Winchester, call sign Hunter. spoke so quietly that Connor had to lean in to hear him. He spoke like he didn't intend anyone to hear him and his eyes never quite met Connor's. For such a good soldier, Wade was oddly timid. Connor had assumed by his accent that Wade was from the Southern United States, so he didn't bother asking where Wade was from. Connor resolved to work on Wade's self-esteem with him when he got the time. After two peer battles Wade was one of only two kids left to only have died in the opening battle with the older kids.

The other was Jinn Matsui, a Japanese native whose call sign of Katana seemed to fit his character. Jinn was not as timid as the other two boys Connor had chosen as bodyguards, and spoke his mind frequently. He was easily the shortest kid in Connor's army, but fierce in combat. Whenever they talked about a battle, Jinn's brown eyes flashed with an edge of excitement, and Connor believed he would never back down from a fight.

With all four in agreement, the three bodyguards unlocked their spears at the same time. Connor would come to find out that the three had sworn an oath that day that they would never allow their commander to get killed in the arena or hurt outside of the arena. As such, they followed him around the OMBIcademy, taking the bodyguard role seriously.

On the Wednesday before Blue Army's third battle, Connor and Wade passed down the corridor where Connor met Cat on his first day, and heard what sounded like fighting. They discovered an unlabeled door around a corner that he had never seen before.

"Wade, have you ever been here?" Connor asked, expecting that the answer was no.

Wade mumbled his reply, "No, I don't think so."

Connor nodded and moved his hand to open the door. As it slid open, Connor saw ten boys wearing Black Army uniforms practicing in this room with their virtual weaponry.

The room was dark, like the boys were standing out in space, complete with stars in all directions. The floor's soft white glow was enough to make Connor feel like he had stable footing. Clearly the virtual elements in this room were designed to make one feel disoriented.

The boys saw Connor too and smiled at each other as he walked through the door.

"I didn't know we could practice in here with our OMBIs," Connor said to one of the boys, whose thin mustache and height suggested to Connor that he was an older kid at the school.

"Yeah, Capretto, these rooms are all over the school, but you need to unlock them before you can come in," said the boy with the mustache and a mop of black hair, in what sounded like a heavy Italian accent.

"Well, how do you unlock them?" Connor asked, curious as the older boys walked his direction.

"You're Mephisto's brother, aren't you? Heard about you. They say you're good," the boy said, crossing the room with a measured stride.

"That's right. I'm Raptor and I'm the best one at this academy," Connor said smugly.

Connor's tone put the older boy on his heels.

"I like that, a lot of confidence. I'm Gladiator, Commander of Black Army 2123," the boy said with a smile. "I'd teach you a lesson about talking back to your elders, but your brother ordered Black Army to leave you alone if we saw you."

Annoyed a little, Connor asked Gladiator again, "So how do I unlock training rooms?"

Gladiator and the other boys shared a laugh and Connor's irritation grew.

"I'll tell you what, Capretto, you spar with me for a minute and I will tell you how."

"Fine, but don't cry when I beat you," Connor quipped.

Wade touched Connor on the shoulder and said softly, "I don't think this is a good idea, Commander. This guy is way older than you and a Black Army commander!"

"So what?" Connor asked, like nothing Hunter was saying mattered.

"Just be careful, he probably has a lot of weapons unlocked and a lot more kills than we do," Hunter said in his thick southern accent, his voice betraying his concern.

Despite the growing feeling of dread at the idea of fighting a kid four years older than him, Connor was touched by Hunter's genuine concern. Were their situations different, Connor might have been friends with Wade.

"You ready, Capretto?" Gladiator asked, squaring off on the opposite side of the training room.

The other boys from Black Army moved out, leaning against the walls, curious to see how their commander would fare against a little kid. They didn't seem to think much of Connor, regardless of whose brother he was.

"Go wait with those other kids. See if you can find out anything useful about Black Army or any tricks that might help us," Connor said to Wade quietly.

Wade walked over to stand next to the older kids. Next to them, one of Connor's best soldiers looked like a little kid. Connor wondered how he looked going up against this boy with a mustache.

Connor closed his eyes for a moment and took several deep breaths. He thought about the times he and William had played together. When Connor was younger, before bed every night, William would chase him through the house either pretending to be a robot that had gone out of control or a zombie that wouldn't die. The scariest times were when they had no "safe zone," which was normally Connor's bed, and Connor would have to run, dodge, duck, and figure out ways to get away from a much faster, larger, and unstoppable opponent.

The memory brought a smile to Connor's face while he steadied himself. Looking back, it had obviously been a trick to get Connor to go to bed on time, but as Connor got better at evading an adult trying to catch him, he could almost play that game all night.

Feeling calm again, Connor visualized fighting this opponent and winning. He imagined how good it would feel to take down a much larger, imposing enemy. When Connor opened his eyes again, he felt relaxed and eager to begin.

"I'm ready, but I have to warn you, on my first day I took out three elites who were all older than you," Connor said with a confident smile.

Gladiator smiled back, not the cocky smile he had been wearing when he had challenged Connor, but a smile masking a re-evaluation. Connor knew he would not be underestimated much in this fight and thought that maybe he shouldn't have reminded this kid that he had already beaten older, better kids on his first day.

"Melee then?" Gladiator said, producing a rapier blade from his OMBI.

Connor noticed that Gladiator hadn't selected anything from his device, but rather swung his arm out and the blade appeared. Resolving to figure out that trick later, Connor considered his available weapons: dagger or fist. Selecting fist, Connor settled back into the martial arts stance he had learned from William when he was seven.

William had taught Connor that stance and how to throw a punch because a kid had been stealing Connor's lunch at school. Connor always appreciated that his stepfather was an advocate of appropriate violence.

"Begin!" Gladiator said in his thick Italian accent.

He came forward quickly, thrusting with his glowing black rapier several times in rapid succession, attempting to score a clean, quick kill.

Taking a few quick steps backwards, Connor's mind was whirling, trying to figure out how he would get close enough to Gladiator to score a hit, let alone a kill.

Connor ran out of room quickly, nearing the wall where he had entered the practice room. His mind raced looking for openings that weren't there. Twice Connor had to use his left hand to deflect the quick weapon that Gladiator was using so fluidly.

It was obvious to the spectators that Gladiator intended to toy with Connor for a while, coming in hard then backing off to dance around and perform slight flourishes with his blade.

A thought came to Connor watching the fluid dance between the weapon and the Black Army commander who wielded it. They seemed as one, the blade an extension of the arm of the boy who thrust it toward Connor.

"Like a snake," Connor said out loud, which caused a crease of confusion on the brow of the boy who was attacking him.

Connor slowed and stumbled backwards against the wall, feigning overbalance. Gladiator moved quickly, stabbing out toward Connor's head. Connor ducked quickly, bringing his left hand up in a hard chop against the wrist of the longer-armed boy.

Shocked that he had gotten hit, Gladiator took several quick steps backwards and grinned at Connor, looking at his own wrist.

"Bene, Raptor," Gladiator said, whipping his rapier back out in front.

Equally shocked, Connor asked, "Isn't your arm supposed to be disabled?" The worry was evident on Connor's face.

"Any commander worth his salt knows to buy some armor upgrades," Gladiator quipped back with a broad smile forming on his face.

Connor turned to his left as if he were going to try to run, Gladiator moved in for the finishing blow. The thrust came at a downward arc toward Connor's heart. Connor's wry smile caused Gladiator to hesitate slightly, but he was committed to his killing blow.

Gladiator knew he had fallen for a tiered ruse as Connor's armored right arm blocked his swing. Connor's left hand came up quickly with an open-handed chop to Gladiator's wrist, disabling the arm that Connor proceeded to grab, before pulling Gladiator down hard into a rapid succession of jabs to the face and chest.

The hits weren't hard enough to cause any physical damage to the Italian's fair skin, but they were enough to disable his OMBI and end the sparring match.

The other boys from Black Army ran over to de-stun their commander as Connor leaned back against the wall, exhausted. The whole fight had taken less than a minute, but he felt like he had been tense the entire time. Wade ran over to where Connor was with a large smile on his face.

"Y'all roped him in twice! That was awesome Connor!" Wade said, forgetting that he was addressing his commander.

Connor let the lapse slide, feeling like this kid was more of a friend at the moment.

"Well, you know what they say, right?" Connor asked.

"What's that … uhh, sir?" Wade replied, toning back his excitement.

"Any commander worth his salt buys some armor," Connor said in his best version of Gladiator's Italian accent.

Connor noticed his OMBI vibrating while he shared in a laugh with Wade. Connor's smile grew as he read the words across the display field.

+3000 Points, mutual combat, 2123 Officer

Showing Wade, Connor wondered aloud, "I guess we get points for a lot of different things; too bad it doesn't count toward my kills."

"Supposin' those are only for bona fide battle kills," Wade replied.

"They are," Gladiator said, getting up from the floor, revived by his teammates.

The other kids from Black Army stood back like they didn't know what to say or do. Clearly they had expected Gladiator to defeat Connor without much effort. The thought made Connor's smile even bigger.

"Maybe next time, if you bring some friends it will be fair?" Connor retorted.

Gladiator smirked as he replied, "Don't get cocky, Capretto. You have your brother's blood, no doubt. I may have underestimated you, but don't think you will always be so lucky."

Connor nodded soberly, admitting that Gladiator was probably right. The fight could have easily gone the other way, had the older boy not underestimated Connor's OMBI upgrades.

"About those doors, Gladiator?" Connor asked, wanting to bring his army in for some training as soon as possible.

"Your brother calls me Jose, I think you can too," Gladiator said with a smile.

"Okay, Jose, I'm Connor."

"Well met, Connor," Jose said with a flourish. "The doors, as you know, stay locked except for some. Mostly commanders' OMBI are given access. I didn't get mine for three years."

"Well, how do I get access?" Connor asked curiously.

"Ah, Capretto, you entered this room, no? Your brother always had higher level of clearance than anyone else; maybe you do too?" Jose said with a questioning look on his face.

"Well this was a big waste of time." Connor said, turning his back on a frowning Jose and his 2123 Black Army squad.

Connor walked out of the room back into the hallway with Wade, who couldn't contain his smile. Pulling up his OMBI's search function, Connor identified two training rooms near Blue Army's barracks and began to walk in their direction purposefully.

When Connor reached the door of the nearer of the two training rooms, he asked Wade to attempt to open the door. Try as he might, Wade could not get the door to budge.

"Move back," Connor ordered as he walked up to the door.

As Connor's hand touched it, the door slid open to reveal a Japanese-style dojo that looked like the one that Connor had in his yard back in Healdsburg, except this one was set out in the countryside somewhere in the middle of rolling green hills. The virtual environment was humid and cool, complete with the sounds of birds chirping outside. Grinning from ear to ear, Connor set off to find the other Blue Army training room.

Opening the door, Connor's jaw dropped. The virtual environment before him looked like an 1800's Spanish warship with boarding planks across to a British Galleon. The environment was huge, and Connor nearly fell due to the motion of the ship's moving in the water.

"This seems like a pretty massive room to hide right next to our barracks without us knowing about it!" Connor said to Wade, who was still standing with his mouth agape.

The sound of gulls crying in the air above and waves crashing against the side of the ship made Connor feel as though he were really at sea.

"We're going to have to start practicing in here. Since we can use our OMBIs, it will be a lot easier to work on stuff," Connor said to Wade, who was staring over the railing of the ship into the ocean below.

"What … what if we fall off?" Wade asked, clearly not feeling at home upon the ocean.

"I don't know, but I bet we'll find out sooner or later." Connor said with a big smile on his face.

"Hopefully later," Wade replied, walking back toward the door to the hallway next to the Blue Army barracks.

~ ~ ~

"A new room was discovered, by a ten-year-old," Roden reported via the video chat window to the UEDF Academy Oversight Committee. While his report was streamed lived to the committee members, their responses came back as text. He never liked communicating with the anonymous committee. Their user names always changed, so he never knew if he was addressing a superior officer or a scientist.

"Another one; how many training rooms is that now?" replied username: AOC3.

"That makes eleven now, Sir," Roden replied with an air of confidence, unsure if he was addressing a man or a woman.

"Understood, Colonel, as long as they are unlocking virtual environment training rooms, our consensus is that limited restriction is still required. Nothing grows in a vacuum, Colonel."
– AOC1

Roden watched the discussion between the ten anonymous members of the advisory board for a few more minutes while waiting for the conversation to end. He had been reporting weekly since the decision to attach an OMBI to the first boy back in 2121.

Since then, he had witnessed a lot of strange things at the OMBIcademy but only reported on the events that he had been asked to. New rooms at the academy were a big deal to the AOC, even if they were virtual environments for training. They always acted like they were surprised to hear that something had changed in the school, as if they didn't know what they had built here.

The bureaucratic speeches and addendums went on for several more minutes while Roden watched the screen. He had decided to not report on the fact that apparently Connor Pereira was able to open every door in the school, regardless of its access level. Roden actually kind of liked the kid and didn't want to see him turn into a pincushion for a scientist any time soon.

When the report session had ended, Roden sat staring at his datapad screen for a long time wondering what it meant. The kid had fire like his mother and his brother before him had been a prodigy in unlocking the potential of the OMBI devices, but Connor had seemed unaware of his growing abilities with his bracer. He had unlocked at least one feature that had never been unlocked before in his first week and now was unlocking doors at the school.

Roden pondered quietly in his observation room on the subject well into the night.

Chapter 9

Changes

A lex spent most of the week-long trip back to Station Sigma thinking about his family, his brother in particular. He hadn't thought much about his childhood since enlisting himself into the OMBIcademy, often focusing on the road ahead rather than the one behind. Spending time with Connor, however, had forced him to think about how much things had changed for them. Connor had grown up a lot. He was surely smarter than Alex remembered him, but his temper and the direct way he described his feelings were something Alex remembered very well.

Marlena had also had a hot temper. Alex had been one of the few people capable of cooling her off. All it took for him was a smile and a joke. Alex had thought about his mom a lot, but never much about the memories that he had of her. He didn't smile or joke very much anymore, except when he had been talking with Connor. His brother's nature seemed to lighten the load that Alex carried somehow. It reminded him of simpler times.

As the PLS-Thunderbird began its docking procedure with Station Sigma, Alex opened his OMBI's messaging application and began to write:

To: William Mercer
Subject: Thank you
Message: Hi William. Sorry it's been so long since I wrote you a letter. Pretty busy being a commander, saving the galaxy and all that. I spent the week before last with Connor and he has really grown! You did a great job raising him. I think Mom would be happy about that. I know I never said it, but thank you. – Alex

—Message Sent—

Alex was surprised to see that the letter was sent immediately rather than stuck pending like it usually was. It used to take two to three weeks before Alex's letters would go through.

As an afterthought, Alex quickly wrote another message.

To: Raptor
Subject: Don't forget
Message: Hey Connor, I know what it's like trying to get an army ready for battles and to do well, just don't forget to write me if you need anything. – Alex

—Message Sent—

Feeling better about reconnecting with his stepfather and brother, Alex was wearing a smile as he got off the Thunderbird. His smile was quickly erased when he saw Colonel Lemmon waiting for him and the other commanders.

The man's face was normally unreadable, but today his scarred right eye looked worried.

"I need all 2121 Army Commanders to assemble in war room immediately," Lemmon said without wasting any time.

Alex nodded and replied with a casual, "Yes, sir," as he separated from his army and walked with the other four 2121 commanders to the war room of Station Sigma.

Unlike the OMBIcademy on Earth, Station Sigma was a fully operational military installation that had real weapons and soldiers ready to defend the planet. Parts of the station were used for supplying and fueling war ships, but primarily it was a hub for Calypso and Titan stations, which orbited the two moons of Jupiter for which they were named. Only a small portion of the station was used for training and housing students.

Alex walked through the metallic station halls purposefully. The walls were white and dotted periodically with small windows that offered a reminder of how lonely and cold life in space could be. Glancing sideways out the windows as he passed by, Alex saw the red surface of Mars, shimmering in the light of the sun. The view wasn't new to Alex after being stationed on Sigma for over a year, but after spending time on Earth, the reminder that he was 140 million miles away made him feel distant.

Entering the war room was always impressive. Normally there were many observing officers watching how the students were receiving and following orders they had received for their mock-missions of assaults on the Gortha or colony rescues. On this particular day, only a handful of guards were on duty, and other than the five army commanders and Colonel Lemmon, the room was mostly empty.

Control panels and monitoring stations encircled the room and in the middle was a large table that served as a holographic display.

Lemmon waited until the door was closed and all five boys were positioned around the table before beginning. Bringing up a holographic display, Lemmon showed ship movements in a binary star system.

"The situation in the outer colonies is growing dire," Lemmon began in a firm voice. "As you may know, we have lost many of them to the Gortha over the last six years. We received a distress beacon from the colony on Atmos XI in the Eagle Nebula last week and have been scrambling to send a recon team to investigate."

Lemmon paused to let the boys in front of him digest the information.

"To get a UEDF vessel out there would take approximately two-and-a-half months to get us into the right cluster, and another several weeks before our normal engines would get to the colony itself."

Lemmon took a deep breath before continuing, "It is our belief that, if the OMBI testing is accurate, we can increase this response time and slipstream accuracy by fivefold or better. We need a response team out there to find out what is going on and report back and to support the colonists if necessary."

Alex was nodding before Lemmon was finished. "I volunteer."

"Understand that I have been ordered by the EMC directly to assess this threat and respond," Lemmon continued, almost as if to apologize.

The man was not kind or personable by any means. But he was obviously uncomfortable with the idea of sending untested children to the front line of a battle.

"I don't require an explanation of my orders, sir. I volunteer Black Army to assess the threat," Alex said coldly.

Slayer's eyes went from Colonel Lemmon's to Alex's as he nodded respectfully.

"Black Army is the best trained," Slayer said with apprehension in his voice.

Behind his green eyes, Alex was eagerly awaiting the opportunity to strike out at the monsters who had taken his mother from him. The fury in his heart would not be satiated until he got revenge and wiped out every last Gortha from the galaxy.

"You are sure that your Army is up to this?" Lemmon asked very slowly, looking Alex directly in the eye.

The wry smile on Alex's face answered Lemmon's question before Alex spoke. "It's not like one of the other armies would do better."

That brought some disgruntled complaints from the other commanders. But Lemmon only nodded to Alex, accepting that what he was saying was the absolute truth.

"Inform your army, you leave in forty-eight hours," Lemmon said finally. "Everyone else, go back to your training. Battles and exercises will be adjusted to proceed accordingly without Black Army. Everyone but Mephisto, dismissed."

As the other kids exited the room, Alex stood staring at the holographic display, studying the ship movements, which did not seem overly aggressive to him.

"You are hereby promoted to the rank of Captain. Your army is officially disbanded from the OMBIcademy and will henceforth be known as Black Squadron. Congratulations," Lemmon said as he pinned a Captain's pin to Alex's uniform.

"Thank you, sir," was all Alex said as he saluted Colonel Lemmon and shook his hand. Alex departed immediately after, his quick steps echoing down the hall away from the command center.

Lemmon looked at the door for a few seconds after Alex had departed, wondering what the EMC could be thinking sending children into battle, even ones as well trained as Black Squadron. Not one to normally question his orders, Lemmon quickly dismissed the thought and went back to his command.

~ ~ ~

In the hallway, Alex stopped and took a deep breath. Thoughts of his family seemed a distant echo as he resumed his march determinedly toward the Black Army quarters. Ignoring the surprised looks of the other kids and airmen aboard the station, Alex kept his mind on the mission ahead.

As Alex approached the Black Army barracks, he stopped for a moment to look at the screen flickering on the wall beside the door to the barracks he had been living in for the last year.

Black Army, Commander Pereira, Alexzander

Alex took a deep breath and put his hand on the screen. He was a little surprised when the screen changed as he touched it.

Black Squadron, Captain Pereira, Alexzander

"Perfect timing as usual," Alex said to himself with a smirk as he entered the room to inform his Army that they had all just graduated almost a year early.

~ ~ ~

The street Connor stood on was vaguely familiar as was the face of the man resembling someone he once knew, though it was mostly covered by a red bandana. The man was wearing an old, brown leather duster that matched a brown leather cowboy hat and boots. His threatening demeanor was fitting for the image of the city crumbling around him.

As he gathered himself he blinked several times taking in a scene that left him breathlessly afraid. The buildings of this city were ablaze, a large bridge was crumbling into a bay, and a massive battle was going on around him between the UEDF soldiers and darkly dressed figures.

The man in the cowboy outfit moved to one side towards Alex, who Connor just realized lay on the ground near him half trapped at the edge of a collapsed building. Alex seemed to be hurt, bleeding and struggling to get free. A UEDF soldier came running around a corner toward the pair and the man in the duster shot him with some kind of modified double-barreled shotgun that had a third under-barrel.

Connor watched the man gun down another soldier who had come at him from another direction, before reloading more quickly than Connor thought possible. The man launched a barrage of fire from the under-barrel toward an oncoming military transport, destroying it completely.

Connor tried to run to Alex but his feet kept getting tied up in rubble and he had trouble moving quickly. As he got closer, he could see that Alex had also been shot in the leg and was attempting to tie off the wound with a piece of torn fabric.

The man in the duster caught Connor's attention as he leapt forward over a broken wall toward Alex and ran at full speed. Connor could see the man's eyes as he got closer, dark blue and as cold as an ocean floor with a look he could only describe as "furious."

Another nearby building collapsed under the fire of some heavy weapon Connor couldn't see.

He somehow managed to get to Alex first and moved to help him up so they could get away from the battle and the crazed cowboy coming toward them. As he reached his hand out, he saw that Alex had a finger pointed toward Connor and then a gun appeared in his hand.

A bright white light started shining around them and Connor couldn't tell where it was from. The rubble on the ground began to slowly float upwards, like gravity was suddenly reversed. The light brightened as the man in the duster got close, so bright that Connor couldn't see.

The wind was screaming in his ears, but over it Connor heard Alex say, "I win" followed by the click of his trigger.

Then Connor fell.

~ ~ ~

Connor hit the ground beside his bed hard. He didn't remember falling asleep the night before. He must have been exhausted after Blue Army's long ocean battle practice. Connor had learned how to temporarily assign different army colors to his squads while in training, and he had worked his army so hard they'd all but collapsed from exhaustion afterwards.

It was still too early to wake up the other kids in Blue Army, only 0348. Connor got up off the ground and sat back on his bunk, trying to hold on to the dream he just had while it ephemerally faded from his mind. He didn't remember much of the dream, only that some cowboy had been shooting troops and attacking his brother.

After a few minutes, Connor could barely visualize the scene at all. Unable to fall back asleep, he read the messages on his OMBI.

Message 1: To Blue Army Commander Pereira. Aaron Michaels, call sign 'Carl', is to be released from the infirmary at 0600, 2121-02-27.

Connor sighed and said to himself quietly, "Aaron Michaels, call sign Carl, returned to infirmary 0630, 2121-02-27."

Irritated by his first message, Connor continued to read.

Message 2: Don't Forget
"Hey Connor, I know what it's like trying to get an army ready for battles and to do well, just don't forget to write me if you need anything. –Alex"
Delivered 2259 2121-02-26
From: Pereira, Alex (Mephisto).

115

Hearing from his brother always made Connor feel better about everything. He hadn't heard from Alex since he departed back to Sigma, and he was worried that Alex would forget to write him.

Message 3: Oh yeah!
"Guess who just graduated a year early!" – Alex
Delivered 2330 2121-02-26
From: Captain Pereira, Alex (Mephisto)

Connor was beside himself. Alex going back to Sigma and graduating within minutes left Connor speechless.

Smiling, Connor wrote a reply.

To: Mephisto
Subject: NO WAY!!!
Message: Well how did you do that? Graduated right into a promotion to Captain? Mom was a Captain! That is so awesome! Of course, now I need to graduate two years early! Ha! –Connor

—Message Sent—

Still unable to fall back to sleep after getting two messages from Alex, Connor got dressed and walked the quiet empty halls of the OMBIcademy.

Not wanting to wander too far, Connor unlocked the door to the Oriental Dojo training room and went inside to relax. The room was peaceful and calming. Outside of a sliding door, Connor saw a peculiar water fountain made of bamboo that, when full, would spill over with a satisfying, *clunk*. As he walked Connor was surprised to find that he could go outside into the Zen garden and into the hills that he had previously thought were merely a backdrop. Looking back at the building, he smiled. It was a small gym up in the mountains somewhere, or at least, a simulation of mountains somewhere which Connor assumed was Japan.

He resolved to ask his bodyguard Jinn if he knew anything about it after he woke up the other kids in Blue Army.

Clunk went the bamboo from the fountain.

Connor sat down to take a moment to think about what had happened over the last couple of weeks. Time moved a lot differently to him now that he was away from home. Every day was full with training and challenges. He had been waking up earlier every day so that he figured he was getting only about six hours of sleep per night now.

Clunk

Connor relaxed his mind and thought about his OMBI upgrades. He'd been thinking about how Gladiator had been able to bring his rapier to bear so quickly in battle and figured it could have something to do with the *Neuro-Sync* option in the *Optimization* section. But to unlock that, Connor was going to need a lot more points.

Clunk

In fact, Connor decided that he couldn't have too many points. Earning them slowly was all well and good, but Connor wanted to be able to bring to bear a wide array of weapons and abilities in every fight. Some of the available HUD options, like *Highlighting* and *Motion Sensor* sounded good to Connor too, especially if he was going to try to be more of a commander, and less of a combatant.

Clunk

What about vehicles? He obviously wasn't going to get trained on those until he was older, but should he be saving points for those? What about the tests? When was he going to be able to finish the classes he was in and get on to more challenging classes that would teach him how to fight?

Thud

Connor was on his feet in a second. Something had changed in the practice room and he felt like he wasn't alone. Looking all around, Connor brought out his OMBI 92FS firearm and surveyed the area.

"Who's there?" Connor asked loudly.

"It is I, Initiator," replied a voice that sounded to Connor like a whisper on the wind.

"Show yourself!" Connor demanded of the voice.

From inside the dojo a shadowy figure appeared, standing calmly and looking back at Connor.

"Who are you, some kind of weird virtual ghost?" Connor asked with an irritated voice.

"I am training optimization program Omega, at your service," the figure said in its strange echoing tone.

"Training optimization? Can you help me unlock some of my OMBI features?" Connor asked.

"I am designed to assist you with all your questions and upgrades."

"Just what I need! What should I call you? Never mind, I'll just call you 'Omega,'" Connor said excitedly.

"Omega?" the program replied.

"Omega. It's just easier to say," Connor said, maintaining his enthusiasm.

"Very well. What would you like to start with?" Omega asked Connor, matching his enthusiasm.

"Well, it's kind of hard for me to talk to you when you're some kind of weird black shadow; can you change into something that is less ... weird?" Connor asked inquisitively.

Omega's image shifted through several different formations as if responding to Connor's thoughts. At first it was a black shaggy dog with big brown eyes that made Connor smile for a second. Then it shifted into the image of the way Connor remembered his mom, which caused him to look away. It finally settled on the form of a little boy about Connor's age with a mop of wavy brown hair and dark blue eyes.

"Apologies, Initiator. Judging by your emotional reaction, I have affected you negatively," Omega said.

"Just call me Connor. Don't worry about it. Did you read my mind though?" Connor asked, not quite understanding what was happening.

"I did not read your mind, Connor."

"You look familiar," Connor stated, still confused.

"I took the form of your closest friend at your age to invoke a sense of trust and familiarity to facilitate my training function," Omega explained.

"My closest friend? Oh, you look like William!" Connor said, smiling.

"Indeed," Omega replied stoically.

"Well, what can we do? I got only a few hours to train. Can you show me how to fight better?"

Omega turned and walked into the dojo, motioning for Connor to follow.

When Connor got inside the gym, Omega asked, "What weapon would you like to begin with?"

"No weapons. I just want to be able to fight with my hands better," Connor said, thinking that bare hands were a good place to start, because he could use that outside of the arena too.

"Come on then, let us begin." Omega settled into a karate stance.

Connor didn't have to be told twice, and so he lunged forward, swinging his arms and legs wildly. Omega moved with fluid ease, dodging each strike deftly without even trying to block.

After a few seconds Omega said, "Hand-to-hand ability ranking, beginner."

Omega's assessment of Connor's ability annoyed him but he accepted the criticism without a complaint.

Omega proceeded to show Connor how to throw various strikes with his hands and feet using the torque of his body rather than just the strength of his limbs. Connor listened intently while going through the exercises he had been taught. He practiced each move as precisely as he could, accepting corrections from Omega.

Connor was starting to feel pretty good about it when Omega asked, "Would you like to take the beginner hand-to-hand test?"

Connor bobbed his head with excitement.

Omega's image flickered for a moment and changed his clothing into the stereotypical karate gi wearing a white belt. The image even bowed to Connor.

Connor returned the bow and took up the stance he had been taught.

The two clashed in a fight of precision strikes and blocks. Omega didn't go easy on Connor, pressing the attack until Connor was near the edge of the sparring mat. Not accepting being completely on the defensive, Connor feigned a stumble and attempted to blindside Omega.

Omega wasn't fooled by Connor's feint and came in hard, striking with his hands and feet, attempting to force Connor out of the ring. Connor fell back beyond the black line. Omega disappeared and reappeared back at his starting position waiting patiently.

"Stop reading my mind! I can't win if you know what I'm going to do!" Connor said with frustration.

"I apologize, Initiator, but I am not reading your mind," Omega said.

Connor growled, "You're lying! You know what I'm going to do before I do it!"

Omega shrugged. "I am incapable of lying."

Walking back onto the mat, Connor burst forward, attempting to force Omega off the mat. He made good progress too, not giving Omega a chance to counterattack. By the end of the exercise neither Connor nor Omega had landed a blow against the other.

"I have to get my army up and over to class," Connor said, sweating from the exercise.

"Understood, Initiator. We will resume your test later." With that, Omega faded away.

Connor smiled. He knew he was going to win, now that he had a break and could think about what he would do next. He still thought Omega was cheating somehow, but he figured he would resolve that issue later.

~ ~ ~

Connor woke up Blue Army right on time to hit the gym. He noticed that he was starting to build more muscle. In fact, even the chubby kids on Blue Army were slimming down with the regular exercise. Connor was glad for it, figuring that sooner or later they would be in a battle that lasted for more than a few minutes.

On their way to breakfast, Connor made an offhanded remark to Ladder that the food in the commissary was tasteless.

"Yeah, tell me about it. Back home, my mom made the best scrambled eggs in the world!" Ladder said.

Never one to let another kid get the upper hand, Connor said, "Yeah, scrambled eggs are good, but if you want the best breakfast in the world, my stepdad would make the best chocolate chip pancakes!"

Connor could just about smell the pancakes being cooked while he was thinking about home.

"I can almost smell them!" Ladder said.

"Funny, I was just thinking that same thing," Connor replied with a smile.

As they got closer to the cafeteria, the smell of chocolate chip pancakes was getting stronger. Connor ran the last few steps through the door.

Surely enough, much to the delight of everyone present, the robotic chef was flipping chocolate chip pancakes. Connor could hardly believe it. Amanda flashed her pretty smile at Connor and Ladder.

"Did you two go and plan this then?" Amanda asked with her thick Irish accent, still smiling.

"Not me," Connor said, shrugging.

"Nor I," Ladder said, returning Connor's shrug.

The three of them proceeded to the line, getting their food loaded onto their trays. When they sat back down Connor thought he would try something new and confide in his lieutenants. He told them about Omega and the training room and about how he was in the middle of a test he wasn't sure how to beat.

As they ate their chocolate chip pancakes, both Ladder and Cat listened intently to Connor's plight, smiling that they were being including in his strategizing. Connor had been keeping everyone at arm's length since he arrived at the OMBIcademy, never really talking about what was on his mind.

Word had spread through Blue Army the moment Connor and Wade had gotten back from the training room where Connor defeated Gladiator in one-on-one combat. Naturally word spread around the rest of the academy before the day was out. Connor didn't really care if anyone knew about his victory, but he certainly didn't want to rub it in Jose's face. Connor did not need more enemies.

Thinking about enemies, Connor asked if either Cat or Ladder had seen Carl since he was released from the infirmary. Both shook their heads, not having anything more to say about it.

They had started discussing how to defeat a sparring machine that could read your mind and predict your movements. Neither of them had any good suggestions. Jinn "Katana" Matsui, who had been following Connor since the gym, taking his turn as bodyguard that day, cleared his throat, indicating he might have something to say.

Connor looked at him expectantly.

"If I may, Commander, I believe that the program is only responding to what it taught you. Maybe if you stop trying to think outside of the box and beat it only on technique and skill you will be more successful," Katana said wisely.

Connor thought a moment on that. One of his greatest strengths was to think outside the limitations he had been given. Reigning in his mind to fight solely based on skill and reactions made Connor feel uncomfortable.

"I guess if my goal is to learn how to fight, I shouldn't try to overthink it, but get used to acting and reacting to my opponent. It's not an arena battle, it's a sparring match," Connor conceded.

He thought he would try winning based on the advice that Katana had given him when he got back into the match.

Connor thanked Jinn for his input and the four ate breakfast together, joined soon after by Wade, Tim, Toby, and Liam. They talked as friends for the first time since Connor had met any of them. Wade even recounted the story of how Connor beat up a kid four years older than him. They all had a good laugh at Gladiator's expense.

Later that day, during a particularly boring story that Sergeant Mullick was recounting in military history class about a personal battlefield anecdote, Connor noticed Cat smiling at him from across the room. She always smiled at him from the other side of rooms. Connor knew that she liked him, ever since the day they had met. But she hadn't talked to him much outside of training sessions. He had no idea what it all meant, but he decided that he would try to be friendlier with the kids he was coming to trust, including Cat.

Although it didn't come easy, Connor was starting to feel like he had some friends. The idea made him feel less alone, like he could afford to care about someone without the fear of losing them.

~ ~ ~

By the end of the day Connor was completely exhausted. But with Jinn following him, Connor thought it might be a good idea to head back into his training session to finish his test.

When Connor got the door open, Jinn found a corner of the sparring room to sit down at and watch.

"If you see anything I can do to improve, let me know, okay?" Connor asked Jinn.

Jinn nodded.

When Connor stepped onto the mat, Omega was waiting for him.

"Resume test, Initiator?" Omega asked in his strangely disembodied voice.

"Resume test, Initiated," Connor said, trying to mimic Omega's voice.

Omega came forward against Connor with a predictable series of strikes and kicks, which Connor dodged and blocked with ease.

Focusing on keeping his mind clear, Connor moved forward with a series of strikes of his own, trying to mimic perfectly the lessons he had been taught earlier that day. Relying on instinct instead of pre-planning, Connor moved and blocked, attacked and defended like he had been doing it for his whole life.

With a clear mind, it wasn't long before Connor started seeing the patterns in Omega's movements. It got to the point where Connor could predict Omega's next strike perfectly. When Omega came forward with a thrusting kick, Connor blocked it deftly and delivered his counter punch, finally ending the match.

"Congratulations," Omega said as they bowed. "You have passed the martial arts test."

Connor checked his OMBI to see that he had acquired another 1,000 points.

Jinn was smiling at Connor from his seat in the corner of the sparring gym.

"So, what is the place? Is it Japanese or what?" Connor asked Jinn.

"It appears to be a traditional Japanese dojo. It is fitting that you are using it for martial arts training," Jinn replied.

"Okay, is there anything you can show me before we go?" Connor asked.

"Probably not more than your sparring programs," Jinn replied. "But if you want any more advice in the future, I'll be happy to help."

"Thanks, Jinn!" Connor said smiling.

The boys walked out together leaving a cold, silent Omega staring at the exit impassively.

Chapter 10

Limitations

Alex walked slowly through the narrow halls of Station Sigma, not in any real hurry to arrive at his destination. After his mission briefing, Alex was ordered to report to the infirmary, where he had to wait for a robotics engineer from another part of the station to show up. The infirmary was rarely used in the training portion of the station, so it was quiet in the lobby without a sign of any other patients or staff.

Alex had sat through a similar procedure when he first arrived at Station Sigma a year before. While waiting, Alex closed his eyes and took several deep breaths. He knew that removing integrated inhibition circuits from an OMBI could be dangerous to the wearer. By the end of the first year, every recruit heard the story of how the first man to wear an OMBI went on a murderous rampage.

The inhibition circuits had been designed by UEDF scientists to slow the bonding of the device to the host. Or at least, that was what the original engineer who had removed Alex's first circuit had said.

No one, as far as Alex knew, was entirely sure at what rate the inhibitor chips should come off, just that OMBIs would only work right when bonded to a child around the age of ten and that inhibitors were set in place to prevent some kind of a mental meltdown.

Alex knew that his first inhibitor chip had been to make sure that an OMBI could only be used in the OMBIcademy training grounds and arenas. Allowing children access to even stunning weapons was a danger that the Academy staff thought prudent to avoid.

Without the first chip, Alex was able to use his OMBI's equipment wherever he went. He and the entire class of 2121 had been warned to not use it unless instructed. But in order for training simulations to continue on Station Sigma, they all had to be less restricted.

Alex had spent most of the last year running through simulations on space combat, connecting to various ships and other vehicles in virtual environments, and practicing attack and recon missions against virtual Gortha ships. Alex lived up to his reputation as a prodigy of OMBI technology, having not failed a single virtual mission, no matter how unbeatable it was supposed to be. It had become a challenge for the station engineers to invent a scenario that Alex couldn't win. One even went as far as to sabotage Alex's vessel, a Ra Class fighter, so that it wouldn't maneuver in certain directions.

It took Alex about eight seconds to repair his ship, giving him plenty of time to dodge oncoming attacks and defeat the Gortha threat.

It all felt like a game to him, one that didn't offer much challenge. In the virtual environment, an OMBI connected a pilot to his ship. Alex had thought he could almost feel his ship's malfunctions and knew instinctively how to repair them. The longer he trained the more comfortable he felt connecting to machines,

When the door to the infirmary slid open, the squeaking brought Alex out of his trance. The door was so rarely used that the maintenance staff had probably neglected to oil the tracks.

The robotics engineer was a 311 Anti-Fire and Medical Robot that had been modified for repairs, which Alex could tell by the green and red stickers stuck to the thing's chest.

The robot walked on two legs, had a broad chest, a small head, and three arms that looked like metallic human hands. Alex knew that they were designed to look somewhat human and operate human machinery. But Alex always thought about how they would function better if they were designed for efficiency rather than to make humans feel more comfortable.

"My last engineer was a human. Do we have human engineers on Sigma anymore?" Alex asked, not really expecting an answer from the machine.

"Affirmative," came the AFMR's reply in its monotone robotic voice.

Alex sighed and set his arm out in the AFMR's waiting third arm.

The machine worked quickly, its other two arms producing tiny screwdrivers and specialized tools that slowly worked to disassemble the device that had been wrapped tightly around Alex's right arm for the last five years.

It took the AFMR about thirty seconds to completely remove the faceplate and disconnect the display. Underneath, Alex watched as the AFMR clamped onto the second restrictor chip in Alex's OMBI and pulled it out. The second it was extracted, Alex felt light headed and slightly nauseated. A rushing sense of anxiety flowed through Alex's chest as he felt more substantial in the chair he sat in. Every limb in his body felt heavy and he became acutely aware of his own heartbeat, which was thumping at a rhythmic pace.

Time seemed to slow down as the machine that had removed his restriction chip was now reassembling the OMBI on Alex's arm. Alex noted curiously that the machine moved with purpose, wasting no time or movement as it expertly performed its task. Watching the AFMR, Alex was forced to reevaluate his opinion of its efficiency. As each screw was returned to its home on his arm, the sense of nausea lessened until it had completed faded with the last screw.

"AFMR," Alex said, which came out sounding like, "Aff-Mirror."

"Captain?" the machine replied.

"Thank you for your service," Alex said respectfully.

"Affirmative," the AFMR replied as it walked to the corner of the infirmary and stood motionless, awaiting its next assignment.

Alex got to his feet and walked slowly back down the narrow halls toward where he was supposed to meet with an observation team to test his OMBI. He didn't have a lot of time to waste, with an eighteen-hour window between his chip removal and his mission start time. He began to pick up his pace, eager to get done with testing and back to studying his mission files.

The test room wasn't far from the infirmary and the observation team was waiting when Alex arrived. The team was comprised of ten men and women standing with datapads behind a wall of shatterproof clear plastic. The rest of the room was large and mostly empty. When Alex had used the room for virtual combat before, it had operated like a shooting gallery. Today, however, the virtual engines weren't activate and the room was empty.

"Now how did I know that?" Alex asked to himself, looking around for some sign that the virtual elements were deactivated. Figuring it was instinct, Alex turned his focus to the observation team.

"Captain Pereira reporting for OMBI testing," Alex said firmly.

"Welcome, Captain," a voice replied from a speaker somewhere in the room. "Inhibitor chip two was removed at 1430 hours; time is currently 1500 hours. Testing will commence immediately."

Normally the voice echoing around the room would have left Alex disoriented, but somehow he knew that the speaker being used was over his left shoulder, and that the voice had come from the second man on the left in the observation room.

Alex took a deep breath, steadying himself for whatever test he would be forced to perform.

He heard the panels opening from the far side of the room as short tubes protruded from them that looked like old maritime cannons.

The first cannon made a popping sound and launched a large red ball toward Alex, which he dove at instinctively, rolling under the object. Alex came up to his feet to see several more red balls launched from different corners of the room at various angles. Dodging the balls was easy for Alex, having performed similar exercises in agility in practice rooms back at the OM-BIcademy.

Alex dove, twisted, and spun away from the red balls that were pouring out of the walls like angry bees from a hive. The room was filling up fast and Alex grinned as his fluid dance became more complex to avoid the red balls.

To make things a little more challenging for Alex, the balls began bouncing off the walls, maintaining their momentum and trajectory until colliding with other balls and bouncing off at new angles. Alex was good at this exercise, but it was quickly getting difficult to find room to move.

Remembering this wasn't a game but an OMBI test, Alex reached through his *Neuro-Sync* application into the device to bring up his melee menu. The two thin curved swords appeared in Alex's hands an instant later. These blades felt more substantial than the virtual blades he had been used to. Alex had chosen them because the hero in a fantasy book he'd once read in William's library had used similar blades and always made him feel cool.

It occurred to him that these blades were made of cold black metal rather than a glowing black hologram. The shock of manifesting a real sword almost cost Alex a red ball to the chest, but instinct and training took over and he became a blur of motion.

He sliced both blades forward into the red ball that almost hit him, and then spinning out to his left. Alex struck out with the blade in his right hand slicing another red ball, which imploded with a satisfying *pop*. Alex grinned as he continued his fluid dance, slicing red balls wherever they got close to him. The room was quickly thinning out when he changed his weapon into an assault rifle that he'd unlocked in his second year at the OMBIcademy.

The scimitars melted away and in their place, the OMBI formed a black SU16 rifle. Alex remembered choosing this particular gun back at the Academy because he had once fired it on a ranch he'd visited with his family back when he was younger. The rush he got from firing the weapon was the same now as it was back then as he took aim through the red-dot sight and began gunning down large red bouncing balls in the test room.

When the last ball popped, Alex released his manifested gun and it faded away back into his OMBI.

"Well, that's new," Alex said, slightly startled at the idea that his virtual weaponry was now real.

Alex couldn't hear what was being talked about in the observation room, but he could tell the observers were excited by their erratic gestures.

The voice came through the speaker again, "No weapon on this next test, Captain, understood?"

"Compliance" Alex said in a voice that mimicked a robot. He wasn't sure why he did that, but mentally blamed it on the time he had recently spent with his little brother.

The mirth he felt faded away as the large door at the back of the test room opened and a large figure moved through. The A25-Combat drone rolled into the room on its heavy treads, which made a terrible screech against the metal floors of Station Sigma. The drone stood twelve feet tall, with a low center of gravity. It looked a lot like a tank with human chest above the turret. Above the main gun, two mini-guns began spinning, setting off a red flag in Alex's mind.

Acting instinctively, Alex brought up his armor menu in his mind and activated all the armor pieces he had unlocked. He felt his OMBI vibrate as black metallic armor formed around his skin. He felt like a Sixteenth Century knight. In front of that armor, the force barrier that Alex manifested glowed black, much like it had when it was merely a virtual barrier.

Bringing it up not a moment too soon, Alex's barrier was put to the test as the A25-Combat drone unleashed a barrage of bullets from the twin mini-guns mounted on the sides of its body. The bullets ricocheted off Alex's force barrier all around the room.

Not to be underestimated, the A25 launched a shell from the main gun that slammed into Alex's force barrier with a clanking sound that reminded him of a hammer striking an anvil. Alex felt his force barrier weaken with the blast that followed and he knew he was going to have a hard time resisting every weapon that was going to be thrown his way.

"No weapons," Alex reminded himself in a sarcastic voice. "How am I going to beat this thing?"

Another barrage of mini-gun rounds came Alex's way and ended the effect of his force barrier. The remainder of them clashed hard against Alex's armor, sending him sliding backwards on the floor toward the wall.

Not wanting to wait to see what the A25 would unleash on him next, Alex took a deep breath beneath the metal helmet he wore.

"What would Connor do about it?" Alex asked himself quietly, thinking that some unorthodox inspiration might be needed just then.

Getting an idea, he reached through his *Neuro-Sync* and activated his HUD's *Thermal Imaging* function. Alex could see that the guns were heating up a lot and put the hot red glow out of his mind. Instead he focused on the central core he thought might be hidden under heavy armor in the back of the machine. The core wouldn't be very hot yet, but the liquid refrigeration would be easy enough to spot as the low-point temperature on the machine.

From there Alex activated the vehicle section of his OMBI > *Robot* > *Unmanned* > *A25-Combat Drone* Unlock for 25000 Battle Points?

Alex was thinking, *YES YES YES YES YES YES* before the OMBI had finished the prompt in his head. Immediately upon unlocking the drone control, Alex began reaching through his OMBI toward the A25's core, asking it to cease fire.

The entire process took less than a few seconds, and the A25 ceased firing immediately. Alex could feel the machine through his OMBI and maneuvering it was as easy as operating the other unmanned vehicles he had unlocked in virtual simulations.

Alex felt a familiar vibration in his OMBI as he earned the points for achieving disarmament of one of the UEDF's best drones. He had long stopped caring about battle points and knew he had several hundred thousand saved up for whatever he needed.

"Well done, Captain," came the response from the Observation team. "OMBI limitation chip two removed successfully. The actualization of previously virtual elements has been activated."

Alex nodded in the direction of the observation room.

"Is there anything else?" Alex asked.

"No, Captain, dismissed," the voice stated as he had expected.

Alex turned to walk out of the room.

"Fri…"

"Pardon?" Alex said out loud.

"Dismissed, Captain," replied the voice in the speaker.

Alex shook his head and turned to leave again.

"…end," echoed the disembodied whisper.

Alex paused again, looking back at the observation room. The staff inside were clearly discussing something and not even looking at him. Alex slowly looked at each person in the room, trying to figure out which one of them was leaning on the microphone. Alex took a deep breath and focused his mind, listening again for the whisper.

His eyes searched the room, quickly finding nothing out of the ordinary.

"I guess I could be going crazy," Alex said mirthfully before turning and exiting the room, leaving shreds of many large red balls and a still A25-Combat Drone behind.

~ ~ ~

It was a cold and rainy evening in Healdsburg, California. The rain had been falling for days, barely letting up at all. The dark days accentuated the dark mood of a man who had been alone in a large house for almost three weeks.

William had started a fire in the large rock hearth in the living room to ward off the cold and to give him something to do with his day. He had chopped the wood for the fire out in the rain, next to a worn-down shed, with an old axe, until the entire cord had been split. The wet wood was hard to get burning, but he managed with the aid of some accelerant he had on hand in the workshop.

One of the calluses on his hand had torn and began bleeding long before he was finished, but he didn't notice it until he got inside and washed his hands in the kitchen sink. The cold had numbed his hands so that he didn't feel the pain until the fire had warmed him up.

Now his hand throbbed, but he didn't give it much thought. He stared into the fire. Its hypnotizing dance caused his mind to drift back over the years to days where he would lay in front of this hearth with his wife, wrapped in blankets and talking about their dreams.

Snuggled up in his arms, Marlena would almost always fall asleep listening to William talk. It wasn't that she'd been bored by what he had to say. She felt so calm lying in his arms, soothed by his tone, it would mesmerize her into a relaxed sleep.

William used to do it on purpose so he could watch his wife while she slept, just for a bit, until her rhythmic breathing would put him to sleep as well. He loved nothing more in the world than to wake up with that girl in his arms.

The thought brought old tears to William's eyes that he worried might never dry up.

The flash from his datapad pulled William from his thoughts and he picked it up to read Alex's message.

Hi William. Sorry it has been so long since I wrote you a letter. Pretty busy being a commander, saving the galaxy, and all that. I spent the week before last with Connor and he has really grown!

You did a great job raising him. I think Mom would be happy about that. I know I never said it, but thank you. – Alex
Delivered 2325 2121-02-28
From: Captain Pereira, Alex

William's mouth formed a slight grin, a smile that didn't quite touch his eyes.

"Captain Pereira?" William asked aloud.

Unable to resist, even in his despair, William drafted his response.

To: Captain Alex Pereira
Subject: Promotion?
Message: Hey Alex! It's really good to hear from you! Nice, making Captain! I don't know what it takes to skip that many ranks, but if anyone were able to do it, it would be you. Thank you for saying that about Connor, I did my best with the time I had. I am really proud of the man you grew up to be, just keep doing what you're doing and give them hell! –William

—Message Sent—

Thinking about his stepchildren training hard to save humanity caused a spark to light in William's heart. It was a feeling he hadn't felt in a long time, not since before Marlena's last mission.

William started breathing slowly, counting to seven breaths, trying to fuel the flame. The sound of thunder from the storm outside only served to stimulate the feelings the man had found. It wasn't despair waiting for him, but determination.

William walked up the steps of the back stairway into his bedroom, where he looked at himself in the mirror. His hair had grown unkempt and was still wet from the rain. His beard had grown whiter than he remembered since the last time he grew it out, serving as a reminder of the time gone by. His eyes had lost some of their luster, but that small spark remained, that warrior spirit that had pushed William through some of the hardest times of his life.

"They deserve better," William said to himself.

He looked at himself a moment longer before putting on his old running shoes and marching downstairs. He knew it would hurt, but right then, he didn't care.

In the dark of night, the fire inside of the man began to roar and, with no other outlet, he ran. He had no path ahead of him, nowhere to go, but he had to feel his muscles burn. It was difficult, but he pushed past the pain and kept moving forward.

Along the long estate driveway, he passed by the first of his sculptures, the imposing figure of Atlas holding the world upon his shoulders. As always when near the titan, William felt a sense of empathy and determination. Even in the darkness, the hulking figure loomed over William, stone eyes staring back at him.

The storm beat down on his face and body, soaking him to the bone with freezing rain, but still he ran. He clenched his teeth and roared out loud to the sound of the storm outside and the fire within.

On a cold, stormy February night, the man felt something he hadn't in years: a fire in his heart.

~ ~ ~

Connor awoke early again to find Aaron "Carl" Michaels, attempting to sneak into an open bunk that he hadn't yet earned. Tiptoeing around other kids, Carl climbed quietly into the bed and rolled the blanket over himself. Connor waited until he had settled in before getting out of his own bunk and proceeded across the room.

"How are you feeling, Aaron?" Connor whispered quietly as he sat down on the edge of Carl's bunk.

Startled, Carl turned around quickly in his bed to stare up at Connor.

"My face hurts," Carl admitted.

"Yeah, it's killing me too," Connor said wryly.

Connor could see Carl scowling at him, even in the low light of the barracks and night.

"I can't transfer or trade you, so we need to work this out," Connor said, trying to hold back from beating Carl back into the infirmary.

"Well, what do you have in mind?"

"I know a way we can earn points together in practice rooms, and as you unlock more weapons and abilities you can get a better score. But points aren't everything."

"That sounds good. Can I have a bunk though? I hate sleeping on the floor."

"I can't go back on my first order now. Only a few of you guys are still on the ground and I'll try to help you guys the most so in our next fight we get you some kills."

"I want a bed though!"

"This isn't a negotiation. You have to earn it. I will work with you so that you're a productive member of Blue Army or I will make sure you don't get in our way. Those are your choices."

"Fine," Carl said quietly. "Can I get a better call sign though? Carl is stupid."

"It's only stupid because you haven't made it cool. It can be cool if you do well, then everyone will be jealous." Connor was making things up at this point, but the notion seemed to calm Carl down a bit.

Connor even heard Carl whisper to himself, "Make it cool," as he walked away.

Connor didn't like the idea of welcoming back a traitor, but if he was going to get stuck with Carl in his ranks, he may as well get it figured out right away.

"One down, two to go," Connor said, making a mental note to himself to deal with the enemies he was forming in the Academy. Thinking then about Gladiator and the rumors going around the school now that Connor had humiliated him, Connor was forced to adjust his assessment.

"Maybe three to go," he whispered to himself.

On that dark note, Connor got back in his bed and tried to fall back to sleep.

Chapter 11

Skoll

"Colonel, the council has decided that your new captain is to pilot the Skoll," General Harruhama ordered from the flickering screen in Colonel Lemmon's war room.

"It will be as you say, sir. However, I am not familiar with the Skoll," Lemmon replied with a look of genuine confusion.

General Harruhama was a weathered man of many conflicts and a consummate warrior. His gray hair and leathery skin gave him the look of a seasoned campaign veteran; however, the Japanese-born general had been ruling the EMC and presiding over the entire UEDF since 2115. It was Harruhama himself who had led the bloodless coup against the civilian government, with the support of the people of Earth.

The General let out a sigh and explained, "Skoll is the name given to the vessel that was discovered when we unearthed the OMBIcademy in 2074."

Feeling like he had been given information just then that was far above his clearance level, Colonel Lemmon stammered his reply.

"Unearthed the OMBIcademy, sir?" Lemmon stammered, unsure of how to proceed.

"Yes, Colonel. Consider this information classified above top secret. I will have a dossier on the Skoll sent to you via a secured line," Harruhama said briefly before cutting the transmission.

Colonel Lemmon was floored by the information he had been given. The man even pinched his arm to make sure he wasn't dreaming. When his datapad flashed with the secured message, Lemmon hesitated to open it. Curiosity got the better of him before his courage kicked in and he opened the file. A video played on his screen as he watched.

Classified: Above Top Secret, the opening screen said.

Images of an oceanic exploration team attaching floatation devices to an underwater structure played across the screen as the audio explained what was happening.

"In 2074, oceanic exploration teams led by the United Earth Defense Force located the object that had been detected at the bottom of the Pacific Ocean one hundred and sixty miles off the coast of Japan.

"It was soon moved to the Island of Kita-Daito and concealed as UEDF science teams attempted to unlock its secrets. Structures and housing were built around the object which is classified as an alien vessel."

The image on the screen showed several huge ships towing the massive structure through the water toward the small island. The engineering of mounting the structure on the island and building around it to make it look like a base was apparently extensive.

"The dating process put the vessel at over two thousand years old. Even though they only had the ability to access a few areas of the ship, UEDF scientists began to unlock its secrets, giving us technologies like slipstream travel."

Lemmon could hardly believe what he was hearing. Like most citizens of Earth, Marcus Lemmon had learned that a physicist named Samson had discovered slipstream travel and other than the Gortha attacks, he had never heard of any alien technology found anywhere, let alone on Earth.

"After forty years of trial and error techniques to access other parts of the vessel, it was discovered that human children, with the assistance of OMBI technology found on the structure, could access rooms that were previously impenetrable. The structure served to function as a training facility from that point on, in order to facilitate its exploration.

"The benefits of children operating with this technology have produced a stronger, more capable soldier. We are learning new information with every new class of students.

Among the discoveries of the OMBIcademy, perhaps the greatest outside of slipstream and OMBI technology was the Skoll, which was discovered in a hangar bay several weeks after the first students wearing OMBI had activated various parts of the facility."

The image on the screen showed a humanoid-shaped vessel that looked to Lemmon like a giant suit of samurai armor with wings. The video went on to an interactive program that showed the hypothetical specifications of the ship, since no one had been able to fly it. None of the specifications could show Lemmon where the cockpit was, if it even had one.

Not liking his orders for the second time that week, Lemmon resigned himself to trusting in the children he had been training and in the wisdom of the EMC and General Harruhama.

Reading the dossier, Lemmon wasn't sure if he should be laughing or crying.

~ ~ ~

"You know who that boy's mother is," Councilman Stahl stated, looking directly at Harruhama.

"I am aware of the situation," Harruhama answered calmly.

"Do you think it's a good idea to send him?" Stahl asked, raising his voice a little.

"Calm down, Councilman. As long as the boy's control chips are in place, we are in control. He is an asset of the UEDF and will perform as required."

As was custom, Harruhama shut off the feed to the other councilmen before any more questions could be asked. He was not a young man and had little patience for bureaucratic debate when he had made up his mind. Everyone who was close to the situation at all was aware that the council had no real power that Harruhama himself did not give.

Looking out his window at the lights of Tokyo below, General Harruhama thought about the wisdom of sending the captain of Black Squadron on his first mission in an untested alien ship. He came to the conclusion, as he had the first time he considered the possibility of something going wrong, that the contingency measures that were in place would be enough to prevent any unforeseen problems.

In his mind, ending the war was worth the risk of losing a single squadron.

~ ~ ~

Connor's sparring match with his growing group of bodyguards was going poorly after only a couple of minutes. Omega had duplicated itself, and Connor - along with Dice, Hunter, Katana, and Carl - were practicing their melee combat techniques with it.

Amanda was watching the match from the sidelines, taking notes on her OMBI furiously in hopes of providing quality feedback for Connor. She watched him move back and forth against his holographic opponent like a gust of wind rolling across an open plain, slamming hard into his opponent's defenses then rolling around them to look for different openings. Slow movements were followed up by quick ones and Connor had fallen into a spinning rhythm of attack and defense.

She watched with amazement at how graceful Connor had become in only a few short days of dedicated sparring, and her respect for her commander's adaptability grew. Connor rarely used weapons outside of his bare hands. He had told her that he liked the idea of being the weapon, rather than using one. She admired his intelligence. There was little about Connor that Amanda didn't admire.

The other boys were having a harder time with their chosen technique. Tim "Dice" Sanz was sweating profusely from his forehead, which shined in the artificial light due to his buzzed head. He was currently using a spear as his weapon, and while he commanded the weapon well enough, his footing was slow and his opponent merciless. As Tim got backed into the corner of the dojo, he lost control of his weapon and was stunned by the spear of the Omega clone that had been sparring with him.

The clone turned and moved toward Wade "Hunter" Winchester, who had opted for a spear that looked more like a trident with three prongs, where the other boys' spears only had one. Wade had managed to keep his footing and fight the clone on even ground, but when the second one entered the fray, Hunter was hard pressed.

Jinn "Katana" Matsui had his clone all but beat, but had gotten stunned when his spear, which looked like a traditional Japanese naginata, got tangled up in Carl's spear.

Carl had actually managed to defeat his opponent through measured advances and calculated movements. His spear was fairly non-descript and he had earned his kill early on in the match after a short lesson from the Omega clone.

After winning, Carl had let out a yell and charged in to help Jinn, which caused the two to get tangled up, costing Jinn his match. Carl found himself facing three spear-wielding clones before the end of the match and though he tried, couldn't move fast enough to avoid being struck.

Connor, working on his intermediate test after only two days of sparring, was clearly frustrated when three clones of Omega encircled him with the long points of their spears stabbing at him. To Connor's credit, he blocked and dodged for several minutes until exhaustion slowed his movement and the clones overtook him.

The match was over when Connor got stabbed, so he didn't go down stunned. He laughed heartily when it was over, lying down on his back on the floor.

"This is pretty fun!" Connor said to his friends.

Amanda shared in Connor's laughter along with the other boys. Jinn was even laughing despite his frustration with Carl. Tim, however, wasn't laughing at all and shook his head as he walked over to join Connor on the floor.

"I cost us the fight," Tim said, his eyes downcast to the floor.

"Well, we did our best. Your moves are good. I think you just got caught up in that corner," Connor said in a rare moment of sympathy.

Sitting down between them, Amanda put her hand on Tim's back and nodded her agreement. "I had my OMBI taking a video of your training, Tim. We'll watch it later and look for ways to improve, okay?"

Tim nodded stoically and sat back on the mat, clearly in deep thought.

"I think it is going pretty good; we're all getting a lot better," Carl said as he walked over to sit down with them.

The other bodyguards had been apprehensive that morning when Connor told them that Carl would be joining them for training, but to everyone's surprise, he'd kept quiet and focused on the lesson. In fact, Carl actually performed better than anyone expected him to.

"You're right," Connor said nodding, "you did really good there, until you lost your patience. I think that's the thing you should be working on most. We have a battle in two days. Ladder has the other squads running drills in the ocean room. I think we'll be ready."

"That reminds me," Amanda said, smiling at Connor, "I should get back over there and help him. Maybe challenge him to a training match."

Connor waved to her as she walked away and turned back around to look face to face with a smiling Wade.

"What?" Connor demanded.

"Y'all know what. She's got it bad for you!" Wade said with a grin.

"You're crazy, we're just friends," Connor said defensively.

Jinn was shaking his head before Connor had finished. "You might want to tell her that, Raptor."

Carl looked a bit confused and asked, "Wait, Cat likes Raptor? I was hoping she liked me."

The other boys laughed a bit at that, since Cat had never looked twice at Carl and the two had never spoken more than a word in passing.

"Sorry, man, but I think she's keen on Connor," Tim said from his seat on the floor.

Connor's face was bright red before the conversation was over. He'd had friends who were girls growing up, even called Mary Atherton his girlfriend for an afternoon when he was eight. But he was not entirely comfortable with the idea that a girl who slept in the same room had a crush on him.

"Well, it's not like I have a lot of time for that kind of stuff. I do have an army to lead." Connor said, obviously embarrassed by the topic.

The other boys nodded along sympathetically. They all knew how busy Connor was on a day-to-day basis, but none of them stopped smiling as they walked of gym on their way to class.

~ ~ ~

When Alex got the order to return to the war room on Station Sigma, he set off immediately. He had been discussing with the other pilots of Black Squadron the responsibility of using an unrestricted OMBI. They'd all agreed to not activate their abilities unless ordered to or in a training session. They all wanted to, since their inhibitors were removed, but Vector had already knifed himself accidentally and would sit in the infirmary while the other thirty-nine boys were out on their mission.

Alex was glad he had Austin to keep the other kids in check while he was away. Austin "Vertigo" Hughes had been the second-best soldier in the OMBIcademy and an expert in technical skill. Alex had tried to get him to bring some style to his tactics, but he often ran formations by the book.

Walking down the narrow white halls of Station Sigma, Alex was glad to have a friend coming with him on his mission. He had earned the trust and respect of the other members of his army and trusted them in turn, but the only boy who Alex considered a friend was Austin. They weren't exactly close friends - Alex wasn't really close with anybody - but they had once shared stories about their families back home, and ever since Alex had felt like they were bonded.

When Alex entered the war room, Colonel Lemmon was nowhere to be found. A hand-written order had been left for Alex with an airman. The note read:

Captain, proceed to docking bay 7 for additional orders.

Not one to think about the significance of a note when an OMBI mail would have done better, Alex walked the halls in the direction of docking bay 7.

Opening the door to the bay, Alex saw Colonel Lemmon standing amongst the crates of supplies that had been left there from a supply ship that had docked earlier in the week. Lemmon was staring at a large object, which looked to Alex like some kind of a giant suit of ancient, black samurai armor with large metallic wings that appeared to be contracted, pulled tightly against its back. Where Alex expected a helmet, the twenty-foot-tall armored suit had horns protruding from the head of a dragon, which glared down menacingly, its mouth locked in a nightmarish snarl.

"Captain Pereira reporting, sir," Alex said absently, as if mesmerized by the armor's deep, black eyes.

"Captain, this is the Skoll. It is a UEDF asset that has been assigned to you for this mission." Lemmon said uneasily.

"Yes sir." Alex's voice quivered, staring at Skoll in awe.

The docking bay was quiet, other than Alex's footsteps echoing off the metal ground as he slowly walked forward.

"I am afraid," Lemmon began, "I cannot tell you how to pilot it."

The tone of sympathy and concern was something that Alex hadn't heard from an adult since he left home. Alex was touched by it, but worried that if his CO was concerned, then maybe he should be too.

"I think I can handle it," Alex said with as much confidence as he could muster.

Alex ran his right hand across the smooth surface of the black machine he was facing. He closed his eyes and let his mind relax as he felt the cold metal against his fingers.

"Greetings, Initiator," something whispered in Alex's head.

Unsure of where it came from, Alex looked at Lemmon, who was staring up at the Skoll, mouth agape.

"Did you say something, sir?" Alex asked, just to be sure.

Lemmon didn't say anything, but looked at Alex briefly and shrugged before looking back at the Skoll.

Alex reached out through the *neuro-sync* application of his OMBI and let his mind search the vehicles section. Oddly, Skoll wasn't listed under the *ground* or *aircraft* menus. Instead, he found it listed on the main menu. Alex psychically looked up the menu on his OMBI to verify his findings.

"I guess this OMBI doesn't know where to classify you," Alex said, speaking to Skoll.

Selecting it in his menu, a familiar prompt appeared, "Unlock *Skoll*: 0 Points." Alex said yes out loud, although he was surprised that unlocking something so large would cost him nothing in terms of acquired experience.

Alex felt his OMBI tighten against his wrist for a moment, and incoherent whispers filled his head. He steadied himself with a few deep breaths and turned to see Colonel Lemmon staring at him.

"Are you all right, son?" Lemmon asked with an edge of concern in his voice.

"Yes, sir. I'm just fine," Alex replied, not sure if he was telling the truth or not.

The look of concern didn't diminish on Lemmon's face as Alex reached out to Skoll. To both their surprise, Skoll turned around and knelt down with its back facing Alex. The panels on its back pulled apart with a screeching sound of metal gears grinding for the first time in ages.

The noise didn't last long as the gears came to a grinding halt. Inside Skoll's body was an upright seat large enough for Alex to squeeze into.

Not waiting for additional orders, Alex stepped onto Skoll's leg and climbed into the cockpit, sliding his body down into the surprisingly comfortable seat. Alex slid his arms and legs out as if he were in the same kneeling position that Skoll was in. When he was settled, the rear hatch shut with the same grinding noise it made while opening.

He made a movement as if to stand up and felt Skoll respond in kind. The entire machine shifted as if it were an extension of his movements. Alex moved to take a step and Skoll took a step. He felt his OMBI pulsing like a heartbeat. Through his neuro-sync, he felt the exchange of data between his bracer and the machine he was piloting. The more data that was exchanged, the more comfortable Alex felt at the idea of going across a galaxy in this ship.

"With your permission, sir," Alex said, hearing his voice echoing metallically inside of Skoll, "I would like to test my manifestations."

Lemmon took several steps back and nodded, stunned at what he was witnessing.

Alex reached out to his OMBI and manifested his scimitar, which he saw appear as a huge version of itself in Skoll's right hand. Alex let the weapon dissipate as he changed his HUD from infrared to thermal, then to highlight mode and motion sensor. He also noticed that he had many more options for all of his weapons and optimizations.

Alex grinned, and while doing so wondered if Skoll's draconic metal face was trying to grin too. Getting an idea, he reached out through his OMBI to the surveillance cameras in the docking bay. He opened a display screen inside of Skoll and began searching through footage. Alex was surprised at how easily he could manipulate closed network security all of the sudden, and figured that he owed it to the recent inhibitor chip removal.

Alex watched through the camera as he moved around the docking bay. Skoll was shiny and black from head to toe, looking like a samurai out of a movie with its armored plating. He noticed that its eyes were glowing bright green, the color of Alex's own eyes.

Kneeling back down, Alex climbed back out of Skoll and stood face to face with Colonel Lemmon.

"Sir, with your permission, I would like to assemble my squad and began my mission briefing," Alex said, filled with confidence from his successful test drive.

Lemmon looked back at him and said "Granted," with the authoritative voice Alex was used to.

On his way out of the loading bay, Alex reached out through his OMBI to the video feed he had captured and took a screenshot, then opened up a message prompt:

To: Raptor
Subject: My new ship!
Message: —*Image attached*— "Guess what I am flying now! Going on a mission to Hades Colony, be back in a few weeks. Keep your eyes forward kid!" –Alex

—*Message Sent*—

After it was sent, Alex got the feeling that maybe he shouldn't have sent an image of a top-secret ship to his brother - or details about his mission. Shrugging, Alex figured he would rather get in trouble and have Connor know where he was, than not tell him and avoid punishment. Either way, no one had said anything about anything being top secret to him, so for now he felt like he had a defensible excuse.

Chapter 12

Learning

Major Sanders stood in the corner of the observation room, absently watching the battle raging below. Green and Yellow Armies from the class of 2125 battled in the Ranged Arena. Sanders watched impassively as the Yellow formations settled into defensive positions while Green started launching crossbow bolts out the backside of the battle-field, which reappeared on the Yellow side of the arena and started hitting the Yellow soldiers from behind.

Green was an innovative army, always finding ways to stretch the rules of the arena combat and sometimes resorting to cheating. The administrative staff didn't punish children for their behavior at the OMBIcademy very often, especially in arena combat. They'd found out early on that letting the children take responsibility for their own actions increased the learning curve and independence of the commanders. They thought of them-selves as guides and teachers, not parents.

So the conversation happening behind Major Sanders was like nothing he had ever heard in the Academy before. The EMC representative from Councilman Stahl's office was sitting across from Colonel Roden, along with a techno-psychologist - a field which had grown since the discovery of the OMBI's potential six years prior.

The representative was a short, balding man whose but-toncd-up whitc shirt was threatening to burst open due to the pressure set against it by the man's ample belly. The techno-psychologist seemed to be in better shape, although not a fit man. He was taller than Sanders and wore glasses that he would remove each time he spoke. Both men had graying hair on different parts of their heads.

"As you may be aware, Colonel, Councilman Stahl has taken a very direct interest in the Academy's progress. You have produced some capable children that may someday be an asset to the UEDF..." The representative paused, breathing heavily and wiping a bead of sweat off his forehead. "... That being said, we have a concern about your methods."

Not intimidated by the Councilman's representative at all, Colonel Roden responded calmly from beneath his immaculate red beret. "What methods are you referring to specifically, Mr. Blumquist?"

"I am referring to the fact that our last report has one of your new students advancing much more quickly than his class-mates. This Connor Pereira has already started taking tests and unlocking advanced techniques after less than a month at the OMBIcademy!" Blumquist was sweating more profusely now. Sanders began to wonder if the man was going to have a heart attack from the mere effort of speaking.

"I can assure you that allowing the students to progress at their own rate has produced the best results in every class. Pereira is a good student, by the reports we've received from his instructors."

"His academics are not in question, I assure you. A finer first year conscript we have not seen. That is, since his brother five years ago. It is his testing and activity scores that have us concerned, you understand," Blumquist said, trying to sound diplomatic. Sanders began to wonder how Roden was able to sit calmly while the fat little man was talking around his point.

"We have not given any of the students in the class of 2126 a test yet, and the neurological reports go to your office before they go to mine, so you're going to have to be more specific," Roden said, irritated that he didn't have data that the Council apparently had.

The techno-psychologist leaned forward with a datapad, which he presented to Roden. Sanders walked over behind Roden to look at the data, as curious about the student as he was about the information the council had. Blumquist watched them both with a slight grin on his face, as though he was about to win an argument.

"What am I looking at...?" Roden began.

"Purvel, Doctor Purvel." the man said with a slight accent that Sanders placed as French.

"Doctor Purvel," Roden finished respectfully, "This looks like a comparative analysis between Pereira and someone else."

"Quite astute, good Colonel. It is indeed a comparative analysis between the Pereiras' first-year scores. As you can see, the boy we assumed to be a prodigy five years ago was way behind where his brother is now," Doctor Purvel finished in a serious tone.

"Why is this a problem?" Roden asked, not looking away from the data.

"It is no problem. According to my analysis, the younger brother has somehow bypassed parts of his OMBI inhibitor chips and begun testing himself."

That statement caused Roden to look up from the datapad at the doctor and the fat man, who was nodding along enthusiastically.

"And how would he do that?" Sanders asked, speaking out for the first time since introducing himself to the two men from Councilman Stahl's office.

The doctor smiled up at Sanders, who was still standing behind Roden's desk.

"That is a good question. We don't fully know. My hypothesis is that he has subconsciously found a way to communicate with his OMBI, and the OMBI has found a way to communicate back with him."

"WHAT?" Roden and Sanders asked together. Roden continued, "I thought that the third inhibitor was supposed to prevent that!"

"It does indeed prevent that, Colonel. It seems as though the boy has found a loophole. The inhibitor was designed to prevent conscious exchange of information between the host and device. As we learned from the initial OMBI testing, the amount of data exchange can cause a normal human mind to overload and shut down. The boy does it on a subconscious level. He doesn't even know that is what he is doing," Doctor Purvel concluded, putting his glasses back on.

"You say he is testing himself? Or is it the OMBI that is testing him?" Sanders asked, trying hard to not sound overeager.

"I won't know before I can do more research, but I believe it is the will of both. That kid has a brilliant mind, no doubt, but it is his heart that's stronger. In our field, we have many names for the subconscious mind: the id, the inner child, the inner shadow, the lower self, the emotional self ... That part of Connor's mind appears to be befriending the artificial intelligence of his OMBI. The device is responding to the boy's 'inner fire,' if you will." Doctor Purvel spoke excitedly, as if he were giving a sermon.

Sanders wasn't sure that sermon was the right word, but it couldn't be far off. He had been told some years ago that the

OMBI was an alien technology and that only a child's developing mind could sync with it properly. But this was the first time that Sanders had heard that the OMBI actually had a consciousness or was capable of friendship. The thought staggered him, and it wasn't long before he found himself sitting in the chair he'd previously rejected.

Roden began slowly, in a level tone, "What does the council propose that we do about this?"

"Nothing! As long as we have the fourth inhibitor fail-safe in place, we can prevent any danger. We want to observe him more closely. We believe his interactions with the OMBI and the OMBIcademy can finally lead us to unlocking more of the secrets of this place. This boy might be the key!" Blumquist said excitedly, sweat now pouring from his forehead.

"I would like a chance to speak with the boy too," Doctor Purvel said. "We need to proceed carefully. Are you aware that the brothers have been sending each other encrypted messages? They have been bypassing the censors and we have been unable to read them."

"We will do something about that," Roden assured the council's representatives. "At the very least, we can find a way to decrypt them and see what they are saying."

Sanders wasn't as confident as Roden that they had a way to do that at the OMBIcademy. Normally, it wouldn't have been a problem, but ever since he had unlocked Connor's ability to send messages freely, they had been unable to read what he'd written or stop him from writing. Even the specialist they had sent for to come and break the decryption had no idea what he was seeing.

"We will also give you the opportunity to perform an evaluation of Connor Pereira. I want to know if he is going to be a danger," Roden said firmly.

"I will make sure you get a copy of my report when I am through; thank you, Colonel," Purvel concluded with a smile on his face.

Sanders walked back to the observation window and watched as the timer on the battle below was running out. It would be another draw, despite the efforts of Green Army to bend the rules. Sanders wasn't sure what to make of everything he'd just heard, but he knew that his life was about to get far more complicated.

~ ~ ~

Amanda watched Connor go through his exercises from the corner of the dojo after Military History that day. Connor seemed to be spending all of his free time in this room now, bringing meals here to eat while watching Omega go through new exercises that he wanted to learn.

She hadn't spent much time working on any personal combat, electing to spend a lot of time studying group tactics that she could teach to her squad instead. She had been studying the maneuvers of Black Army since she discovered how to access the battle feeds from previous years on her OMBI a week before. Her favorite subject was Mephisto of course, since his record was nearly perfect.

His tactics were always quickly implemented and fluid, like water rushing down a river, adapting to anything his enemies had thrown at him. She had been sharing her findings with Connor most days. One feed in particular had caught their attention. It was a battle back in Alex's first year in which two of his squads inexplicably moved to the back of the melee arena and sat down, waiting for Alex to get slaughtered. Running forward into Red Army's charge with only two squads, Alex wore a huge smile as he cut their ranks with a curved sword that he had been using since his fourth battle. The end of the feed showed Alex standing triumphantly, surrounded by more than a dozen stunned soldiers. Connor wanted to know more about how Alex had dealt with the treacherous squads. Obviously he had earned their respect back somehow.

Seeing the feeds of his brother's victory always seemed to make Connor push himself harder. When his exercise was finished, Connor came over to sit next to Amanda, sweat glistening on his face.

"You're learning faster than anyone I've ever seen! Three days and you're testing for advanced hand to hand. It's incredible, Connor," Amanda said in her thick Irish accent.

Connor was beginning to like the way his name sounded when Amanda said it. It sounded cooler to him in her accent than in his head.

"It doesn't feel like it's only been three days. I think I could do better if I had more time to practice!" he said, stretching his legs.

"Still, how are you learning so fast?" Amanda asked.

Laughing, Connor just shrugged.

"Omega, how am I learning so fast?" he asked his holographic instructor.

Omega walked over and sat down next to Connor and Amanda, as if he were one of their friends. It was the first time either of them had seen Omega behave like a human instead of a program.

Omega replied as if reading from a textbook, "Your OMBI device syncs with your brain and body, Initiator. As you perform techniques properly, your body is acquiring abilities. You refer to it as 'muscle memory' and you are adapting to it at a rate accelerated by your OMBI."

Connor shrugged to Amanda and said, "There's your answer, if that makes any sense to you."

Amanda nodded thoughtfully and shrugged back at Connor. Not really interested in the answer as much as she was in hearing Connor talk, she slid her hand over an inch until her index finger was touching his hand.

Connor looked at Amanda without pulling his hand away and blushed in a light shade of red. Neither of them could explain the connection they were building, but both of them understood they felt happy when they were together.

The vibration of Connor's OMBI ruined the moment between them, causing Amanda to pull her hand back and ask, "What is it?"

Connor stood up and stretched his back and checked his OMBI's display.

"Awesome, one month in and I get a psych evaluation!" Connor quipped. Obviously annoyed, he continued sarcastically, "Because I've got so much free time and all."

Amanda laughed at Connor's sarcasm and the two shared a smile as Connor offered her a hand to help her off the ground. Walking toward the door together, Connor's OMBI vibrated a second time.

"You never get a break, do you?" Amanda asked, still smiling.

Message 2: My new ship! "Guess what I am flying now! Going on a mission to Hades Colony, be back in a few weeks. Keep your eyes forward kid!" –Alex
Delivered 1430 2121-02-28
From: Captain Pereira, Alex (Mephisto)
—Image attached—

"How did he attach an image? Cool!" Connor said to Amanda as they both looked at the screen. Amanda had to touch

Connor's hand in order to see his OMBI display, but neither of them minded the proximity anymore.

When the image opened, Connor's jaw dropped. The large suit of what looked like some kind of ancient samurai armor with wings was the coolest ship he'd ever seen.

"That is so awesome!" Connor said to an amazed Amanda.

As they passed through the door, Connor looked over to her and said, "Oh man, I want one!"

The door had shut. Omega still sat where Connor and Amanda had been sitting, staring impassively at the door that they had just exited. The holographic image flickered quietly.

"Yes, Initiator," Omega said to the empty room.

~ ~ ~

"This is getting out of hand," Major Sanders said into the communicator in his quarters on the upper levels of the OMBIcademy.

"What are you referring to specifically, Major?" came the eerily distorted voice.

"Roden is acting strangely. I think he's beginning to doubt the EMC."

"Watch him closely. If he means to defect, I want to know about it," the dark face said menacingly.

"Of course, I will report on it immediately," Sanders replied quickly.

"How are the boys progressing?"

"Alex's records were sealed when he returned to Sigma, so I'm not sure about him. His brother has been growing faster than we anticipated; even the council's techno-psychologist came in to evaluate his progress."

"Alex's records were sealed because he was promoted. The council's interference won't slow this down if Connor is growing as fast as you say," the voice said as if the speaker already knew what Sanders was reporting on. "Any word about what is happening with William?"

Sanders thought he detected concern through the distortion. "I don't think you have to worry about him becoming a threat. What can one man do?"

"Don't underestimate him, Major," the voice said harshly.

"I understand. I will be sure we continue to monitor him," Sanders said before the communication ended.

~ ~ ~

The psychological evaluation began in a practice room that Connor had never been in before, over by Yellow Army's barracks. This particular setting was rolling green hills that bordered a rocky coastline. The green grass swayed in the blowing wind and the rocky shore below produced the calming sound of waves breaking.

Connor sat on the grass staring off into the ocean on what felt like a summer afternoon. When Doctor Purvel arrived, Connor didn't turn around to address him; instead he kept looking out at the vast ocean ahead of him.

"Hello, young man. My name is Doctor Purvel, but you can call me Julius if you like," Doctor Purvel said in a friendly tone.

Connor didn't turn around, watching the water glisten in the sun as he replied, "Connor Pereira."

"It's nice to meet you. You have come a long way in a short time; how do you feel about being away from home?" Purvel asked, maintaining his distance and non-threatening posture.

"Fine," Connor replied as if Purvel were annoying him.

"I can see that you have made a lot of friends here, Connor, and have been working hard to be a good commander. The United Earth Defense Force appreciates commanders who take their role seriously," Purvel said as he took a few slow steps in Connor's direction.

Connor was quiet.

"Connor, I want you to tell me what you are feeling in this place." Purvel sat down beside Connor.

"I like it. It reminds me of when we used to go to the ocean," Connor said quietly.

"You mean with your family, yes?"

"Yes…"

"Do you miss your family?"

"Yes."

"Connor, some of the council have been wondering how you are learning so quickly. Is there anything you want to tell me about that?"

"I'm just using what you guys gave me. I want to do my best," Connor stated.

"Why do you want to do your best?"

Connor took a deep breath before replying, "I want to end the war so Alex and I can go home."

Doctor Purvel put his hand on Connor's shoulder and asked, "Can you show me some of the things you have learned at the Academy so far?"

Connor shrugged and reluctantly got up off the ground. He began by manifesting the virtual weapons that he had unlocked, followed by some of the martial arts forms he had been studying.

"Impressive. You have learned a lot in a very short time, Connor. Can I share something with you?"

"Okay," Connor replied.

"Your brother was also a fast learner. He's been making the other children at the Academy look stupid for years."

Connor laughed at that.

"But your brother didn't learn as fast as you are learning."

Connor shrugged.

"Do you think the other kids feel bad that they can't learn as fast?"

"I don't care," Connor said, getting tired of wasting time talking to this guy.

"Connor, I want to know how you feel about being the best."

"Your opinion of how good I am doesn't really matter to me. I don't feel anything about it. I'm getting bored, can I go?" Connor asked, looking quite bored indeed.

"Just one more question, Connor. What do you think of the Earth Military Council?"

Connor knew that this kind of question was dangerous. He and William used to talk about the council's mandate to make it unlawful to speak negatively of the council or their decisions. Bored and irritated that he was wasting time, Connor decided to be as honest as he possibly could.

"I don't think of the Earth Military Council at all."

"What do you…" Purvel began, but Connor stopped him with an upraised hand and began walking toward the exit.

"Nope. You said one more question," Connor said as he left the room.

"So I did," Purvel conceded.

~ ~ ~

Connor was halfway back to the Blue Army barracks when he came around a corner and almost bumped into Marcus Ramirez, who he hadn't seen much of since his first day at the Academy.

"Sorry," Connor said insincerely as he tried to move around Marcus.

The older boy put his arm out, blocking Connor's path.

"What?" Connor said, having spent all his patience for the day on his psychological evaluation. "I'm in a hurry."

Marcus looked at Connor so intently with his dark eyes, that Connor wasn't sure if he was going to talk or try to hit him. In either sparring match, Connor was sure that he would win.

"I want to use the practice rooms too," Marcus said quietly.

"They are all around the Academy; go find your own!"

"I don't know how to open the doors," Marcus said, sounding defeated.

"Don't be a baby, it's easy. You just have to walk in, and just know that the door will open."

"What do you mean by that?"

"I mean just what I said, walk through. If you think it might not open, it won't," Connor explained, unsure why anyone would try anything if they expected to fail.

Marcus removed his arm and let Connor pass.

"If you're lying to me, kid, I am going to come find you," Marcus threatened as Connor walked away.

"That's a good way to end up in the infirmary," Connor shot back, leaving a very frustrated Marcus Ramirez behind him.

~ ~ ~

Fully suited up for his mission, Alex climbed back into Skoll for the flight to Hades Colony. The other thirty-eight members of Black Squadron that were fit for duty were assigned to ten Anubis Fighters that included a pilot, navigator, and gunner as was required, even with the benefit of OMBI interfaces. Very few Anubis Fighters had less than a three-man crew, and those were highly specialized and rare, like the Tizona.

The other eight pilots operated Ra Fighters to fly escort to the two large Battle Frigates from the First Fleet.

It was enough firepower to level a small planet, which caused Alex to worry a bit about what command thought he might encounter out there. His mission briefing documents contained vague information about Atmos XI, but nothing about the expected number of Gortha ships.

Piloting Skoll was easier than Alex expected it would be. The controls, as it turned out, were almost useless because Skoll responded to Alex's thoughts. Alex maneuvered through the docking bay and out into the vacuum beyond with seamless ease. He learned quickly to not fight the movements of the machine around him, but to flow with them like water finding a path through rocks. The more he felt like he was moving normally, the better Skoll responded.

Alex had no point of reference for moving through space or activating a slipstream, but his zero-gravity training had prepared him well for what to expect. It required only a slight modification of how he imagined propelling himself through space to gain the poise required to move around.

When Black Squadron assembled outside the main docking bay, Alex heard many jealous moans and complaints over his communication system from the other soldiers of his squadron. Alex only laughed in response.

After meeting up with the two Assault Frigates from the First Fleet, Alex was ordered by the commander of the UEDF Griswold to open a wide slipstream to the Eagle Nebula.

Fortunately, Alex's OMBI was a step ahead, already syncing up with the Skoll's slipstream drive. He sped through the menus with the speed of thought, selecting the Eagle Nebula from a list that included several areas of the Milky Way Galaxy that Alex had never heard of. Alex even had options on how long the trip was to take and which planet he wanted to arrive at.

Not wanting to make a mistake on his first mission, Alex set the timer for eighteen days and selected Atmos XI as his destination. Taking a deep breath, he engaged the slipstream drive and was pulled through the rift in space-time toward Hades Colony on the furthest journey from home he had ever taken.

Chapter 13

Secrets

By the end of Connor's fourth week in the battle academy, he felt extremely comfortable with his routine. He had been working hard to keep his mind off the things that haunted him: the home he left behind, his brother off on some mission using experimental hardware, and, most of all, the dreams he had about his mother dying. They were coming back.

He wasn't sure what had started those old dreams up, but he didn't like waking up in tears each morning hours before his alarm was supposed to sound.

The battle with Green Army had been nearly a shutout in the melee arena the week before. Connor expected some rule bending from the warning that Alex had given him a couple of weeks prior, so he had his team moving aggressively. Green Army seemed to think that they would be able to set physical trip-wires that they had stolen from a utility closet near the arena entrance of the school. They never even got the chance.

Blue Army, with three squads moving fast, swept behind Green while they were still getting set up. Cat's squad, along with Connor and his body guards, formed a line to crush Green Army between the two groups. So complete was their devastation, Blue Army only suffered two casualties. It would have been bad for Blue Army, but Connor had spotted soldiers from Green Army milling about two days before, and when he pulled up a station schematic and found out the nature of the utility closet, he pieced together their plan himself. Connor only got two kills in the battle, but he figured it would be better for morale if he let his army do more of the damage and play catch up to his points.

Connor also found it interesting that his OMBI was starting to offer vehicle upgrades and unlocks, even though he wasn't supposed to begin vehicle training for another two years. Connor toyed with the idea of using a training room to brush up on his vehicle skills, but he had so little time in the day as it was, he decided to put it off.

Everyone in Blue Army was anxious for their first battle with Black Army, since they were supposed to be the best army in the school, regardless of class. They talked like they were lucky to have that battle put off so long so they could train more, until Connor reminded them that Black Army would be training too- and probably getting help from older classes.

To their credit Blue Army had been working hard, sometimes even having squad versus squad battles without Connor even being there. His lieutenant choices seemed to be working out well, with Cat and Ladder keeping a good rapport with their squads. Manzar and Skulls were not as good at leading, but they were both good fighters. Connor had been working with them on their leadership skills on the side and they were both making admirable progress.

On the day they were to fight Black Army, Connor almost missed the fight, having been working on his martial arts mastery test. He had almost switched over to another weapon, but something about martial arts training kept Connor's focus better, and he really liked the idea of building a skill that would help him outside of the training room when he didn't have a sword or gun handy.

Running to the arena entrance, Connor met up with his army just in time to lead them into the arena. Cat glared at him as he ran by, forehead covered in sweat.

"You're almost late, commander," Cat said as he ran by her squad.

"Then I'm right on time," Connor replied with a grin.

"Well, how was it? Ladder bet me my dessert that you would need two sessions to pass that test. I bet him you'd do it in one," Cat said wryly.

Connor zipped up the jacket of his uniform and whispered quietly, "You won," followed by a boyish grin that made Cat's heart skip a beat.

Focusing on his army and still slightly out of breath from his run, Connor spoke quickly as they were moving into the arena lobby.

"We have defeated Yellow, Red, and Green armies without any problem at all," Connor began, ignoring Carl's wince at the mention of the Red Army match.

"Now we're going to face Black Army, who we all know has a reputation for winning every time they fight. Today, however, they are going to lose for the first time in OMBIcademy history!" Connor shouted with conviction.

A cheer went up through the ranks of Blue Army and all of them believed in what their commander had said.

As the lobby spun and moved to set up for the battle, Connor began cycling through his OMBI to look for potential upgrades that would help him in the coming battle. He had wanted to save up for the *Neuro-Sync* application; however, he hadn't unlocked a lot of different weapons to switch between, so he let it pass.

Connor hadn't activated his OMBI's score function in a few days, and had completely forgotten to upload his score from the Green Army win, so the score in the lobby still read 30:0. When

Connor opened up his points tab, he was extremely surprised to see that he had 27,900 points available to spend.

Passing the intermediate, advanced, and master martial arts tests had given him 18,000 points that he hadn't yet spent.

Smiling, Connor thought it might be fun to bring something new into the fight, depending on the arena that was selected.

~ ~ ~

When the ranged arena prompt came up on the lobby screen, Connor shared a nod with his Lieutenants. They had been practicing for this in the training rooms and even earning a few extra points running mock battles, to unlock some weapons. Connor had been telling his army to not unlock anything until the equipment was needed, so they could remain more versatile and adaptive.

Every squad had at least three members with firearms unlocked, including all of the lieutenants and Connor's bodyguards except Tim, who had unlocked and been training with throwing weapons. All the other members had unlocked crossbows to use for this fight.

When the red door opened, Connor wasn't surprised to see that this ranged arena was different from the large wall and two towers he had battled against Red Army in two weeks before. This time the landscape was like nothing Connor had seen.

He appeared to be standing on one side of a large chasm in dense forest. Tall green trees and the sounds of birds added ambiance to the serene landscape. Blue Army moved quickly to the edge of the tree line, spreading out and awaiting orders. Connor spotted a rope bridge that spanned the sixty-foot gorge near the center of the arena.

Blue Army was still taking cover when the barrage of gunfire began from the opposite side. Black Army was already in position. From his vantage point, Connor couldn't see a single member of Black Army on the opposite side. Some members of Blue Army were trying to launch attacks at the tree line, but according to the scoreboard, which was floating above the bridge, it didn't look like they were doing any damage.

"If this ends up as anything other than a draw, I'll be surprised," Carl stated from his hiding place behind a nearby stump.

Cat was nodding from her position beside Connor before Carl had finished his statement. "I think he's right," she said anxiously, "I don't see any way of winning a firefight in this kind of a location."

Connor thought quickly, ordering Ladder to have his squad fall back and begin launching arrow volleys toward Black Army to keep them looking up. Manzar and Skulls moved their squads to flank the bridge, preventing anyone from gaining a foothold on the Blue Army side of the arena.

"I'm not playing to tie. I want to win!" Connor said furiously to himself, unable to think of an idea that would give his army an advantage.

He wasn't sure where the thought had come from, but somewhere in the back of his mind while he was trying to visualize an outcome where he would win, Connor saw himself using throwing explosives out toward the other side. Unfortunately, Connor had nothing on his OMBI that indicated that he could even use explosives.

"Dice, what throwing weapons do you have?" Connor asked.

"Knife unlocked, hatchet, shuriken, and javelin locked," Dice replied without even looking at his OMBI.

On impulse Connor unlocked *throwing weapon* from his OMBI's ranged section and was excited to see a new option appear: *explosives*.

Connor was smiling when he unlocked the section, despite the 5000-point price tag they carried. These options were far more expensive than he would have liked, and he resolved to work on long-range planning in the near future.

Connor read through the options carefully: *dynamite, grenade, rocket launcher,* and *mortar.* He looked across the chasm, nearly taking a bullet to the head while figuring the distance to be within his throwing range.

Connor unlocked *grenade* for 4000 points and glanced out again, unable to see any Black Army soldiers still. He remained frustrated.

"I don't think lobbing grenades around is going to help us much," Connor said to Cat, as he looked up at the timer counting down: 40:40 35 minutes.

"Isn't there a HUD option that someone can use to help us see where Black Army is?" Cat asked insightfully.

Connor was scrolling through menus by hand before Cat had even finished speaking. *Infrared, thermal, highlighting, zoom,* and *motion sensor.*

The idea that there was an infrared ability made Connor wonder if he was going to be fighting in the darkness any time soon. He figured that it wouldn't help in this scenario anyway and moved on down the list.

The *motion sensor* was appealing to Connor, although the cost made him wondering if thermal imaging would be adequate for the task. In the end he stuck with *thermal,* thinking that having more points for now would be better in the long run, until he could master more tests, anyway.

Connor was delighted after he activated his thermal vision. He could see the members of Black Army entrenched on the far side of the chasm in small groups, well concealed. A few had even begun attempting to climb the trees on the other side to get a height advantage on the hidden squads of Blue Army that were near the ravine edge.

He manifested his virtual grenade, which was glowing blue in his hand, pulled the pin, and threw it as hard as he could to the far side of the ravine. A second grenade took the first one's place in Connor's hand and he threw it as well. By the time the third explosive was airborne, the first was just detonating.

Chaos ruled the other side of the chasm with members of Black Army scrambling to get out of the way of the explosive barrage Connor was sending their way. The soldiers of Blue Army were laughing at first, but quickly began launching virtual arrows and bullets at the enemy troops, who had broken cover to run from grenades.

Connor's arm was getting tired after a few minutes but he didn't let up, throwing grenade after grenade into the largest concentrations of Black Army troops he could see. In the end, with a very sore arm, he watched as the last soldier on the opposite side got blasted while attempting to hide behind a bush near the back of the arena.

Looking up at the scoreboard, Connor felt a swell of pride. The reputation that Black Army had of being unbeatable was shattered in thirteen minutes with a complete shutout.

Connor had thought his team picked off most of the stragglers and was shocked at the effectiveness of his explosives. He earned thirty-four kills in the match, and after five matches, Connor was up to 66:0.

Before he'd even started to leave the arena he was drafting a message. Knowing Alex was on a mission, he wasn't expecting a reply anytime soon, but he couldn't resist.

To: Mephisto
Subject: Shut out!

Message: Guess who just shut out Black Army in his first match against them! 34 kills too! Next time can you spend a little more time training these hissers so I have something to do other than baby-sit for 13 minutes?

—Message Sent—

Connor's left arm ached from throwing grenades and he was sweating from the activity. Blue Army cheered exuberantly as they collected their points for winning.

Instead of walking out with his army, he walked across the bridge, which didn't fade away like the trees and chasm when the virtual elements of the battlefield disappeared. Looking over the edge, Connor saw that the ground was only about five feet down and wondered what would have happened if he'd jumped in during the fight. He figured he would earn a death or something and resolved to figure that out in a practice room instead of an arena match.

When he got to the other side, he addressed the first Black Army soldier he found.

"Where is your commander?" Connor demanded, Cat and Skulls coming up behind him.

The kid was shocked. Normally soldiers from different armies didn't communicate much. They had different gym and lunch times and only rarely interacted in the halls.

"He should be waiting at the exit ramp," the kid said, seeming unsure of whether or not he should be talking to someone from another army.

It wasn't hard for Connor to spot the commander without the virtual trees obscuring his view. His black uniform with gold braid on his wrist seemed to fit the boy's hawkish features. Connor walked up to the boy and extended his hand out.

"I'm Raptor, commander of Blue Army 2126," Connor said.

The boy glanced at his lieutenants, who only shrugged slightly in reply.

"Annihilator, commander of Black Army 2126," the boy replied, matching Connor's gesture and shaking his hand.

Connor could feel the calluses of the boy's fingers, marking him as someone who had grown up working with his hands. The commander of Black Army had a sharp nose and narrow brown eyes. Even his hair was bird-like, standing tall and combed back.

"I won't patronize you by saying it was a good match. We may not be on the same team, but when we graduate we will be on the same side, so next time really bring it!" Connor said, challenging the boy's ego.

Annihilator smiled at Connor unexpectedly.

"Your brother said that you would be the first commander to ever beat Black Army in a fight. We all expected it sooner or later. Didn't think it would be a shutout on our first fight though," Annihilator said with an undignified chuckle.

It was Connor's turn to smile.

"Listen, this is a waste of my time if it's going to be like that. Mephisto did you no favor by telling you that. This is a game that you came into expecting to lose, so you lost. You are Black Army; you're not supposed to lose, ever. Keep that in your head the next time we fight and we'll see what you really are made of."

Connor turned and walked away back to his own exit ramp, leaving behind a frustrated Annihilator.

When they were past the bridge, Skulls spoke up.

"Your challenge there is going to make it hard to beat them next time."

"Good! We won't get better if it only takes me to win what should have been a hard fight!" Connor responded with frustration mounting in his voice.

Cat looked at Connor suddenly with lines of concern forming across her ginger features.

"What is it, Connor?" Cat asked, using his name rather than call sign.

Tears rimmed Connor's chocolate-colored eyes as he stopped and looked at Amanda.

"Sometimes there are fights you can't win. You just do your best and no matter what you still die! Well I'm not going to die like my mom did. I am going to figure out how to win no matter what! But I won't ever be able to do that if this is as hard as it gets!" Connor was screaming by the end of his speech, tears flowing freely from his eyes.

The kids exiting the opposite side of the arena had stopped and were staring back at Connor, who was sobbing. Amanda grabbed Connor and pulled him close. He tried to struggle for a moment, then broke down in her arms. The other soldiers of Blue Army were stunned and uncertain of what to do.

"I'm sorry," Amanda whispered in his ear while running her fingers through Connor's brown hair.

Carl grabbed Manzar and moved across the bridge, ushering the kids from Black Army out their exit, saying that the show was over.

Ladder, Skulls, and Dice went about clearing out Blue Army while Hunter and Katana moved away, keeping other kids from getting anywhere close to their commander.

Everyone in the OMBIcademy knew how Connor's mom had died. She was considered a hero in the UEDF. To a soldier, everyone felt sympathy for Connor at that moment, crying tears he had held in for a long time.

When the arena was clear and Connor had calmed down a bit, Amanda kissed him softly on his cheek. Connor's face flushed a brighter red, but he smiled and looked at the ground.

The moment was interrupted as a voice came over the Arena speaker system, booming from the ceiling high above.

"Clear the arena, Blue Army."

Connor and his friends walked slowly up the ramp to the exit as they began talking about how cool grenades were and what other OMBI unlocks might appear by combining different battle applications. Connor's eyes were still red, but by the time he reached the door, he was laughing with his lieutenants and bodyguards about shutting out Black Army.

~ ~ ~

From high above, Colonel Victor Roden watched the friends walk out of the ranged arena, feeling a rare tug of sympathy for the Blue Army commander. He'd heard every word of the exchange between Connor and Annihilator as well as Connor's breakdown. While the emotion touched Roden, something about what Connor had said sparked a troubling thought in his mind.

The official story of Captain Mercer's death at the hands of a Gortha surprise attack was released after a black box recording had been recovered from the colonization freighter Andromeda when it returned to earth. The report suggested that the Gortha appeared out of slipstream, surrounding the freighter, which got away only through the heroic efforts of the Tizona.

Like everyone else, Roden accepted the report when it was released, and joined in mourning the hero who had saved two thousand colonists.

Roden walked over to his datapad and opened the files from 2115 and began reading. For twenty minutes he went over the data, looking for discrepancies. The report was much like he remembered it, but a search for the black box video from the Andromeda came back, "Classified: Above Top Secret." He made several attempts to open the file using various usernames and access codes, all of which came back with access denied.

Frustrated but resourceful, Roden began looking up information on the survivors of the incident; two thousand participants in the conflict who were sleeping in stasis pods during the journey.

No results found.

Roden took a deep breath and began looking up crew manifest for the Andromeda. Of the twenty-three crew members, all were listed as MIA. This included Captain Armando Velez, who had supposedly issued a statement praising the heroism of the pilot who had saved him and his ship after returning to Earth.

The suspiciousness of the missing crew caused the colonel's chest to tighten with anxiety. Troubled by what he might find, Roden began the process of looking through the passenger manifest, which had a list of names, occupations, and addresses for each of the passengers before the mission to colonize the Hourglass Nebula. He began searching each passenger individually for current locations and occupations, but was interrupted as his desk communicator buzzed.

Roden's left hand tapped the communicator as his right hand began copy and pasting classified documents into an outgoing message. The official report, crew dossier, passenger manifest, and encrypted black box video were transferred to the message as fast as Roden could move them.

"Yes?" Roden answered, trying to sound calm.

"A man calling himself Operative Three from the EMC here to see you, sir," the administrator replied, her voice shaking slightly.

Roden took a deep breath and worked furiously, typing a message on his datapad, which read simply, "Something not right. My ability to investigate compromised. Good luck."

He'd heard of the EMC operatives before, but had never met one and had hoped he never would.

"Send the operative in Lucy and get some lunch; you've been at it all morning. That is an order." Roden didn't normally order his administrator around and made sure to emphasize the statement.

He could hear heavy footsteps moving outside the door to his observatory lounge. Without the benefit of encryption or an open network, Roden knew he was going to have to think of something quickly, something outside of the box.

The thought gave him an idea as he accessed the OMBI data of his students. He knew he couldn't access Connor's OMBI, as it had closed off the data stream to the Academy, but he wasn't out of options. Hands working furiously, Roden typed transmission commands.

To: Captain Alex Pereira > Immediate Forward > Connor Pereira > Immediate Forward > William Mercer > Send

Quickly deleting his outgoing message, Roden began a new message, attaching random quotes on success that he found quickly.

To: Captain Alex Pereira
Subject: Success
Message: Here is that quote I told you about Captain. Good luck in your career! Sorry if you get this twice, I think the first one was an error.

"The heights by great men reached and kept
Were not attained by sudden flight,
But they, while their companions slept,
Were toiling upward in the night." – Roden

—Message Sent—

The door opened. The man who walked in was not tall; in fact, he had no real extraordinary features about him at all. His face was plain, as were his clothes. If Roden had seen this man walking on the street, he wouldn't have looked twice. The man's walk betrayed his skill and confidence though, moving with no waste of motion, purposely striding forward with the measured steps of a killer.

"What can I do for you, Operative?" Roden asked, not moving from his chair.

The man stopped and stared at Roden. He gave no explanation as he produced a small capsule from his pocket and placed it in front of Roden on his desk.

Roden looked up at the man with a resolved look on his face.

"Three. Operative Three. You have been snooping in a dangerous place, Colonel. I am here to make sure that you stop," Operative Three said in a cool voice.

"Then, this is the painless option?" Roden asked quietly, nodding to the capsule on the edge of his desk.

The operative nodded slightly and waited.

There would be no interrogation, no trial, and no funeral. Colonel Victor Roden had known the path he'd started down was dangerous when he began looking for the truth behind the story of the incident of 2115. He hadn't expected General Harruhama to send an assassin, or that they would arrive as quickly as they did. He'd heard of officers who questioned the leadership of the EMC going missing, but he never put much stock in the rumors until now.

Clearly his searches had been monitored and he could only hope that the data he sent through Alex and Connor's OMBIs would become encrypted like their personal messages had without putting the two boys in jeopardy. It was a gamble, but if Harruhama was willing to kill him for even looking, he knew that the truth was something terrible.

Roden took a deep breath and picked up the capsule on his desk and placed it into his mouth. As it dissolved, the poison was released into his body. Roden felt it move quickly through his blood, making his veins feel as though they were aflame. The pain was intense, long-lasting. His insides began to shut down one organ at a time, painfully melting away over the course of several minutes.

Operative Three watched with a satisfied smile as the colonel who had sought information that could usurp General Harruhama's leadership writhed in pain upon the floor of his office. There was no painless escape for traitors of the UEDF. When the man finally stopped moving, the operative collected the datapad and non-OMBIcademy files from Roden's desk.

"The traitor Roden has been removed, sir," the operative spoke into his wrist communicator.

"Understood. Return to headquarters immediately," came the expected reply.

The EMC assassin turned and slowly walked out of the room.

Chapter 14

A Long Way to Run

In the days following his emotional breakdown, Connor didn't feel quite himself. He had been bottling up frustration and pain since his birthday and never really vented it. He was glad for his friends then, and realized just how close he had gotten to them. In the evenings after his classes and workouts, Connor would sit up late with Cat, holding hands and talking about where they had come from.

Connor loved it when Cat talked about Ireland. She was passionate about her homeland and had loved being there. Connor told Cat about Healdsburg and the places he visited with his family. He found out that Cat had been drafted because of her extraordinarily high testing scores. When she was nine she had begun taking high school classes and received her draft notice two months after her tenth birthday.

"I had a week after my notice before I was required to report to duty," Connor had told her.

"That would have been better. Knowing it was coming was agony. I couldn't finish my classes on time, and my parents were so clingy!" Cat had responded.

The conversation did make Connor change his perspective about things a bit. A long goodbye might have been harder on both him and his stepfather. During those nights they talked, Connor told Cat a lot about his time with William and also the memories he had of his mother. He even told Cat about his recurring dream of her death.

During the days, the lieutenants would rotate between running drills in the training rooms and practicing with Connor in the dojo. Connor's bodyguards also rotated in with the regular army and personal workouts, since they wanted to be knowledgeable about the formations and tactics the army was using. Connor was always around for the first practice but would move into personal training as the day went on, preferring solitude and close friends to leading.

The rumors that Colonel Roden had disappeared didn't affect the classes or training schedules much. But the day after he went missing they had received an OMBI message that a new Head Commander was being selected for the OMBIcademy and to continue with their normal schedules.

On the third day after the battle with Black Army, Connor noticed the date while reading an OMBI message about changes to the commissary schedule. March 13th! Connor drafted the letter immediately:

To: William Mercer
Subject: Happy Birthday!
Message: Sorry I couldn't be there on your birthday, William, hopefully it turns out better than mine did. I miss hearing from you. I am doing well here. I have a lot of friends. Write me back!
– Connor

PS: How do you know when a girl is your girlfriend?

—*Message Sent*—

That morning Connor was in the dojo early, opting to go in alone to start some new training. When he arrived, he saw Omega standing on a hill far away from the dojo, staring off into the distance. Connor jogged up to where the training program was standing and looked out to see a picturesque valley and green hills beyond.

"What are you looking at?" he asked, curious about the program's strange behavior.

"Where am I?" Omega asked Connor.

"You're in a training room of the OMBIcademy," Connor replied.

"Understood, Initiator," Omega replied, seeming satisfied with the answer.

"What's out there?" Connor asked, pointing to the hills beyond.

"I don't understand your question."

"What's over that hill? And another thing, why do you always call me Initiator?" Connor asked inquisitively.

"We have never been over that hill, so I do not know. I call you Initiator because you are the architect of my function."

"What?" Connor asked with a chuckle.

Before Omega could answer, Connor started running down the hill. When he got up to the top of the next hill he looked back to see Omega standing where he had left him.

"Come on!" Connor yelled.

Omega manifested next to Connor, startling him.

"So you can just teleport around," Connor stated more than asked, looking out at the rolling hills from his new vantage point.

Staring across the lush countryside on what felt like a summer day, Connor decided he was going to see how far he could go. He began running in the direction he had started without a thought of looking back. He kept his eyes forward at the endless horizon ahead.

He ran for what seemed like hours, pushing past his fatigue and achy legs. Omega matched his pace, floating by Connor's side as he ran. Eventually the hills flattened out and Connor came upon a pristine coastline. The blue water was a brilliant contrast to the green grass, and Connor climbed down a steep, rocky hill until he was next to the water. Stripping off his exercise uniform into his underwear, Connor jumped into the water, which felt cold against his skin. He swam and played in the surf while an impassive Omega watched from the beach.

Coming back to shore after a few minutes, Connor laid on the sand and marveled over how real it all felt. Getting an idea, he accessed the vehicle section of his OMBI. Not wanting to spend any points, Connor thought a moment.

"Omega, I want to test beginner motorcycle skills," Connor said, not really sure what would happen.

Omega turned around and two small dirt bikes appeared on the beach. On the coastline ahead, a series of red and blue flagged gates appeared from the sand.

"We race to the end on beginner difficulty. On your word, Initiator," Omega said, moving to the red dirt bike.

A big smile appeared on Connor's face as he put his exercise uniform back on and walked over to the blue dirt bike. Connor had ridden small dirt bikes a couple of times with some friends back in Healdsburg, enough that he didn't need to be taught the controls. He got on and started his engine, revving the motor a couple of times for good measure.

"On your marks, get set, GO!" Connor yelled as he put the bike into gear and pulled the throttle back. Omega accelerated quickly and pulled ahead of Connor through a narrow part of the route before moving away, toward the first red gate.

Connor didn't really care that much that Omega was ahead, and wouldn't have minded running this test over and over again with how much fun it was. But for good measure, he decided he would do his best. Taking a deep breath of ocean air, Connor dropped the gear to catch up.

The two passed through the first few gates with Omega in the lead, but Connor was gained ground, albeit slowly. He hadn't spent any time learning the techniques he would be required to know to win, but he was still making pretty good time through the course.

As they approached the final gate, Connor put his head down and pulled as hard as he could on the throttle. He wasn't watching his opponent as he crossed the gate, but the buzz on his left forearm indicated that he had earned some points.

As they come to a stop, Omega looked at Connor and said, "Congratulations on passing the beginner motorcycle test."

Connor beamed.

"That was fun, Omega. Let's take our bikes back up to those fields and keep riding!" Connor said, forgetting about his classes and obligations.

"Affirmative," Omega replied.

Connor rode up a broken trail carefully until he was back up above the coastline on the green fields. The two sped along in the cool ocean air over some hills above the rocky coast line. For several minutes they rode on. Connor laughed as he enjoyed the sense of freedom he felt riding on the back of the dirt bike.

It was Connor who stopped first, coming to an area he'd seen before. It was the rocky coastline he'd come to for his techno-psychological evaluation. No one else was there beside Connor and Omega, but Connor recognized the area because of the curious arrangements of wildflowers that were growing in that spot.

"Is this another training room?" he asked breathlessly.

"Yes," Omega said in his impassive voice.

"How is that possible?" Connor asked, stunned by Omega's answer.

"Training rooms are open areas surrounded by hardware which produces a wireless data stream, connecting it with other rooms."

"So between the two rooms I travel as wireless data? How does that work?" Connor asked, unable to fathom what he was hearing.

"Your mind is not ready to process the information required to explain molecular-data transportation between two points," Omega said calmly.

"Fine," Connor snapped, irritated by Omega's condescending answer. "But where was I in between the dojo and here?"

"The distance between two points is relative to your perception, Initiator. In your case, you felt five point seven miles traversed between the dojo and this shoreline. The actual linear distance is nine hundred and seventy-two feet, three inches."

"Explain that, like William would!" Connor demanded.

Omega's image shifted and the little boy that Connor was talking to grew in front of him to appear as the man who had raised him. The impassive tone of Omega's voice changed into the familiar sound of his stepfather's voice.

"You think that other places are far away on the world. But when you look at a globe, the distance between you and the ocean is less than the tip of your finger. On a map of the solar system, the distance between you and Alex would be the size of your thumb. On a map of the galaxy, everything you know or have ever seen - no matter how far away - is right beside you," Omega said before reverting back to his usual childlike form.

The alarm on Connor's OMBI went off before he had a chance to ask the ten other questions he wanted to at that moment. Military History class was beginning soon and he had to go.

"I have a lot of questions to ask you later!" Connor said, moving to the exit point he knew was near Yellow Army's barracks.

"Yes, Initiator," Omega said as he watched Connor leave.

~ ~ ~

Connor wasn't the only one who noticed that he'd left from a different place than he entered. Since his humiliation over two weeks prior, Johnny Perez had been trying to figure out a way to beat his old friend, who seemed unbeatable in the arena.

Johnny had been asking around and studying Connor's patterns. When Johnny's spy reported that Connor went into the training room he always occupied and ended up in class without coming back out, Johnny thought he was being lied to. But then he began to wonder if maybe there was something he hadn't thought of.

He thought about trying to ask Carl to help him again, but a week after the battle he had tried that and almost got into a fight. No one else in Blue Army seemed interested in talking with him, let alone sharing information about Connor. Even the older classes, where he knew Connor had some rivalries, weren't open to the discussion.

He had been staring at the door of the training room for nearly an hour when, by luck he noticed Connor walking back to his barracks out of the corner of his eye. He returned to his own barracks shortly after to weigh his options.

Johnny was feeling very frustrated sitting on his bed when his OMBI flashed a message that he was summoned to the observation lounge of the OMBIcademy to report to the new Head Commander.

Sure that he was going to get expelled or executed, Johnny dragged his feet the entire way to the lift that would take him up to the upper levels of the Academy. The airman at the door to the lift looked down at Johnny menacingly after sizing him up and selecting the observation room for him on the lift's keypad.

When the door opened on the upper level, Johnny almost didn't step out. The administrator saw him though, and waved him forward. Reluctantly, he proceeded from the elevator, which closed behind him, leaving him trapped in a place where he didn't want to be.

"Are you Johnathan Perez, call sign Mouse, commander of Red Army 2126?" the administrator asked impatiently.

Johnny nodded slowly, frowning the entire time.

"Wait over there," the administrator said, pointing to some chairs on the side of her desk.

Johnny's shoulder slumped as he sat down and waited for what seemed like forever. Sweating from his forehead, all he wanted to do was to get back into the lift and head back downstairs to the safety of his barracks, where he had a whole army around him instead of up here where he was exposed.

"Head Commander Setzer will see you now," the administrator said as if she had just announced his execution.

Johnny walked slowly through the doors into the observation lounge that looked down upon the various battle arenas of the academy. The man standing in the room wasn't very tall, but his well-muscled form made Johnny think of a bull getting ready to charge. The man's bald head shined with the reflection from the ceiling lights as he stared at Johnny from across the room.

Stopping before the man's desk, Johnny remembered to salute before standing very still and clenching his fingers.

"So you're the mouse?" the man asked quietly in a baritone voice.

"Yes. Commander of Red Army 2126, Sir." Johnny replied quickly with all the confidence he could.

"Relax kid, I have been getting reports about your activity. You've been spying on your classmates."

"No, sir, I am just spying on Connor, uh, the commander of Blue Army. No one can beat him and I am trying to find a way how," Johnny replied timidly.

"Yes. I am aware you two used to be friends. Why don't you tell me about him?" Setzer asked with a stern look on his face.

"He always leaves me behind and he tricks me into looking like an idiot. I hate him! I think he is cheating. All he does is practice all the time so no one else gets a chance to win," Johnny ranted, gaining confidence as the man in front of him nodded along.

"According to your reconnaissance, how do you believe you can beat him?"

"I can't! Not even Black Army had a chance against him! I tried to beat him by, um, planting spies in his army, and even then he won! But it wasn't fair! He has too many points!"

"So you need more points, or more troops?" the man responded in a level tone.

"Yeah, if we had more points or a bigger team, maybe," Johnny replied angrily.

The bull-like man's sinister grin chilled Johnny to the core.

"What do you think about this?" the man said, sliding a datapad Johnny's way.

Before Johnny was a plan as dark as the man across the table's smile. Johnny read it over, looking at the diagrams, and smiled.

"Can we really do this?" Johnny asked excitedly.

"I thought you would enjoy that. I will notify the other commanders. You are dismissed," Setzer said with finality.

Johnny walked out of the Head Commander's office feeling great. He couldn't wait to tell everyone the plan that he and the Head Commander had come up with to beat Connor in a fight.

~ ~ ~

Back in the Head Commander's office, Major Sanders wasn't happy. He and the new Head Commander didn't exactly see eye to eye on how to run the Academy, and he had been growing more and more uncomfortable ever since finding Colonel Roden dead on the floor, apparently having suffered a massive heart attack.

"Is it really necessary to stack the deck against the kid so much?" Sanders asked Setzer as he walked over from the window. Sanders was sure that Johnny hadn't even seen him, being so focused on the plan and the imposing new Head Commander.

"What's the matter, Sanders, you got a soft spot for that kid?" Setzer replied while going over the former Head Commander's documents.

"I recruited him personally, sir. He is good, maybe the best we've ever produced. But this plan is overkill."

"Ha! So you do have a soft spot! This kid thinks he's better than everyone else and I want to take him down a peg or two. No one should think that highly of himself, you know?"

Sanders turned back toward the observation window to hide the disgust on his face.

~ ~ ~

William had spent birthdays alone before. After he started living on his own half his life ago, he would often work through those days, not really caring one way or the other. But after spending some with a family that he loved, being alone was particularly difficult. Marlena would always take him out to dinner and make sure he had cake, whether he wanted it or not. She was the kind of woman who thought birthdays were special and meant to be celebrated.

Prior to receiving the message on his datapad, William didn't even know what the date was. He had been pushing himself through the pain and loss every day. He'd even restored the old Triumph motorcycle that he had in his garage, which he had begun riding to clear his head. He had just gotten back from one such ride, still dressed in cold-weather rain gear on a drizzly day in Northern California, when the datapad lit up to inform him that he had messages.

The two messages from his device were sent about three days apart from Connor. He decided to read the latest one first, since it seemed far more festive.

Message 2: Happy Birthday. "Sorry I couldn't be there on your birthday, William, hopefully it turns out better than mine did. I miss hearing from you. I am doing well here. I have a lot of friends. Write me back! – Connor
PS: How do you know when a girl is your girlfriend?"
Delivered 12:25 2121-03-14
From: Pereira, Connor

With a big, genuine smile on his face, William sat down on a bar stool with a bottle of water and began to draft his reply.

To: Connor Pereira
Subject: You just know
Message: Thank you for the birthday message, Connor. I really appreciate that you reminded me that I'm getting older. I'm happy to hear that you're making a lot of friends, your mom always used to say that everyone was drawn to your light. As for the

other thing, if you have to ask, I think you might have a girl-friend. – William

—Message Sent—

Message 1: No Subject "Something not right. My ability to in-vestigate compromised. Good luck"
Delivered 1315 2121-03-10
From: Connor Pereira > Captain Pereira, Alex > Colonel Roden, Victor *—3 documents, 1 video attached—*

Curiously, William studied the string by which the message was sent. He had met Colonel Roden at his wife's funeral years before and remembered the man vaguely. He was the only person in attendance wearing a red beret, or any kind of a hat at all. He remembered that the man offered sincere condolences with tears in his eyes.

A red flag went off in William's head when he read the short message a second time. He opened the attachments and began sorting through the puzzle of what he was reading. He followed the same path Roden did, but didn't attempt logging into the black box video. Instead he began looking up the names of the crew who had been on the Andromeda to find out when and how they went missing. Slowly he began compiling a list of crew members who had news stories related to their disappear-ances or rewards for information from their families.

Men and women from all around the world were part of the colonization efforts, but seven of the twenty-three crew members of this particular ship had come from parts of California and Or-egon. Captain Armando Velez was an Argentine who had come from Buenos Aires, where William's brother-in-law currently lived. He had drafted a half-page message to him when he decid-ed against sending it. If what he was beginning to suspect might be true was true, William thought his messages might be monitored.

With his list of seven crew member addresses that were within driving distance, William packed his bags and strapped them to the Triumph motorcycle and began strapping his cold-weather gear back on. Taking enough cash to not be tracked by using credit services, he got on his bike purposefully and began to ride.

Chapter 15

Echoes of Yesterday

"**W**e were right about Roden," Sanders said to the dark figure when he established contact.

"I received the report that he was eliminated for seeking out the truth of the incident of 2115," the distorted voice replied.

"Well that's that then."

"No. You need to find out what he was looking at that was worth dying for, Major. We cannot make mistakes like this anymore. If there is unrest against the UEDF, we must act upon it more quickly!"

"I understand," Sanders said as the transmission was lost.

Sanders thought quietly in his dark room for a long while before laying down to unsuccessfully try going back to sleep.

~ ~ ~

With only two days to go until the next match, Connor had been approached by the commander of Black Army 2126, two Yellow Army lieutenants, and one teacher about the new Head Commander's plan to launch multiple armies against him during the next match.

When he first heard it, Connor began devising ways for his squads to hold off entire armies, depending on the layout of the arena. As more information came forward, he started to find the entire situation humorous. Sure, no one had been able to beat him, but after only a couple of months of trying, they had resorted to trying to cheat. Connor wasn't surprised that Johnny had been unable to keep the secret that the Head Commander had given him. He was, however, a little surprised that the other army commanders seemed to find it as distasteful as he did.

Sitting in the dojo with his four lieutenants, four bodyguards, and Omega, Connor told them all about what he had discovered about the connections between the training rooms. Figuring that these were supposed to be the brightest kids on earth, Connor thought he might get an answer about how he could physically teleport through a virtual landscape.

Cat had the only plausible hypothesis, indicating that there may be some tunnels below the school that continue the virtual landscape physically until reaching the other training rooms. Connor wasn't sure about that, but he began to discuss the theory of what the space in between the rooms might look like without any holographic elements anyway.

Before they went too deep down the rabbit hole, Connor began training with them in a target practice range he had Omega set up across the virtual environment. Connor even had Manzar bring in the Blue Army squads one at a time to get some target practice. The shut-out win against Black Army gave each member of Blue Army a cache of at least 2,000 points, which Connor had them save for firearm upgrades.

Having learned to shoot at seven years old at a ranch he had gone to with William, Connor began running through the firearm tests and even had Omega begin giving tests to Blue Army soldiers who were ready. Connor breezed through the beginner, intermediate, and advanced handgun tests, leaving his army and friends in awe. He then began working on rifle tests, which he passed as easily. The other soldiers weren't as skilled, but as Omega gave instruction, the children of Blue Army began to pass tests and collect upgrade points.

"We should have been doing this the entire time," Skulls had said to Ladder, who nodded in agreement.

"Yeah, I hope that none of the other armies have figured out how easy it is to unlock stuff when you train in it," Carl had added to the conversation.

"It's too bad we don't have more time in our day for this stuff; in a couple of months we could unlock everything on our OMBI," Dice said to Connor.

"I'm not so sure about that," Connor said thoughtfully, "These tests get pretty hard. I think we're supposed to take years to unlock them."

"If that's the case, why are you unlocking everything so fast?" Dice asked, suddenly very serious.

Cat chimed in before Connor had a chance to reply, "It's because he's a quick study. I'm glad he's our commander and not one of those other guys."

Giving up his place at the range to one of the soldiers from squad 3, Connor sat down against the corner of the dojo watching his army train with a satisfied grin. Watching his friends helping Omega give instruction to the other kids, Connor felt good about his chances in the upcoming battle. Going through his OMBI menu, Connor asked Omega what he suggested against an army that outnumbered his 4:1.

"I have no information regarding successful tactics in a one-sided battle," Omega said in his impassive voice.

"If I was a coward, I would suggest waiting out the timer, focusing on defense," Katana chimed in from his place near the end of the range.

Omega glanced at Katana with what Connor thought was a grin. Shaking his head at the absurd notion, Connor asked, "What are some famous one-sided battles?"

The wall of the dojo flickered slightly and a screen appeared in its place.

"In 1936, during a thirteen-day siege…" Omega began.

"During the Texas Revolution, one hundred and eighty-two Texans and volunteers held the Alamo against two thousand-four hundred Mexican soldiers. Next," Connor said, shrugging to Cat, who was looking at him with a big smile.

"I've been paying attention in Military History class," Connor lied. He had known a lot about military history before ever coming to the OMBIcademy.

"June, 1876…" Omega started.

"Battle of the Little Bighorn, Custer's last stand. Next," Connor said, shrugging again.

"480 BC, Greece…" Omega began again.

"Battle of Thermopylae," Connor replied quickly, taking it as a game.

Omega recited dates more quickly.

"Sudan 1898."

"Battle of Omdurman."

"Poland 1939."

"Battle of Winza."

"1610."

"Klushino."

"2115."

Connor stopped. No video played on the screen, but behind his eyes he could picture his mom dying in a dozen ways protecting the Andromeda from the Gortha attack.

"That's enough," Cat said to Omega, who stared at Connor blankly. Everyone had stopped their target practice and was watching Connor, unsure of what to expect. The training room was deadly silent except for the sound of wind blowing through the valley.

After a moment of silence, Connor lifted his head and got up off the ground. "The Hourglass Battle that began the Gortha War, where one ship defeated dozens of larger alien vessels while rescuing two thousand colonists and twenty-three crew members."

Connor grinned at Omega and said, "March 15th, 2121, the battle of training room eleven, where Raptor, Commander of Blue Army, kicks the virtual training program's butt in the grandmaster martial arts test."

Omega stared at Connor a moment then shifted into the image of a grown man wearing a karate gi. The man then multiplied until seven clones were surrounding Connor's position.

The other soldiers of Blue Army backed off and formed a semi-circle inside the walls of the dojo, watching with anticipation for the battle that was about to ensue.

Connor took seven deep breaths, closing his eyes and visualizing himself taking down the virtual opponents in a blur of motion and finishing the grand mastery martial arts test. He kept his eyes closed, listening to the wind sweep down the valley, through the grass and around his skin, onward out to the rocky coast he had discovered. He allowed himself to feel the wind's gentle caress until he began to sway like a tree in the breeze.

When he opened his eyes, he could see only the seven opponents surrounding his position. So absolute was his focus that when the clone directly behind him began to move, Connor was already acting.

Connor moved forward two steps, as if he were charging the three clones in front of him, and then, like the wind, changed direction into the two to his left, sending a barrage of fists and kicks into them before throwing himself into a backwards roll beneath the charge of the two clones coming from behind.

He came to his feet between them and threw his arms outward, aiming for center mass before spinning behind the clone to his right, using it as a shield against the four coming at him from the other side. Using the momentum of his spin and the shoulder of the clone as leverage, Connor leapt into the air back out toward the four clones charging in, kicking out several times at the middle two before spinning back around to the back of the clone he had grabbed for his jump.

The two clones he hadn't made contact with yet came on with blinding speed that seemed to be getting faster with each second of the fight. Remaining focused, Connor blocked the barrage, which he knew wouldn't end if he didn't make a move.

Feigning right, the clone on his left moved in for an attack. Connor dropped low and swept his leg out behind him, catching the clone off balance as it charged. He continued the momentum of his sweep and brought his leg back out high, catching the clone in front of him with a hook kick across the neck, sending it spinning to the ground.

Connor turned around to see the clone that he had swept getting back up quickly. Wasting no time, he charged forward with a furious onslaught of kicks and punches. Unable to defend against the boy's fury, the clone collapsed back onto the ground. Connor turned to attack again but found himself facing the passive face of Omega no longer wearing a gi.

"Congratulations, Initiator, for completing the Grand Mastery Test of the Martial Arts."

A cheer went up among the ranks of Blue Army before Connor realized what he was hearing.

Cat threw her arms around Connor and whispered into his ear, "Most one-sided fight I have ever even heard of."

Connor hugged her back, finally comprehending his victory. The entire fight felt slow to Connor, every move and reaction measured. He had moved like wind: letting himself flow through the battle, striking forward in powerful gusts, and rolling around obstacles. Calming down, Connor realized that the fight had lasted only two minutes, but he felt his body aching as if he had been fighting for hours.

Checking his OMBI, Connor was delighted that he had accumulated 52,300 points. Sitting back while the soldiers of Blue Army walked by to congratulate him, he felt a lot better about his chances in the coming battle. Cat sat next to him as they leaned against each other watching the soldiers train. Some were even attempting various tests for skills that they believed they had, prior to getting training, with mixed results.

Closing his eyes, Connor took a few deeps breaths before nodding off to sleep with a grin on his face.

~ ~ ~

It was the third attempt with the same result. Showing up at the address of the former crew member of the Andromeda left William growing more resolved in his purpose. On the first day of his trek, William stopped by an apartment in San Francisco to find a crew member's former girlfriend who said she hadn't seen the man in over six years, since he had left for the Hourglass Nebula Colony, in fact.

When he inquired about the story of the Andromeda's escape, the girlfriend didn't have an answer, saying that after she heard the news she expected to get a call, but nothing ever came through.

Later that same day in Monterey, William had to ask around to find another crewman's mother. She was an elderly woman who had been troubled ever since her son had been reported missing shortly after his return to earth from the Hourglass mission. She had neither seen him nor heard from him since before he left.

It was the next day in Santa Barbara that William encountered a strange man who insisted that his daughter was still in the Hourglass Nebula and had been sending transmissions to Earth for years under an alias. Unfortunately the man had no evidence and said he had deleted the records to avoid being tracked.

Watching the ocean roll by on his way to San Diego, William's mind started working through the problem while the sound of the motor rumbled in his ears.

The image was still fuzzy in the man's mind, but it was coming clearer with each passing minute while he worked through the details of the missing pieces of the puzzle ahead of him.

Cruising at seventy miles per hour down I-5, the possibilities of silencing an entire frigate's crew sat heavy in his mind. He had never trusted the global government and saw the truth through a lot of the holotube news' misleading announcements. But he knew that some truths were dangerous. Some might change his perception of reality and some might destroy him.

With that cryptic thought in his head, William drove through streets he was vaguely familiar with, having spent a part of his youth exploring the southern California coast. The cool ocean breeze reminded him of the times in his life when his passions were naïve and simple.

As he pulled up to the house in La Jolla, he was surprised to see that it had been burned out. The charred remains of a once-beautiful home with an ocean view were left like an ancient ruin at the end of the long driveway.

The black gate had been rusted shut, but William climbed over it, walking down an old stone path. As an architect he had an eye for seeing potential in places, and this place must have been beautiful in its prime. Rows of gardens that once might have been the pride of the people who lived here were now left untended and overgrown. Straight ahead the door still hung crooked upon its hinges, swaying noisily in the cool breeze.

He followed the broken path up to the house and walked in through a burnt hole in the wall to look around. The house wasn't huge, but it was sizeable with a simple, open floor plan. Nothing compared to the Mercer estate, but it had a charming quality of refinement and detail. An old marble fireplace still stood and William imagined the events that might have been held in front of it, where a family might have entertained guests or enjoyed birthday parties.

Shaking away his projections of the place, William continued through rooms looking for some indication of what had happened here. While rummaging through what appeared to be the study, he caught a glimpse of a smaller house beyond a dried-up pool. It appeared to still be standing, if a little worn. As he walked through the backyard and descended a short flight of stairs to the other house, he realized that this house was inhabited.

It made sense to William for a house in this area and for a property of this size to have a caretaker of some kind. But if the occupant was in charge of property maintenance, he had surely renounced his duty long ago.

William knocked on the door firmly, listening for signs of life beyond the windblown door. He heard a rustle of movement from inside, slow steps moving toward the door.

When the door creaked opened, William stood face to face with an elderly bald man who wore thick glasses and stood slightly hunched over. The smell of the room beyond was foul, William realized, taking a step backwards before introducing himself.

"Good day, my name is William Mercer."

"Oh, hello … What can I do for you?" the man replied in an unsteady voice, as if he hadn't spoken in years.

"I'm curious about what happened here," William responded firmly.

"A fire, two—no—three years ago."

"Do you know what happened to the family living here?"

"They were taken away by some men before the fire."

"I see. Were the men UEDF? Did they set the fire?"

"They didn't wear uniforms, but now that I think about it, they did seem to be soldiers of some kind. They set the fire when they were leaving."

"I understand. Do you know why they came here? Did it have anything to do with a man named John Michaelson?"

"This was his parents' house. He signed up to colonize another world and left. They were staying in contact via long-range transmission. Mrs. Michaelson always seemed so happy when she heard from her son," the man said, staring distantly off toward the ocean.

"You mean they were in contact before the colonization ship was attacked?" William asked, dreading the answer he was about to hear.

"Attacked? Oh, yes. He told us about that attack, when the UEDF tried to turn on them. He talked about that for years. We never could figure out why they did that."

William was trembling violently staring hard at the man.

"Do you mean the Gortha attack?"

"No. I don't know anything about no Gortha. What John told us was that the UEDF ships turned on him, but some of the other ships helped them escape."

His fists and teeth were clenched with rage.

"Listen to me very carefully. Is John Michaelson still alive on the Andromeda?"

"He was three years ago, but I couldn't tell you if he was still alive."

"Thank you, Mr…"

"Rehnquist. I am the caretaker," the man said proudly.

"Rehnquist. I appreciate your time."

William turned and left the property as fast as he could walk. Getting on his Triumph, William began heading north with anger fueling his tired body. He felt a deep sense of worry for Connor and Alex, who were now in the hands of their mother's killers.

Steadying himself with a few deep breaths while he rode fast toward home, William Mercer felt his mind slip over the edge.

~ ~ ~

Coming out of a slipstream after two-and-a-half weeks, Alex felt slightly disoriented. The process of traveling through folded space actually seemed to go a lot faster than the amount of time that had passed to other people in the galaxy. It was an uneasy feeling coming back into normal space time, but Alex shook it off after a couple of seconds. It was hard for him to fathom that what felt like an hour had actually been much longer.

Alex's OMBI messages came up on his main screen, which he read briefly. He wasn't sure why Colonel Roden had sent him anything; he wasn't close with the man, nor did he speak with him since transferring from the OMBIcademy to Station Sigma over a year before. Shrugging it off and reading Connor's message about the Black Army shutout, Alex laughed. He didn't believe it, of course, but he knew that his little brother was capable of it.

With a happy thought in his mind, he set his auto-pilot toward the binary star just ahead of him. He had achieved a much closer slipstream jump than he'd thought he would and proceeded to fly for an hour at normal engine speed in the Skoll until he got close enough to send a communication to the Atmos XI colony.

"Hades Colony, this is Captain Pereira of Black Squadron in response to your distress beacon, please respond."

Alex knew it would take a while at this distance for him to get a reply from a normal communicator. With nothing but time to kill, he formed up with the rest of his squadron, which was escorting the larger frigates toward the distressed colony.

Chapter 16

The No Win Scenario

Connor didn't feel like he had slept for that long in the training room. But when he awoke he was alone. A red flag went up immediately in his head. There was no way his army would have abandoned him and left him there. Moving to the exit, Connor discovered that he was locked in, and that the door had been welded shut.

Panic welling in his chest, he called out for Omega but got no reply. He walked outside of the dojo and was surprised to see that it was nighttime. It had never been night in the virtual environment before, no matter what time he'd gone in. Troubled, he began walking toward the exit on the other side of the green hills that came out near Yellow Army's barracks.

After getting to the top of the first hill, Connor accessed his OMBI to manifest a dirt bike to cross the distance more quickly. The motorcycle appeared in front of him and, as he climbed on, he noticed a large shape out of the corner of his eye.

Turning his head, Connor saw a large machine on the hill on the opposite side of the dojo from where he was. It looked like some kind of military robot armed with guns and missiles. Curious, Connor rode his motorcycle around the bowl-shaped valley toward the idle machine.

When he got close enough, he recognized the A25-Combat Drone because he used to play with the action figure after it was introduced in 2119. This drone appeared to be deactivated and left in place for him to find. Connor got off his motorcycle and tried to activate it with his OMBI. When he touched it, the activation and upgrade options appeared on his screen, so he began the process of reactivating the powerful drone.

As it powered up, it began to fade away from his sight like the memory of a dream after you're awake. Watching it disappear, Connor had a profound thought.

"I'm dreaming," he said out loud as the wind rolled over the grassy hills.

Leaving his motorcycle, Connor decided to run across the hills, gaining speed with every step until he was moving faster than even the motorcycle would carry him. Grinning at the realization of his dream, he began jumping over the valleys to the hills beyond, going high into the air before landing perfectly on the other side.

He was laughing now, enjoying the boundless existence of the dream he couldn't seem to wake up from. It wasn't long before Connor found himself flying short distances before landing and jumping into the sky again. He wished he could capture the feeling of flying somehow and share it with his friends.

Down below where he was flying, Connor saw a familiar red truck near a picnic table and floated down to it. It was the same truck that William had when Connor first met him, even though he vaguely remembered that he sold that truck years ago. He closed his eyes for a moment, and when he opened them it was daytime again. Looking back to the picnic table, he saw the familiar faces of his family.

William moved with purpose as he spread out the baskets of food and drinks he had brought for the picnic. His blue eyes were full of the luster and happiness that Connor hadn't seen in years. Alex looked the same way that Connor had last seen him, a well-muscled and confident man. He was listening to music through headphones while singing along out loud as if he were on stage somewhere in his mind. Then there was his mom, as beautiful as he remembered her. She was wearing a sun dress and smiling at Alex's performance; she really did have a stunning smile. Connor walked over to the table and sat down, looking across the food at his mother's almond-colored eyes.

"What is it, Tonns?" Marlena asked him, turning her attention away from Alex.

Connor almost started to cry as he put a pout on his face and got up to sit on her side of the bench. William was laughing at Alex, who had started laughing too as both began to sing off key to one of Alex's favorite songs.

"Oh, my baby," Marlena said to Connor with a soft, sympathetic voice, putting her arms around Connor and pulling him close. He knew it had to be a dream, but he let himself enjoy the warmth of his mother's embrace. He had forgotten how it felt to know the security and love of her touch.

Connor looked up into the eyes of the woman who had given him life and said quietly, "I miss you, Mom."

Her eyes rimmed with tears and she smiled at her little boy.

"I miss you too," she said, looking at him right in the eyes. "I am very proud of you."

Tears began to flow from Connor's eyes as he pulled her in close.

~ ~ ~

The OMBI alarm went off, pulling Connor from his dream, his pillow wet with tears. Connor collected himself and took a few deep breaths before activating the barrack lights and waking up his sleeping army.

It took Connor a few minutes of quiet reflection before he was ready to address his soldiers. When he was composed he stood up, putting on his blue commander uniform.

"Today is the day we show the new Head Commander and all of the OMBIcademy just how tough we are," Connor said loudly.

"They thought they could stack the deck against us and expect us to roll over and die. Well we won't die, not today, not ever! Today we will show them all that no matter how badly they want it, Blue Army will not go down without a fight!"

The soldiers of Blue Army were cheering as Connor finished the speech, roused and ready. By the time the OMBI alert came through that they had a battle, Blue Army had already exercised, eaten breakfast, and were making their way the training rooms. The alert didn't give them a lot of time before the match, so Connor lead them back to their barracks for a short rest.

Cat sat at the foot of Connor's bed while he lay on his side, discussing choke point tactics with his commanders, who sat on the floor in front of the bed. It felt more like a morning with friends than a pre-battle briefing. Connor had wanted to keep his army relaxed before the battle, thinking that tension wouldn't serve anybody.

When it was time to go, Blue Army lined up quietly in their squads and Connor led them out the door into the barracks common room. They were all taken aback when they entered the room, as the older members of Blue Army were waiting for them to wish them luck. Everyone in the OMBIcademy had heard about the battle by now, apparently.

"Happy hunting out there," Flayer said to Connor as he shook his hand.

"We'll be back in an hour to tell you all about it," Connor replied with a smile that Flayer returned.

Blue Army marched out of their barracks to the sound of applause and cheering from the three years of older soldiers who had come to show their respect.

Marching through the cold metal halls of the OMBIcademy, Connor couldn't contain his smile. He wasn't sure how he was going to do it yet, not knowing which battlefield he would be placed in, but he felt confident that his troops were well trained and eager to show their stuff, never mind being outnumbered four to one.

As they passed through the gate of the arena lobby and sat down, Connor stared at the prominent display, reading it quietly.

#1: Raptor: Connor Pereira 66 Kills / 0 Deaths
#2: Mephisto: Alex Pereira 1246 Kills / 1 Death
#3: Vertigo: Austin Hughes 723 Kills / 7 Deaths
#4. Slayer: Anthony Ramirez 685 Kills / 20 Deaths

As the room moved into place, Connor thought back to when he had first reconnected with his brother in this place and had fought with Alex in the melee arena, and wondered how he would do against Alex now if they were to fight again.

Relaxed and calm, Connor smiled over at Cat, who was smiling back at him. He still had no idea if this girl was his girlfriend or his lieutenant, but just then he didn't really care. For Connor Pereira, Commander of Blue Army, it was enough to just smile.

~ ~ ~

The red door opened to reveal that the starting conditions were going to be bad. Blue Army moved down the long ramp into the very center of an arena Connor hadn't been to before, the Massive Assault arena. The area he was supposed to defend was an old building up on a small hill with a stretch of flat ground between it and a fence line on three sides, and a small river on the fourth.

"Let's call the river side 'south,'" Connor said to his lieutenants, who nodded as they took positions.

On the west and north sides, the fence bordered a small forest providing cover to attackers from those directions, and there was a large hill on the east. The only saving grace of the defending area was that the small structure that looked like an old adobe house was surrounded by a waist-high rock wall on all sides. The house had a couple of windows and provided a lot of cover, but the roof was gone in most places.

Connor heard the other armies moving to surround him before he saw any soldiers. He knew they would be moving quickly and thought they might give each other some problems, being more used to fighting against each other rather than with each other. Connor hoped that the chaos would benefit his position. William had always told him, "The more you are outnumbered, the more chaos is your ally."

Connor ordered his bodyguards into the house along with Squad 2 and Cat to provide covering fire in all directions. Apparently, in Massive Assault all weapons were valid. He then positioned Squad 3 on the north side behind the rock wall, Squad 4 on the east side, and Squad 1 on the west. Using the river as a barrier, he asked Katana and Dice to watch it from the back of the house to make sure that it didn't get forded.

"We may be taking a tie today, Connor," Cat said to him quietly when they were in position.

"I don't play for ties," Connor replied confidently.

Red Army came over the hill from the east side, running down toward the fence line, screaming as they charged toward the Blue Army position in a wave of eager kids.

Connor watched their predictable charge and trusted in Skulls to halt it with a hail of gunfire, which he heard after a moment. Their momentum slowed, Red Army began returning fire from the bottom of the hill where they were taking positions behind the slats of a wooden fence.

Black Army moved down through the trees on the north end slowly, spreading out and taking cover while putting pressure on Ladder's squad with a steady stream of gunfire.

Yellow Army became a problem from the west when volleys of arrows began raining down on the roofless house. Fortunately they were poorly angled from the distance they were fired and thus, easy to avoid. The volleys did, however, keep Squad 2 watching the sky and taking cover. Connor figured it would only be a matter of time before some of those arrows found flesh.

He didn't know where Green Army was, but he suspected they were looking for a way to use the river to sneak up behind the adobe structure to force Blue Army to scatter.

Connor began to feel overwhelmed. He shut his eyes for a moment and took a deep breath to steady his nerves. "One thing at a time," he said to himself in his head.

Opening his eyes he used his OMBI to unlock and manifest a Dragunov sniper rifle and stabilized it on a broad windowsill, facing the east side of the arena. Connor scanned the battlefield, putting the shouting of his commanders out of his mind and letting go of anxiety caused by the yellow arrows that were raining down. With deep focus, he became a hunter stalking its prey. Searching the enemy faces, he finally found what he was looking for.

~ ~ ~

Johnny was at the top of the hill to the west side of the structure, afraid to run down through gunfire to join the other half of his army. He stood up to get a better view, thinking that his reserve squads could start using the height of the hill to their advantage and fire into the building.

Something flashed and caught his eye, which made him peer toward the house. He realized his mistake too late when the sniper bullet slammed him in the chest, sending him down to the ground, stunned on the edge of the hill. Unable to shift his weight, he slowly began to roll down the hill toward the fence.

~ ~ ~

When the commander of Red Army went down and began rolling, one of the lieutenants at the top of the hill moved to help and took a sniper shot to the face for his troubles, causing him to collapse too. A second lieutenant got up to sound the retreat from the fence line and took a sniper bullet to the throat for the effort.

Red Army's final lieutenant did everything he could to stay low and move from the fence line over to the treed area to the north where he could find some cover. Connor tracked him from the window and sent him down mid-run with a shot to the leg. Exposed, the soldiers of Squad 3 stunned him as he was trying to crawl to cover.

Without leadership, Red Army began to scatter. A few soldiers held positions at the top of the hill and the fence line, but most started trying to find better cover from the sniper rifle by fleeing into the wooded area to the north. Connor could hear the confusion it was causing for Black Army and the suppressing fire from the north subsided a bit.

"Green Army in the river!" Katana shouted from the doorway to the south. Releasing his Dragunov and using his OMBI to manifest a grenade, and threw it into the river where Katana was pointing. Connor couldn't see green in the water, but he trusted his friend's eyes and tossed out three more grenades before spinning back toward the window to the west.

The splashing explosions made Connor smile while he moved. He knew that he still had a problem, but he hoped a few grenades would slow down their progress or make them think twice about attacking from that direction.

On the west side, Connor yelled out to Squad 1.

"Manzer, Yellow is using a lot of bows. Charge in there with some melee and hit them hard, then circle behind Black Army if you can!" Connor said, loud enough for him to hear, but not so loud that he might give away the plan.

"Cat, take your squad and back him up," he continued, looking into her green eyes, "and be quick."

Squads 1 and 2 moved quickly to the west as Squad 3 provided covering fire to the north. Connor turned his attention back on the problem he was having with Green Army to the south, throwing several more grenades into the water.

"What's the situation back here?" Connor asked Katana.

"I don't think you got them with those, but they did move back so I think you bought us some time," Katana replied, itching to get out into the battle.

"Calm down and be patient; there are plenty of enemies around still," Connor assured his battle-hungry friend.

Connor looked up at the scoreboard hovering quietly high above the battlefield. 152:38, 40:00 minutes to go. He did a double take and stared a moment at the clock.

"No timer on this match, I guess it's all or nothing," Connor said to Katana and Dice near the back door. "I shouldn't have sent Manzar and Cat so quickly. Katana, go and help them. Hit hard and get them back here."

~ ~ ~

Jinn Matsui didn't need to be told twice to get out into a battle. He produced his long naginata from his OMBI and ran off to the east at full speed into the cover of the trees to the west of the house as quickly as possible, avoiding random fire from the Black Army position to the north.

Jinn made his way quickly and saw soldiers from Squad 2 moving up ahead. When he moved beyond the trees into a field, he increased his speed. Forty strong, Yellow Army's archers were quickly trying to switch to melee weapons as Jinn, Cat, Manzar, and the other fifteen soldiers of Squads 2 and 3 charged into their lines.

They struck hard, doing some damage before Yellow Army had a chance to get prepared. For a moment Jinn thought they were going to overwhelm Yellow, until he heard a shout from the south and turned to see Green Army, at full strength and moving in their direction rapidly, firing guns into the fray.

Jinn noted with a sense of disappointment that Green Army's holographic bullets weren't affecting Yellow Army at all.

"Connor said for you to pull back," Jinn relayed to Cat and Manzar, who both immediately ordered their squads into retreat.

Moving back to the tree line at a run, Jinn stopped and put his back to a tree near the edge of the field, waiting a few moments. Yellow and Green Armies were right on the heels of Squad 2 and 3 when they hit the tree line. Jinn watched the first few enemies run by before he moved. Spinning out to the left, he nearly ran into the Yellow Army soldier who was running right at him and sent him to the ground with a slash from his mighty naginata. Not hesitating, Jinn ran forward against the current of enemies slashing out left and right, downing several enemies before they even realized what he was doing.

Moving back toward the commander of Yellow Army, Jinn seemed to move like a tornado of devastation. What troops he didn't stun he disabled, striking out at whatever limb was within his reach. He gained ground on the Yellow Army commander and had almost reached him when he felt himself stiffen up.

The virtual smoke from the Green Army commander's handgun wafted into the air as he walked over to where Jinn fell, looking at the devastation the boy had caused.

"Looks like you got ten of us, not bad," the Green commander said, "but not enough."

~ ~ ~

Katana's distraction gave Cat and Manzar enough time to get back over the fortifications and select ranged weapons to halt the charging enemies behind them.

Connor noted that both squads were significantly weaker when they returned and quietly cursed to himself for sending them out. He also noted with a touch of regret that Katana hadn't made it back. Looking at the scoreboard, Connor felt a sense of frustration. 127:32, 40:00 minutes remaining.

"It won't be long until they just rush in here and kill us," Dice said, as if reading Connor's thoughts.

"I know," Connor replied more harshly than he intended.

"Already Green and Yellow are working together and you just know that Black Army commander is recruiting Red Army troops," Dice continued.

"I know!" Connor said more forcefully.

"They have every advantage. I'm surprised the Head Commander even gave us fortifications. If he wanted a one-sided fight, he could have just given them tanks and attack-drones," Dice finished, sounding as frustrated as Connor.

"This isn't helping, Dice, just shut..." Connor began, but stopped as he got an idea.

"Shut what?"

"Never mind, I have an idea," Connor said, working through his OMBI menus feverishly.

~ ~ ~

Annihilator wasn't happy about having to work with three other armies that he had beaten in order to fight Blue Army. He lost badly, but now that he understood how Connor thought, he figured he might beat him in a rematch. He had gone to Connor when Johnny sent him a message with the orders from the Head Commander of the OMBIcademy. He told him of the plan in hopes of creating a more even match so it didn't feel so dirty.

Looking at the scene below, the Black Army Commander didn't feel less dirty about it. He had taken up the position at the top of the ridge to the east of the compound that Blue Army was defending in order to survey the battlefield. His officers were going about recruiting the Red Army soldiers that they could find, gathering their strength while Green and Yellow worked together putting pressure from the other side.

To their credit, Blue Army had held their position fairly well and inflicted a lot of damage, but now that the armies were merging it would only be a matter of time before they were crushed between the superior forces. The merged armies on the opposite end were pushing forward and putting a lot of pressure on the western side of the compound when Annihilator reluctantly gave the order for Red Army to charge in with melee and Black Army to follow up with guns and explosives, which he had learned how to unlock after the last battle he had fought with Blue Army.

The jaws of the greater force were closing in fast when a rumble shook the ground. In horror, Annihilator watched the A25-Combat Drone manifest on the west side of the structure. It arose slowly from its crouching position with a screeching sound as it slowly surveyed the field.

Then it unleashed hellfire.

~ ~ ~

The mini guns made a grinding sound as they spun, which hurt Connor's ears a little bit being so close to the drone. His order to the A25 was simple: "Kill them all." The virtual ammo was cutting down trees to the west of the structure as the A25-Combat Drone moved forward against Yellow and Green armies.

Connor ordered Cat and Manzar to use it as cover and follow it along the river to pick off anyone who managed to avoid that thing's overwhelming firepower. The other two Blue Army squads held their position as the enemy charge came in from the east, getting a couple of shots off before engaging in melee with the overly aggressive remnant of Red Army. Connor switched to his rifle and began picking off soldiers who were running down the hill and out of the woods to ease the pressure on his front lines.

He felt like he was making some progress, too, until a glowing black stick of dynamite came flying through the roof of the house. Diving out the south side of the building, Connor avoided the blast that managed to take out Dice and Carl, who had been standing next to him at the time. The virtual structure collapsed in on them with a resounding crunching sound.

Connor got up on his knees and crawled behind the building for cover. He knew that if he could hold out, the A25 would win the fight for him. He doubted many of the other soldiers in this fight had weapons that could damage that thing's armor.

Holding out would be a problem though. With his army engaged in melee combat with Red Army and Black Army's explosives damaging only his troops, Connor knew it wouldn't be long before his position would be lost.

Taking a cue from Black Army, Connor selected his grenades and began throwing them into the engaged troops on his front line, figuring he should even out the battle with the remnant of Red Army before focusing on the bigger problem. The plan worked well. Connor was closer to the action than the troops from Black Army who had elected to use cover and continue shooting and throwing explosives from the tree line.

As the numbers thinned out on both sides, Connor knew he was running out of time. He looked at the scoreboard. 46:14, 40:00 minutes remaining. The odds were still heavily against him, and if he went down his team would lose the benefit of the A25, which had stopped advancing on Yellow and Green and had begun moving back his direction, shooting missiles into the wooded area at Black Army's entrenched location.

Using the explosions as a distraction, Connor slipped back into the river and began swimming to the east.

~ ~ ~

The shock in the observation lounge was shared by everybody in attendance. Head Commander Setzer's mouth hung agape, unsure of what to say about what he was witnessing. The most one-sided humiliation he had ever arranged and the boy was putting up an amazing fight.

Major Sanders was standing off to the side of the room, his lip curled up in the man's version of a smile while he watched the devastation on the battlefield below. He didn't interact with the other people in the lounge, only watched and wondered just what this boy's future held.

Colonel Setzer had invited members of the Academy Oversight Committee to watch the battle in order to show them that he was getting things back in order after Colonel Roden's disappearance. The ten members of the committee were also stunned by what they were seeing, unsure if they were supposed to be cheering or booing the event. They watched over video from the corners of the world where they lived and made decisions from the safety of their desks. Their images displayed on the various screens in the room matched Setzer's expression almost exactly.

Setzer spoke after a long period of silence, breaking the tension in the room.

"The boy puts up a good fight, as we all expected, but it is just about over. Black Army has a reputation, you see; they never lose and are still in the fight in great numbers."

"If you keep saying it," Sanders said quietly, "you might even believe it after a while."

~ ~ ~

Connor emerged from the water to see Cat leading Squads 1 and 2 back through the wooded area to the North of their starting position. He didn't see Manzar go down, but he figured if he wasn't on the battlefield, he was out of the fight. He didn't get much of a count on her troops, but they were working well with the A25, using it for cover and moving up, not letting it get hit from behind.

Hunter, who Connor had thought went down with the adobe house, was over on the back side where Connor had jumped into the river, shooting what looked like two pearl-handled pistols at anyone he saw, hooting and yelling as loud as he could. Grateful for the distraction, Connor moved up the hill, climbing toward the top to where he had taken down Johnny with his first attack of the match.

Connor peered over from behind a lone rock to see the commander of Black Army standing with four other Black Army soldiers which Connor figured were some kind of guards, like he had. Moving low and quietly, he came up behind them like a phantom, selecting his fist attack from the OMBI.

He hit the group like a bowling ball, scattering them in every direction. Two of the Black Army guards were down in Connor's opening assault and one went rolling down the hill. The other one tried to shoot Connor with a handgun only to have Connor close the distance faster than the bodyguard would have believed possible, slamming his fist into the guard's stomach and putting him out of the match.

Face to face with Annihilator, Connor smiled like he was addressing an old friend.

"Better, but still not hard enough," Connor quipped, flashing a boyish smile.

"Ha! I was hoping I would get a chance to face you one on one," Annihilator said, producing a broadsword from his OMBI.

"So you want a shot at the title, eh? Okay, let's dance." Connor tried to sound cool, but found himself laughing at the attempt.

Annihilator came on quickly with the sword offering measured thrusts to test his opponent. Connor danced back on the balls of his feet, producing no weapon other than his fists. He was aware that the Black Army commander was fairly well trained with the sword, given his poise and confidence with the weapon.

Connor fought defensively, choosing to gauge his opponent's strength and let him tire out a bit before coming on with the attack. Deflecting the blade with his open hand, Connor felt like he could continue the fight forever. Still Annihilator came on, slashing and stabbing, trying to gain ground any way he could with the longer reach.

Hearing the A25's guns slowing, Connor realized it was out of targets and it was time for him to end this match. Feigning a stumble backwards, Connor drew Annihilator in close before reversing his momentum and catching the Black Army commander's blade between his hands. Using the strength of his arms, Connor pushed the sword back, forcing the pommel into its wielder's face with a resounding, "oomph."

Connor struck out with a left-handed chop that landed squarely on Annihilator's neck. Immediately the virtual elements of the arena started fading and the soldiers who were stunned started getting back up.

Connor offered a hand to Annihilator, who accepted it graciously.

"I have to hand it to you, you put up a good fight!" Connor said, chuckling at his own pun.

Annihilator, despite his frustration at losing, laughed along with Connor. The two boys walked down the hill to rejoin their respective armies, talking about the ebbs and flows of the battle and how they had both felt at certain turns and events. They shook hands at the bottom of the hill, Annihilator offering congratulations to Connor on his win.

Cat ran and jumped into Connor's arms, offering him a big hug before standing back to make room for his other friends to come congratulate him. The commanders of Yellow and Green Armies left immediately, not wanting to say anything to anybody. Johnny tried to tell Connor how he had been planning to help him out in the fight but got accidentally shot in the first few minutes. Connor, surrounded by true friends, would hear nothing of it. He shook his head then walked away.

Blue Army carried Connor back up the ramp on their shoulders chanting, "Rap-tor, Rap-tor" all the way back into the arena lobby. They placed their OMBIs on the pad and updated their scores before sitting down for the slow ride back to the main OMBIcademy halls.

Chapter 17

Deception

On the opposite side of the galaxy from his brother's victory, Captain Alex Pereira was awaiting his reply from the Hades colony when his long-range scanner picked up an incoming vessel heading toward his convoy.

"Incoming vessel, this is a United Earth Defense Force convoy. Identify yourself," Alex said into his communicator.

Alex's head pounded as the squeal on the line pierced his mind. The voice sounded surprised at first, and then started barking commands in a language Alex couldn't make out.

"Is anyone else picking up this communication? I'm getting gibberish."

The commander of the battle frigate UEDF Griswold responded, "We are receiving orders from command via slipstream that we are to eliminate hostile Gortha ships."

"Again, I am receiving only gibberish; can anyone identify the ship?"

Alex's eyes ached when he tried to physically look at the ship, even though it was far off. He tried to scan it with Skoll's sensor but his arm cramped up so badly he couldn't even make a fist.

"Check your premises," a whispering voice said inside Alex's com.

"Captain, this is Vertigo. I'm also receiving gibberish and, what's more, I cannot seem to scan or identify the ship"

"Vertigo, I'm experiencing the same thing. Is it jamming us?"

"I don't know, sir. My head feels like it's on fire."

"Black Squadron, this is Commander Worthington of the UEDF Frigate Griswold. Our orders are to eliminate all enemy vessels in the system."

"UEDF Frigate Griswold, this is Captain Pereira of Black Squadron. We are unable to identify any enemy vessels, please advise."

Alex attempted to reach through his OMBI to magnify his vision and help him see the incoming ship better, but felt tremendous pain for the attempt, like someone kicked him in the back of the head. The pain was so intense, he could hardly see out the window of Skoll at all.

"Sir, something isn't right," Vertigo said in a concerned voice. "I can't focus. Are we being ordered to attack?"

"...not as it seems," the whispering voice said in Alex's head.

"What does that mean?" Alex asked aloud.

More vessels began to appear on the long-range sensor. Skoll's HUD started flickering and Alex could hardly see the area in front of him.

"Hold your pattern, Vertigo," he said, barely able to focus.

"Captain, this is Commander Worthington; you are ordered to attack the incoming vessels."

"Sir, I cannot even look at them, something is wrong with my squadron's equipment. What is the ETA on contact, sir?"

"Thirteen minutes, Captain. Pull it together."

"Trust your instincts," the voice whispered.

Alex didn't hesitate. He immediately reversed the direction of Skoll and sent himself flying toward the Griswold with incredible ease and coordination. Looking back toward the Griswold, Alex's pain immediately subsided.

"Griswold, this is Captain Pereira. I am coming into docking bay seven with an emergency medical condition. Have a 311AFMR standing by."

Alex increased his speed toward the Griswold's docking bay until the last minute, when he fired reverse thrusters and landed without awaiting authorization.

Setting a timer on his OMBI, Alex disembarked onto the hard metal ground of the frigate. Twelve minutes. He ran through the decontamination field, almost colliding with a deck hand in the process.

He encountered the AFMR in the hallway outside the docking bay and began accessing it with his OMBI for a full brain scan. Eleven Minutes. The AFMR's scanning process took three minutes of Alex standing in the hallway before it came back with no abnormalities.

"Dammit" Alex cursed. Eight minutes.

Alex accessed the AFMR again, ordering it to check his OMBI inputs. When he mentally issued the command, he collapsed in agonizing pain. Alex looked hard at his OMBI, thinking that it was malfunctioning somehow. Each time he tried to order the AFMR to access it, he collapsed again in writhing pain.

Opening a com port on his OMBI, Alex said, "Austin, I need you in docking bay seven, now!"

"Affirmative, Captain," Vertigo replied from the com.

Six minutes.

"Attention all Black Squadron, hold fire until further notice." Alex said, confused by the situation and concerned by what was happening.

"Belay that order Black Squadron; you are now under the direct command of Commander Worthington of the UEDF Frigate Griswold, you will proceed with attack."

"No!" Alex yelled to the impassive machine in front of him. He led the AFMR into the docking bay where he waited for Vertigo.

Five minutes.

The larger Ra fighter flew in through the open bay port.

"Gortha Capital ships on mid-range sensors, all ships prepare for combat," Commander Worthington said into an open com.

Four minutes.

Austin was by Alex's side after running from his Ra fighter over the metal floor of the dock.

"Kind of a bad time to need a checkup," Austin stated.

"I need you to access this AFMR with your OMBI, spend your points if you have to. I need it to open my OMBI and inspect the inhibitor chips, and every time I try it backfires into my brain." Alex said quickly.

"Unlocked and commencing," Austin replied in his level tone.

The AFMR began disabling Alex's OMBI while both boys watched it work.

Three minutes.

"Inhibitor chip, performing as designed," the AFMR responded in its robotic voice.

"What is the function of the third inhibitor chip?" Alex asked it.

"Access denied."

"Austin, can you access it?"

"I can try."

The AFMR began to speak after a second. "Third inhibitor chip designed to prevent incoming data from external sources, allowing only outgoing data to process."

"What? Oh man, what about the fourth inhibitor?" Alex asked, looking at Austin, whose face looked as surprised as Alex's.

The AFMR spoke, "Fourth inhibitor chip designed as failsafe. Purpose: Control incoming data perception. Secondary purpose: Disposal of operator."

"Well crap!" Alex exclaimed, shocked. "Austin, make this thing remove my fourth chip.

"Two Minutes.

"Working on it."

The AFMR began disabling Alex's inhibitor chip. Alex could hear footsteps coming down the hallway and looked at Austin.

"Can you hold them off while this thing works?" he asked.

"What is this about? I don't understand, Alex."

"I think the UEDF is controlling what we see, which is why we cannot identify those enemy ships, and I have to find out why. I can't do that with this chip. Hold them off, then I will get your chip off."

"You are going against orders?" Austin asked plainly.

It hadn't occurred to Alex that his friend, who had been beside him for more than five years, was acting because he thought he was obeying orders.

"I am," Alex said honestly.

"I'm not sure I can let you, Alex; this is too important. There are Gortha out there!" Austin said, his voice full of uncertainty.

One Minute.

The AFMR removed the chip and Alex felt the wave of nausea from his attempts at controlling the machine subside. If he would have had time, he may have removed the third inhibitor too.

"I'm not sure you can stop me. But you're right, this is too important. Let me remove your inhibitor and we can go find out what is really out there," Alex pleaded to his friend, who had moved to block his way.

The security detail that came down to apprehend the rogue captain arrived, coming through the door behind Alex and fanning out around him.

"Please, you're like a brother to me, just stand down," Austin said in a rare moment of emotion.

Alex's armor appeared around his flesh and two curved swords appeared in his hands as he replied.

"I can't do that. I hate the Gortha as much as anybody, but there is a reason why the UEDF is controlling us and I need to find out. You helped me so I owe you one, but please don't do this," Alex said quietly.

Austin's armor appeared around his body too, and a long spear appeared in his hands just as the counter on Alex's OMBI hit zero.

~ ~ ~

The battle outside of the Griswold was chaotic. The smaller Gortha vessels moved quickly but held their fire at first. The three larger vessels moved in to square up against the two assault frigates. It was Black Squadron that fired the first shot, unleashing a barrage of missiles upon the nearest Gortha capital ship, which looked like a large horned fish.

The Gortha ships responded in kind, unleashing what weapons they carried toward the heavily armored frigates.

The battle was greatly one sided with all the Anubis and Ra fighters piloted by Black Squadron doing heavy damage to the

Gortha ships. One smaller Gortha ship, that looked like a spiked bird, sped ahead to engage the entirety of Black Squadron directly.

The Black Squadron ships scattered and engaged the Gortha fighter, attempting to box it in as it maneuvered close and sped along the length of the larger frigates. It turned in mid-flight, without altering its forward momentum, and launched several missiles at Black Squadron before turning back around and flying away. Two of the missiles connected to Anubis fighters, who took light damage from the attack.

No one in Black Squadron was able to land a shot, despite their OMBI enhanced piloting and gunnery skills. The battle raged across the darkness of space in the dim lights of the binary star. The entirety of the highly trained and enhanced Black Squadron chased and attempted to outmaneuver a particularly nasty Gortha ship that they couldn't manage to keep up with.

~ ~ ~

The Griswold lurched forward, throwing the security detail off balance. Alex, using the distraction, spun into motion, sliding his twin blades in and out of human flesh for the first time in his life. The seven men who had come to apprehend him were lying on the ground bleeding out from their wounds within seconds.

Alex spun in time to catch the spear thrust between his scimitars and forced it away. A few quick steps forward put Alex inside of the range of the longer weapon, which Austin let go of, manifesting a shorter sword and shield within an instant to block the incoming attack.

Alex changed the direction of his charge toward the sword arm of his friend, smacking his smaller blades against the larger one several times, pushing it out wide before coming back with a double slash that was deflected by Austin's shield.

Dancing a few steps backwards, Alex looked at Skoll beyond where Austin was standing, eager to get back outside where he belonged.

"I can't let you go, you know that," Austin said, studying Alex's glance.

Alex took a few steps to his left that Austin matched. Frustrated, he had an idea. He didn't want to have to kill his friend to get outside, but he knew he had to a take a chance if he was going to keep it non-lethal. He moved close to the 311AFMR and when Austin moved to intercept him, he pushed it over with all his strength, diving into a backwards roll.

Austin moved to intercept, stepping over the AFMR. As Alex came to his feet, he reached out to the medical robot through his OMBI and forced it to overload, causing a small explosion that sent Austin flying back onto the ground.

"I know it, my friend," Alex said to a barely conscious Austin as he ran past him to Skoll.

Climbing through the back of the ship, Alex settled in and walked over to where Austin's Ra vessel was resting. Producing a large battle axe in Skoll's hand with his OMBI, Alex swung several times to disable the engines of the attack ship before flying out through the airlock on the docking bay.

~ ~ ~

The scene outside was utter chaos to Alex. Without the inhibitor chip altering his perception, he saw a different scene before him than he expected. None of the enemy ships were Gortha ships. They were UEDF ships from the Third Fleet that had been reported destroyed in a battle with the Gortha.

"Black Squadron, stand down immediately," Alex said.

Static

Frustration began to well in the young man's heart. He wasn't sure why he was being lied to, or what it meant that the UEDF had sent him to attack the Third Fleet. The weight of his responsibility to Black Squadron and the deceit of his commanders left Alex's mind reeling.

Then he saw it. Black Squadron was flying formations, trying to box in another Anubis fighter, one that Alex would recognize anywhere, a ship he hadn't seen in over five years. Alex was looking at the Tizona.

~ ~ ~

At that same moment on Earth, William Mercer was sitting at his computer after spending the entire day working under his house. He opened a picture folder he had vowed he would never look at again: a family vacation from 2114.

The pictures of the road trip he took with his family brought tears to his eyes. He scrolled through them one at a time, immersing himself into the memories of the time they had gone to the ranch in Montana. William had taught the boys about gun safety and how to shoot on that trip. There were many pictures of Marlena too, her beautiful smile putting even the most epic scenery to shame.

William took a deep breath, and for a moment he remembered how it felt have his wife in his arms. The smell of her hair as he breathed in, her warm body pressed against his like they would never let each other go. In his mind, he felt himself brush her cheek with his fingers and then press his lips against hers, tasting the passion of her kiss. For that moment, William Mercer felt at peace.

Then reality came crashing down like bolt of lightning. He closed the file and moved his hand over to a more dangerous file that he knew he would not be able to access: the Andromeda black box video.

Chapter 18

Hati

The morning after his epic win, Connor was sitting in the training dojo with Cat, talking about the battle, when the message came through on his OMBI. It was the first anonymous message that he'd ever received.

Message 1: Black Squadron has gone dark in Eagle Nebula, all members KIA or MIA. *Delivered 0915 2121-03-18*
From: Anonymous

Connor had to read it a second and third time to make sure he understood what he was reading. Tears welled up in his eyes while he had Cat read it to make sure he was reading it right.

"I'm sorry, Connor," Cat said sympathetically.

"Sorry for what? Alex isn't dead. No one can beat him!" Connor snapped.

Cat was silent, stoically accepting the tongue lashing from Connor.

"I cannot sit here," Connor said as he got up to run, leaving behind a tearful Amanda.

He began to run, needing to feel the wind dry his tears as he sprinted in a direction he had never gone before. He ran hard, ignoring the pain in his legs and lungs as he moved over green hills.

When his legs gave out, Connor collapsed and screamed as loud as he could. He cried in the grass, unable to shake the feeling that he had just lost his brother forever.

Omega appeared beside him, staring impassively as Connor rolled on the ground in emotional agony.

"Why did he have to die? Why him?" Connor yelled.

"Whom, Initiator?" Omega replied quietly.

"Alex! His squad is missing or dead in the Eagle Nebula. He's probably out there right now, dying in space, and I can't do anything!"

Omega stood quietly for a moment.

"Untrue."

"How do you know? He could be suffering!"

"I do not know. My response was to your other statement," Omega said with an uncharacteristic explanation.

"What do you mean? What can I do about it?" Connor asked, sniffling.

"We can go to the Eagle Nebula."

"What are you talking about, you stupid program? How can we get to the Eagle Nebula? You can't even leave this stupid room."

"Investigation. Hati. Untrue."

Connor had to think back to his rant to figure out what Omega meant.

"What's Hati?"

"He is our vessel, Initiator."

"You aren't making sense! He is a vessel? Our vessel? I don't have a vessel!"

"I am. He is. He is. We do."

Connor was quickly getting frustrated with Omega's unclear responses.

"Show me, idiot," Connor said, bottling his anger for the moment.

Omega continued on in the direction Connor had been going. Connor pulled himself to his feet and began walking after the program. Each painful step led him onward toward the goal somewhere beyond the holographic horizon.

Eventually Connor and Omega came to a rocky outcropping at the edge of an aspen grove. The wind rustled through the aspen, causing their leaves to dance, reflecting the light of the artificial sun up in the sky above. Omega moved to an overgrown hackberry patch where he stopped.

Connor walked beside him, following Omega's eyes off into the bushes and the rock face beyond. He thought he saw what could be a small opening between the rocks.

"What's in there?" he asked quietly, not taking a step.

"Destiny," Omega replied cryptically before dissipating, leaving Connor standing alone wondering what he meant.

Connor stood staring at the rocky cave beyond the berry bushes for a long while before moving. He was afraid of where he was going and what would happen when he got there. Tears began to flow from Connor's eyes when he realized that fear was stopping him.

He went to his OMBI and activated his location application, thinking about his brother. To Connor's surprise the line between them appeared to his vision from his feet straight into the cave ahead of him. Renewing his resolve, Connor took a step forward.

"Is this a dream?" he asked quietly to the wind.

Walking through the overgrown bushes, Connor could feel their branches scraping against his arms as he forced his way to the other side. He didn't hesitate, walking into the dark cavern knowing that if he stopped, he might not be able to muster the courage necessary to continue. Activating his OMBI, Connor spent the 2,500 points to unlock the "Infrared" HUD option and began walking downward through the narrow rock hallway.

With his visual enhancement active, Connor could see well enough in the darkness. The pathway ahead sloped downward through the natural cavern, the narrow halls offering little room to maneuver as he squeezed through some areas, keeping his eyes on the path ahead. He ducked and climbed through stone obstacles for several minutes, continually progressing deeper into the cavern until the path ahead of him widened and looked more worked.

Connor wouldn't call it man-made by any stretch of the imagination. The worked cavern ahead looked like it had been clawed out by the talons of a dragon from a fantasy story. The deep scars in the stone made the boy pause and take a deep breath of musty air before moving forward into the deeper halls.

The air was still and humid as Connor walked through the cavern, which got wider with every step he took. He could feel sweat begin to form on his forehead as the hall expanded outward into a great room. The room was massive, expanding upward beyond his enhanced vision. The ground, covered in the rubble of what could have once been stalagmites, was uneven and cracked in many places.

The room seemed brighter to Connor than it should have been, so he released his infrared to find that the cracks in the floor were producing their own light, a bright reddish glow from below. Connor moved up to one of the larger cracks and looked downward. Far below him, he could see the hot glow of magma churning, the molten stone giving the cavern a nightmarish quality.

Ahead at the far side of the room, Connor could see a large wooden door that looked unnatural in this place. As he walked ahead, around the large crack in the floor, a dark form loomed ahead of him. He almost collapsed when it rose from the ground until he realized that it was his own shadow, created from the light of the magma.

He took a deep breath and moved forward, the dark form mirroring his steps ominously. The ground before the door evened out and Connor made his way toward the ramp, his shadow following him every step of the way. Then he stopped. He was far enough away from the light source that the shadow should have dissipated by now. Getting a bad feeling, Connor turned his infrared back on.

Immediately he regretted his decision as the white glowing eyes of his shadow were staring back at him. The dark form contorted and shifted, moving to block him from the exit of the room. As it grew, great dark wings sprouted from its back and a long tail whipped out into the stone wall, causing the ground to shake. The shadow had become a giant dragon.

The beast roared so loud, the cavern shook violently, sending Connor to the ground. Thinking he would surely die in this place, he curled up on the ground tightly.

"Coward boy, you are not ready!" the beast roared.

Connor hadn't expected the thing to talk, and certainly not to judge him before eating him. Irritated, he got to his feet.

"I didn't realize…" Connor began unsteadily "… that character assassination was a necessary requirement of food preparation."

The beast roared and bellowed in laughter that caused the room to shake again, almost sending Connor back to the ground.

"The little bird has wit!" the dark dragon roared.

"Uh, thank you?" Connor replied, looking around for some kind of escape.

"There is no escape," the beast said suddenly as if it were reading Connor's mind.

"So I cannot go forward and I cannot go backward," Connor stated absolutely.

"You always have been observant, Little Bird," the beast grumbled, looking off into the distance thoughtfully.

"What do you see?" Connor asked, unsure of how to proceed.

"You, Little Bird, I have been watching you."

Connor's mind worked furiously, trying to figure out what was happening, how this great shadow beast has been watching him.

"Solution in the problem..." a whispering voice said in Connor's head.

The thought came from the back of his mind as he looked at the dark lines from his feet that led toward the monster in front of him.

"You are my shadow," Connor stated more than asked.

The dragon's great maw formed into a nightmarish grin, showing rows of great teeth that were the size of swords.

"I guess I had a lot more darkness than I thought," Connor said to himself thoughtfully.

The monster roared furiously, causing fear to ripple up Connor's spine, and he cried out. Taking a step backwards, Connor's terror only increased as the dragon got larger.

"You are not ready!" the beast roared again, seeming invigorated by its gain in size.

Connor took a deep breath, trying to steady his resolve. He had come a long way and was not going to let a quirky shadow manifestation stop him from what he came to do.

"Solution in the problem..." Connor whispered to himself, realizing what he had to do.

"Alex is out there still, and I don't have time to be afraid of you anymore," he said with as much bravery as he could muster. "So the only choice I have is to accept you, me, us ... whatever."

The first step was difficult, but he somehow managed to take it. The beast roared but got a little smaller as Connor moved away from the light behind him, giving him confidence to take another step.

"I'm afraid of bigger kids sometimes. I'm afraid of the dark. I'm afraid of dying. I'm afraid of being alone. I'm even afraid of Amanda!" Connor admitted to himself as he took another heavy step toward the great roaring beast, which diminished with every step closer Connor took.

"I'm afraid when people put high expectations on me. Afraid of failing. I'm afraid of you too."

Another heavy step forward.

"I'm lazy sometimes because I'm afraid of taking responsibility for my success. I like getting stuff because it makes me feel like I have more value."

He took two more steps, saying out loud the things he somehow knew he was hiding in himself. The dark parts of himself that he could see in the eyes of the great monster ahead of him. With every step closer, the great dragon appeared smaller.

"I'm afraid of being loved, because I'm afraid I'll lose it. I'm afraid of loving since my mom died, because of the pain I might feel losing someone I love again."

He was getting close now, walking into his darker self. The beast tried to reach out for him and Connor reached back, embracing the darkness with full acceptance.

"I get angry and frustrated easily because I don't like when other people waste my time with their expectations of me. I want to be my own person."

They were the same size now. Connor moved forward with full acceptance of the darker side of himself until his shadow was again in the form of a boy silhouetted on the white door ahead of him. Together the boy and his shadow reached for the handle of the door and pulled it open, moving as one into the room beyond.

~ ~ ~

Connor had never been to this part of the OMBIcademy before and judging from how dusty it was, no one else had either. The dark metal halls got darker when the door behind him shut. He activated his OMBI, which cast the soft glow of his interface into the darkness ahead, letting him see a short distance ahead.

Unsure of which direction to begin, Connor set off to his right, walking fearlessly down halls that curved slightly off into the darkness. Many of the old doors and side passages were labeled in a language he wasn't familiar with. Some of the doors opened as he walked by them, reacting to his presence.

One of the rooms that looked like a supply closet had a thick musty smell to it. Looking inside, Connor saw many old cords and strange tools that looked like they might be for maintenance.

Another room looked like a medical bay with four operating tables in the corners and several unfamiliar instruments. There was no sign of any 311 AFMRs or any tracks in the dust. Looking back down the hall he had come from, Connor felt good seeing his own footprints, knowing that he could find his way back if necessary.

A third room reminded Connor of the Blue Army barracks, except there were several inactive stasis pods where the beds would normally be and the common room looked more like some kind of a locker room. Connor attempted to open one of the lockers, but couldn't figure out the strange locking mechanisms.

Continuing down the curved hall, he finally found what he was looking for. The label on the passage didn't look like anything he had seen, but he moved through the portal to investigate. A ramp sloped downward from the door, connecting the upper walkway to what appeared to be a hanger bay.

He knew that if he was going to find a ship of some kind, this would be the place. But the fact that these corridors and rooms had been abandoned a long time ago left Connor with the feeling that he wouldn't find anything at all.

The cold metal walkway reminded Connor of areas in the OMBIcademy, but knowing that no one had walked in this place since before the dust had settled made him wonder if he was even still in the academy at all. The light of his OMBI reflected off something on the far side of the room, but he couldn't see anything beyond a few feet in front of him.

He walked on the upper catwalk along the side of the room until he found a spiral staircase that took him to the lower level of the bay. The ground floor was flooded by a few inches of water that soaked his pants above his boots, getting his feet wet too. Worse, the water was extremely cold as Connor waded through the darkness, stepping on what he hoped were old parts.

Out of the corner of his eye, Connor spotted a small U-shaped vessel that was partially submerged and looked like it would need some work before he could fly it. Gaining confidence that there was indeed spacecraft in this hanger, he trudged forward through cold water that rippled out from him off into the darkness.

Ahead, the faint image of a giant knight in white armor gave Connor pause before he realized what he was looking at just at the edge of his vision. A few steps closer and his theory was confirmed. It was a battle suit ship like the picture Alex had sent him three weeks before. But unlike Alex's dragon-faced, black samurai-looking suit, this one was white and appeared more like a medieval knight. Blue stripes rolled down the vessel's shoulders over what looked like metallic wings on its back. Curiously, it had three wings on one side arching out to the side and four on the other.

The thing's face looked like the head of a wolf snarling down at Connor. He hadn't noticed it when he first approached, but as he got closer Connor could tell that the vessel was kneeling down. Connor touched the cold metal leg and felt a curious vibration in his OMBI that he thought he might have imagined.

"Hati," Connor said quietly, remember the strange name that Omega had given the object of his quest.

"Welcome, Initiator," spoke a whispering voice at the edge of Connor's consciousness.

Almost falling back into the water, Connor was a little shocked to hear anything in these halls other than his own splashing footsteps. Steadying himself with a deep breath, he walked around to the back side of Hati and climbed up into the open cockpit, settling in. When his legs were in place, Connor slipped his arms into the open slots, which caused the rear hatch to close around him and the HUD appear.

"Okay, now how do I stand up?" Connor asked, not seeing any controls in Hati. He tried hard to budge the legs but couldn't get the machine to respond to his movements. He sat there for a few minutes, taking several breaths and trying to steady himself. He imagined himself in the training room, altering the world around him on a whim.

In his mind Connor saw himself getting up into Hati in the training room and moving it around as easily as walking. When he opened his eyes, he realized that Hati was standing and had taken a few steps forward.

"I don't know how I'm going to pilot this thing with my eyes closed," Connor said sarcastically. Relaxing again, Connor kept his eyes open as he tried to imagine what it would feel like to walk, moving the entire suit, and how easy it would be. Awkwardly Hati took a few more steps forward while Connor focused on not thinking about moving, but trying to feel how it would be to move.

Trying to use his subconscious motor skills instead of his conscious mind, Connor found that it helped if he put his conscious mind to work on something else, so he began to sing. The song wasn't good, but he kept singing as if he were on stage in some great hall, belting out cat noises to a song he didn't know the words to, but enjoyed the beat.

Hati began to pick up speed, the external lights on its hull giving Connor a better image of the room around him. Meowing as he made his way to the exit, he pushed a large red button on the wall only to be thrown back by a wave of water that flooded the entire hanger bay. The massive doors let in the water quickly, and soon Connor was completely submerged. Fortunately the seals on Hati were air tight and it apparently had working life support. Connor was glad that he tested it in water before testing it in space.

Lifting himself to his feet, Connor imagined himself flying through the water toward the surface and up into the sky beyond, higher and higher until he broke out of the Earth's atmosphere. Hati responded by lurching forward into the dark water ahead, deep at the bottom of what Connor presumed was the ocean. Gaining speed, Hati progressed upwards for what seemed like minutes to Connor, until the light of the sun was visible from beneath the waves.

Hati burst free from the water on a cold winter day somewhere in the world that Connor was unsure of, since he couldn't see any land around him. As Hati climbed into the sky, Connor could make out the shape of a landmass far away and, the farther up into the atmosphere they went, the more geographical masses formed a map in Connor's head.

Placing his ascent somewhere in the Northern Pacific Ocean near Asia, Connor turned his focus and meowing song to getting higher into the sky. Once outside the atmosphere, he looked back over his shoulder at the Earth, floated quietly in the endless night of space and smiled.

"Look, everyone, today I am an astronaut," Connor said dryly inside the suit he was wearing. He was starting to get the hang of distracting his mind and letting his subconscious do the work, but as a boy who was used to thinking his way in and out of problems, it was very uncomfortable. He had no idea what he would do if he had to perform any complex maneuvers or engage in combat, but with purpose in his mind Connor activated his OMBI's location function.

The soft blue image appeared in front of him, pointing up from where Connor was looking. He rotated his suit and began the process of trying to imagine how a slipstream was supposed to work. He imagined the line on a piece of paper, with a picture of Hati on one end, and his best interpretation of the Eagle Nebula on the other. Meowing a song about a gambler he had heard once, Connor imagined what would happen if that paper was folded in half, bringing the two points together.

Chapter 19

The Fine Line

The man he had been was gone. The holotube news report had been playing a story on the latest Gortha attack all morning - the annihilation of Black Squadron and one UEDF Battle Frigate. Apparently the survivors of a disabled Frigate had sent back a report and requested aid that would be months in arriving through a standard slipstream.

He wasn't even sure a Gortha was a real thing anymore, but he knew that Black Squadron was his stepson's command and held no illusions that he would be able to see the boy ever again. William Mercer had lost a lot to the UEDF. In fact, he had lost everything to them.

A man with nothing to lose was no longer a man, but a dangerous and unpredictable beast.

He heard the footsteps in the hallway leading to the study even though they were almost imperceptible. He had been sitting alone in the silence for hours, and the slight vibration in the floor was the anomaly he had been waiting for. He struck one key on his datapad and set it down.

"Surely an architect is not so dangerous that the EMC would have to send an assassin," he said to the figure he knew was on the other side of the door to the study.

"Surely an architect with such keen senses may be more than an architect," the sarcastic reply came.

"I'm unarmed. You can come in; the EMC has taken everything from me now, except my life. But I suspect that you're here to remedy that problem," William said, trying to sound defeated.

The door opened slowly and a nondescript man walked into the room. He was clearly wearing some kind of armor beneath his plain clothing and had many weapons within his reach that he was no doubt quite skilled with. Looking at him, William thought he would never be able to identify this man in a crowd as anything more than just a man. These assassins were trained well to blend in.

"Just one? I'm offended," William scoffed indignantly.

"There is an entire squad already inside; you should be flattered. Apparently someone thought highly enough of you to send me with backup. But looking at you, maybe I should be the one who is offended."

"Touché," William replied, leaning back in his office chair from behind his desk.

"This can either be painless, or it can hurt. It is up to you, Mr. Mercer." the operative said, setting a white capsule on the desk.

"I've heard that operatives are rare and highly trained," William said, playing to the killer's ego.

The man bit. "Indeed, there are only three of my class in the whole of the EMC. But I digress; what will it be?"

"Right to the point. Very well, I choose pain. But before you proceed, I have something to share."

The assassin wasn't in any hurry and it had been a long time since he'd spoken to anyone even approaching intelligent. He let his curiosity get the better of him.

"What could you possibly have to share, that you think I would even be remotely interested in?"

"This."

William placed a datapad, which had a countdown timer, on the desk. The timer display read fifteen seconds and was counting down.

"You should really learn to notice when someone is stalling," William said with a sinister smile growing on his lips.

The assassin pulled a gun from his sleeve faster than William could blink and pointed it at William's head, which caused the man to burst out laughing.

"Shut it down," the assassin demanded, failing to see the irony of threatening death to a man who he had been sent to kill.

"Sorry, no off switch on this one." William laughed so hard that he fell out of his chair.

The assassin turned to run, jumping into a nearby window, which he bounced off of like a rubber ball, causing the man he had come to kill to laugh even harder. Getting up and keeping time in his head, he ran back the way he had come. Realizing that the windows might all be shatterproof, he made his way to the front door. He found it quickly but realized that it had been nailed shut.

Not bothering to inform the squad that had entered the house of their impending peril, the operative dashed up one flight of stairs, back to the one open window on the second floor that he had entered from. Counting in his head, he realized that the distance to the window was too great and he would not be fast enough to reach it. Still he ran, knowing that there was no chance for him.

The perfect killer, caught in the perfect trap.

The explosion rocked the fertile valley of the Russian River. The sculptures of carved stone gave way and burst apart, causing stone to rain down for miles around. The glorious tribute to the heart of man's greatness was gone in the blink of an eye, engulfed in the flame of retribution.

It would be a long time before history would recognize the event for what it was. Eventually it would be known as the first explosion of the "Free Man Revolution," and it certainly wouldn't be the last.

~ ~ ~

Hati came through the fold in space-time at the edge of a field of destruction. Many pieces of ships were floating listlessly in the emptiness of space, including the hulking shell of a large battle frigate. The light from the binary star system cast dark shadows on the ruined vessels. The scene made Connor think of a graveyard.

He had no idea how to work his sensors, but he began quietly meowing a song from the Twenty-First century he knew from watching reruns of old holotube shows. He couldn't not physically see the second frigate that had been on the mission with his brother, nor could he see any enemy vessels around him, so he relaxed a bit as he started searching through the hollow tombs of his brother's squad.

He found several pieces of Anubis fighters who had been torn to shreds, but by what looked like cuts from a sword rather than explosions, projectile, or laser weapons. Inside a few of them Connor saw the frozen remains of their pilots, their faces locked in horror.

It was hard for him to think of them as sixteen-year-old kids under his brother's command. Using Hati's strong arms, Connor began to gather the remains of the ships that had been destroyed and put them together, bending the metal of their hulls so that they stayed in one place. He figured it would be easier to search around if he didn't end up checking the same ship twice.

Once all the smaller ships had been accounted for, Connor went through the frigate. Many cold corpses floated through the halls, quietly spinning in their macabre dance. He began to feel nauseated and chose to leave the giant mausoleum-frigate in search of some evidence of the whereabouts of his brother.

Among the remains of Black Squadron, Connor could only confirm seventeen deaths and assumed that the others must have been captured. Also absent from the field was the black samurai ship that his brother had been piloting.

Unable to stay amongst the wreckage any longer, Connor began flying toward the binary star system, looking around desperately for the planet that was supposed to have the colony on it. He realized it was going to be impossible to spot a small planet in the vastness of space, so with no working sensors, Connor tried his OMBI's location function again.

The blue line was pointing to the far side of the blue star ahead of him and Connor moved Hati that direction for what seemed like hours before deciding to try to slipstream to the other side. He imagined space folding again and moved through the rift.

When he emerged other side, the blue line was pointing behind him toward a small planet that Connor could barely see. His sanguine eyes stayed focused on the planet as he moved forward until the blue line moved again, this time directly below him, out into the vastness of space.

"No!" Connor shouted, assuming that his brother must have just been taken through a slipstream to some unknown part of the galaxy. He began to well up with fear. He believed that Alex was alive, but now he had no idea what system he might be in or where he might go from there. Frustrated, he continued toward the planet, looking for something that might tell him where to go next.

Despite how fast Hati could move, it took a long time before he got to the surface of the planet. He landed hard on the sandy ground of a wasteland with large crystalline formations emerging from the ground.

"No life could exist here; this can't be a colony," Connor said to himself, trying to fathom a way anyone would be able to survive on such an unforgiving surface. He had landed approximately on the side of the planet where he had seen the blue line pointing before it had switched to deep space, but couldn't figure out where to start looking for a settlement.

Lifting off the sand into the air, Connor moved Hati around, scanning the surface with his eyes in a probing pattern, back and forth, looking for any sign at all that this place had ever been colonized.

Quickly getting frustrated, Connor almost gave up the search when he fortuitously saw the opening to a cavern near the base of a large mountain.

"Oh, they might live underground here, that makes sense." He started making his way toward the cavern's entrance.

It was large enough for Hati to walk upright -if not fly through - and stayed large, deep into the core. Apprehensive about a second visit into a scary dark cavern, Connor looked for any signs that there may be a colony in here or any signs that there had ever been one.

Deep in the cavern, he saw what looked like an old hulk of a colonization freighter, and even saw the ship's name on a panel near the top of it that was still intact.

The Argos

"Okay, Argos, now where are your people?"

Going deeper into the caves, Connor started seeing the bottom of the large crystalline formations that were protruding downward from surface casting many different-colored lights all over the cave walls. They were a beautiful contrast to the dark walls of the cavern.

After almost twenty minutes of progressing through the cave, Hati emerged over a frozen lake, which had large blocks cut out of it on the far end. Flying over to where the ice had been harvested, Connor landed Hati at the edge of the lake and opened the rear hatch, hopping out onto the hard ground. The air smelled like wet stone, which Connor liked as he took a deep breath while stretching his aching body.

Looking around, Connor didn't see anybody but saw some machinery and tools down a short path that led to a small building. Running down the path and opening the door, Connor found a boy who he would have guessed was three years older than him by his size. The boy's back was to the door and he was listening to music on some kind of a portable player.

Connor tapped the boy on the shoulder, which sent him jumping up into the air.

"Oh my god! Why did you do that?" the boy said in a strange heavy accent that Connor had never heard before.

"I'm sorry! My name is Connor. I'm looking for my brother."

"And I thought I knew everybody here. I'm Abe Malavich. Who is your brother?"

"His name is Alex Pereira, he is a captain, he…" Connor stopped talking as Abe's face went white.

"Come with me," Abe said, leading Connor out the door at a run.

The two boys ran through several smaller passages that led out into larger caverns. The caverns were surprisingly well–lit, almost as bright as a cloudy day on Earth.

After they had trekked for a few minutes, Connor and Abe came to a house that was carved into one of the crystals and oddly reminded Connor of home. Abe walked right in the front door and called out.

"Dad, there is a boy here looking for his brother, Captain Pereira."

Connor heard movement from the next room as a hardy-looking, older man came through the door. The man stopped and looked Connor up and down curiously.

"You look like him," the man said quietly, "—and her."

"Do you know where my brother is?" Connor asked in haste, missing the comment's full meaning.

"They all left, didn't say where," Adam Malavich replied levelly.

"Alex is alive, right? His squadron was shot down in space," Connor said, pleading for good news.

"Yes, he is alive. I know about his squadron, damn shame."

"What happened up there?"

"I don't know the details really. We were approached about lending our resources to a coalition of colonies to maintain survivability without interference from Earth," Adam explained. "Then the UEDF sent some ships in and attacked the people who we were talking to. My fault really, I sent a distress signal when I couldn't identify their ships. I thought they were Gortha."

Confused, Connor knew that he wouldn't get any real answers from this man about what happened to Alex and why he would have gone with some kind of a colony independence faction.

Connor tried to get more details, but the man didn't know much about the Independents or whether or not Alex was a prisoner. The details he did have about the arrangement he had come to with the Independents he kept to himself, saying that it was probably better of Connor didn't know.

Connor was frustrated when he left, walking with Abe back to the frozen lake where he had left Hati. The boy offered no more information than his father did. As he boarded Hati, Connor waved at the kid.

"Thanks for nothing!" Connor fired as a parting shot while he began his journey through the cavern back outside.

The kid frowned as he walked back into the workshop where Connor had met him.

~ ~ ~

Flying back outside to the bright surface of the planet, Connor thought about where he would go next, not really feeling good about staying here now that his brother had left. He had the idea that he might be able to help the other frigate, so Connor slipstreamed back out to the wreckage of the battle and began looking around for anything that would tell him where the other ship had gone.

It was by sheer luck that Connor found it on the far side of a moon that was orbiting a gas giant in the system. The Griswold looked bad. Connor wasn't even sure that it had power until he got close enough to see a repair crew trying to patch gaping holes in the hull.

Connor moved to help, but he realized that there wasn't much he could do. When the terrified repair crew began to scatter Connor thought that the best thing he could do was slipstream them all back to Earth. He waited until the crew had gotten back inside, since he wasn't sure that an exposed human could even survive a slipstream.

He flew around the ship once for good measure to make sure no one else was outside, grabbed the Griswold by the edge of an open docking platform, and imagined himself and the much larger frigate on a piece of paper with a line drawn between it and Earth, and then folding the ends together.

Epilogue

In the weeks following Connor's return from the Eagle Nebula, he had been interrogated seven times, been put through two psychological tests, and spent a week in a military prison cell. He had begun to think that he would be imprisoned forever when an escort arrived to take him back to the OMBIcademy.

When he had first brought the Griswold back into the Sol system, the rescue crews arrived from Station Sigma within hours. In the meanwhile Connor had been working with Hati to keep various large gaps from venting air out by bending the metal together and smoothing it over with Hati's strong metal hands. He wasn't sure if he was helping, but the idea of doing nothing didn't sit right with him.

When the crews arrived, he had been taken by cargo transport back to Earth with Hati in tow. He wasn't sure where the transport had taken Hati after that, but Connor was taken immediately to a military prison facility for questioning.

He told the truth to the interrogator as best he could. He didn't know where he had found Hati and got called a liar for trying to explain how the training rooms might be connected. That seemed like a minor detail compared to the weight of what had happened in and around Atmos XI. One interrogator even tried to convince him that the colonists were under Gortha mind control, which didn't sound right to Connor at all.

When they asked about Alex, Connor didn't know what to say. He ended up telling them that he thought that Alex might be dead, but gave no details on how or why he thought that.

The psychological evaluations were both followed by medical exams of his brain function and OMBI. He wasn't sure why they were examining his arm so much, but Connor let them do it without complaint. They opened it up and were examining some large chips that Connor thought they called "Inhibitors" before giving him a clean bill of health.

When they finally sent him back to the OMBIcademy, things had changed a lot. The first change was that he had been transferred to Green Army. The scoreboards had been removed and the new Head Commander had issued a rule that he would decide who the army commanders would be. Connor wasn't one of them, but did get selected by Green Army's commander as a lieutenant after a short discussion about Green Army tactics.

The other big changes were that the training rooms had been welded shut "until further notice," and Connor had also been put on probation, so he had to attend weekly evaluations by a techno-psychologist. Connor was positively miserable and tried to write a letter to William, which came back "no such address" after a day. He had tried to write Alex too, but got the same response from his OMBI.

With opposite schedules, Connor didn't see his friends from Blue Army at all for two days until he had been walking down a hall and saw Cat and Manzar walking together. When he had stopped to say hello to them, they both put their heads down and kept walking, like they were afraid to talk to him.

On his third day back, Connor was laying in his bunk when he heard the whisper. He thought it was his imagination at first, but when he closed his eyes he heard it again. It sounded like faint voices on a breeze in his mind ... He wasn't sure of all they were saying, but the one word he could make out definitively was a word he had heard a lot: "initiator."

~ ~ ~

When the fire had finally gone out, the 311 AFMR began a body count of the explosion, trying to gather data on the scope of the disaster. Rubble had been removed each day and the holotube news had reported it as a gas line rupture on the estate of the well-respected architect, during a routine investigation by military authorities. It was hailed a minor tragedy for a week, until the next major sporting event drama unfolded and by the time the body count had been established, most people had forgotten about it.

So complete was the destruction that the AFMR had trouble putting together a final body count, coming up with an estimate between eighteen and twenty-two on its first count. The count included an entire squad of special operations soldiers who were declared KIA. The twenty bodies of the soldiers were found in two groups near two entrances of the estate's main house and were so badly destroyed that they only way they could differentiate the remains was by guessing.

The final body, which had been declared the body of William Mercer, was found near a stairway at the back of the house and was buried at the Oak Mound Cemetery on April tenth, 2121. The eulogy was given by a priest and the funeral was attended by fourteen people, including two brothers who hadn't talked to him in years, one brother-in-law who had spoken to him last when he had called to wish Connor a happy birthday, and an old high school friend who happened to live only an hour away.

It went by quickly and the memory of the man slowly faded from the minds of those he had once known.

~ ~ ~

"The boy has been released from custody and put back into the OMBIcademy under probation as you instructed. I had to pull a lot of strings," the image of Major Sanders said through the communicator's flickering display.

"You did well, Major. I won't forget how much you have helped me in this. But we're still only getting started," she said in a melodic voice, before the distorter altered it for the transmission.

"There is one more thing. It's about the boy's stepfather…" Sanders said in a cryptic tone.

The woman's chest tightened suddenly, unable to breathe as she responded, "Tell me."

"The EMC tried to have him eliminated. There was an explosion at the estate that killed him and an entire special ops force. I'm sorry," Sanders said, not sounding confident that he should be apologizing.

"I see." Then she ended the transmission.

It was a cool day on Aeris VII, which had become known by the Independents as the Hourglass Colony. She had landed the Anubis fighter on a high shelf in the mountains, near a communications array that she had built for long range transmissions.

The pain built up inside the woman from the pit of her stomach as she looked at the picture she had placed on the instruments of the Tizona long ago. She felt the tears welling up while she looked into the dark blue eyes of the man who had stolen her heart ten years prior. The caption of the picture read, "My Boys."

8,000 light years away from the funeral, the dark-haired woman of peerless beauty uncontrollably wept.

End

About the Author

Born on a snowy morning in LaGrande, Oregon, Joseph Mackay was raised with two brothers in Placerville, California. A born adventurer, Joseph has lived in an RV full time and off the back of a motorcycle, has flown a helicopter and enjoyed skydiving, has been a burlesque performer and an opera singer. When not writing, he enjoys playing bass guitar and singing in his band, playing with his dog "Mimi," watching Giants baseball, and preparing for his next adventure.

Interested in contacting me?

Please direct all emails to josephmackay@gmail.com

Want to stay current with the latest news and releases?

Check out: www.josephmackaybooks.com

www.ingramcontent.com/pod-product-compliance
Lightning Source LLC
Chambersburg PA
CBHW071135170626
46809CB00002B/635